THE PERFECT MARRIAGE

JENEVA ROSE

Print ISBN 978-1-913419-65-3

To Mom
My biggest supporter
My proudest fan
My favorite memory

PROLOGUE

Did he love her? He loved the way she looked at him—the way her bottom lip trembled and her foot quaked when she orgasmed. He loved the way her long chestnut locks fell in front of her doe eyes as she rode him and the way her slender back curved into a crescent moon when he thrust her from behind. Did he love her? He loved parts of her. But the question isn't whether or not he loved her. The question is... did he kill her?

1

SARAH MORGAN

"**N**ot again."

The disappointment in his voice fills the room and hangs there like a light fog, clouding us from one another. I take in a deep breath, removing the haze, and let it out just as quickly, clearing the path back between us. I don't need to look at him to know his eyes are disheartened and his lips are pressed firmly together. I don't blame him. I've disappointed Adam again. I run my hands over my golden blond hair taming any flyaways. It's wrapped tightly in a perfect bun. It's always wrapped tightly in a perfect bun. I slide a white blazer over an emerald-green blouse and straighten out my pencil skirt. My eyes meet his, locking us back into place.

"I'm sorry." I tilt my head down, avoiding his gaze to lure him toward me. He takes the bait, walking to me, his six-foot-two stature towering over my petite body. He puts his hand to my cheek, lifts my chin, and kisses me softly on the lips. Every hair raises on my body. After ten years of marriage, Adam still does that for me. After ten years of marriage, I still do that for him—disappoint, I mean.

"We were supposed to leave for the lake house yesterday. You said you'd be able to today."

I break our embrace and begin packing up my briefcase, my sense of responsibility outweighing my levels of sentiment. "I know, I know. It's just I have so much work to do and a huge closing statement to prepare for."

Adam walks to the door frame of our master bedroom and leans against it. He folds his arms in front of his chest. There's nothing more that I want at this moment than to be wrapped up in his arms rather than wrapped up in a messy court case, but there are some things even I can't control.

"You always have so much work to do. There's always a big case you're working on." He narrows his eyes at me playfully but in a somewhat accusing way, as if I were now on trial.

"Someone has to pay the bills." I give a small smile. That lands. He shakes his head so slightly I almost don't notice it, but I need to acknowledge it. I place my hands on his shoulders. He pretends he won't lean down to meet my lips, but I know he will. He can't resist me, just like I can't resist him.

He smiles, but his game of tug-of-war only lasts a few seconds before his body bends toward me. Our lips meet again —this time more passionate. This time our mouths spread, our tongues swirl, his hands run up and down my back. I consider calling it all off at that moment. I'll quit the firm. We'll sell this house, and we'll move to our lake house in Virginia, just the two of us running hand in hand into our own fairy tale.

But reality sets back in.

"I have to go," I whisper into his ear as I pull away. I'm always the first to pull away. Someday, we'll be everything I always knew we would be but someday isn't today.

"But it's our tenth anniversary tomorrow." He frowns. He still has the boyish charm I fell in love with, and it would be annoying if I weren't also smitten by it.

4

"I'm going to try to make it there tomorrow." I take a step back from him, surveying his disappointed face, the damage I've done.

He lets out a huff. "After ten years, you'd think I'd be used to you doing this... but I'm not." Adam rubs his chin as if he's contemplating what he'll say next. "I'm just really fed up with it, Sarah." He lowers his head and shakes it.

I close the space between us and bury my face into his chest. "I'm sorry. I know I've disappointed you. But regardless, after this case is over, I'm taking a week off work. I've already talked to Kent." I look up at him with doe eyes, hoping he'll be happy with this news.

He lets on a small smile. "Is this a real promise or a Sarah promise?"

I lightly pat his chest. "Oh, stop."

He grabs my hands and pulls me in for another kiss. "I'll stop when you stop." He smirks. I kiss him again.

"Oh, I almost forgot." From the closet I pull out a small wrapped box and present my gift to him. "I got you something."

He looks at it and then at me. "You shouldn't have," he says taking the perfectly wrapped present. We had agreed after our fifth anniversary, we weren't going to do gifts anymore, but I couldn't help myself. I know I've been neglectful, but this was my small way of making it up to him. He pauses for a moment and then carefully unwraps the gift. He lifts the box open unveiling a Patek Philippe grand complication watch with alligator band and a gold face. His mouth drops open.

"I've been looking at this watch for years... but this, this is too much," he protests while admiring the intricacies and design of the watch face.

"No, it's not—it's ten years of marriage." I pull the watch out. "Look at the engraving."

He flips it over and on the back is engraved, *5,256,000.*

JENEVA ROSE

Adam looks to me. "What's that?"

"That's how many minutes are in ten years." I plant a light kiss on his lips.

"You counted?"

"I'm always counting." I laugh as I help him put the watch on.

He holds out his wrist admiring it. "Is this so I can keep track of every time you're late or stand me up?" he teases. I roll my eyes at him.

"I'm kidding."

"No, you're not." I tilt my head. I know he's not kidding.

He lowers his arm and returns his attention to me, placing his hands on my shoulders, running them down my arms. "You're right, but I love you anyway, Sarah." He kisses me hard.

After untangling ourselves from a passionate kiss, we make our way down to the kitchen, a large and modern space with stainless-steel appliances, cream-colored cupboards, and granite countertops. I set my briefcase on the island and rummage through the fridge for fruit and water. I take some sliced pineapple and a glass bottle of San Pellegrino, which should tide me over until I send my assistant on a lunch run.

Adam pours two cups of coffee and places one beside my black Bottega briefcase. He removes the used coffee filter from the machine and walks to the garbage, pressing his foot on the pedal to open the lid. Just as he is about to discard the refuse into the can, a brief glittering of silver catches his eye.

"What's this?" Adam reaches down into the trash, pulling out the source of the luminescence. A torn envelope with a card inside.

"Your mom sent us an anniversary card," I reply without looking up from my phone.

"And you just... threw it away?" He crumples up his face.

6

"I read it. Acknowledged it. Digested it. What more do you want me to do with it?"

He pulls the card out of the ripped open envelope, and reads it aloud, "I can't believe you lasted ten years! Happy Anniversary, my darling Adam and Sarah. P.S. Where are my grandchildren? Love, Mom."

He smiles and walks to the fridge. "That was nice of her." He begins searching through drawers for a magnet to secure his prize to the front of our stainless-steel fridge. I roll my eyes as I watch him add a piece of garbage to the refrigerator.

"What are you going to do today?" I change the subject. I'm just going to let this one go, and by this one, I mean his mother. I pick up the cup of coffee and bring it to my lips. It burns, but a good type of burn, like the small fires we sometimes need in our lives to remind us that we are alive.

"Well, now that I have nothing but time on my hands..." he says with a chuckle while looking at his new watch. I let out a small, polite laugh for his terrible joke. "I'll probably head up to the lake house and get some writing done. Daniel needs more pages before he can pitch the book."

I nod and take another sip. "The last ones you sent were wonderful. Your agent is going to love them. Make sure you send me your newest ones."

"Do you mean that?" He skeptically raises an eyebrow.

"I mean everything I say... especially, about you." I wink.

He sets his cup of coffee down and closes the distance between us, standing behind me with each hand on the countertop. He nuzzles and kisses my neck while pressing his pelvis into my butt. I giggle like a schoolgirl.

"Come tomorrow. Just for the day."

"I'm going to try, even if I can just spend a few hours with you."

"Do more than try. We've had the lake house for over a year, and you haven't spent more than a night up there."

"I said I'll try." I take another sip of my coffee.

He groans into my neck. "Please."

"I'll do everything in my power to be there tomorrow, and you and I can finally christen that lake house." I playfully back into him. He pulls me in tight and kisses my neck.

"Now that is a plan I can get behind." Adam turns me around to face him and runs his hands all over my body.

"Thank you for being patient with me." I raise my chin so our eyes can meet, giving him my most bashful puppy-dog eyes to convey as much sincerity as I mean to express with my words. His eyes lock with mine.

"I'd wait a lifetime for you and then some." He kisses my forehead, the tip of my nose, and then my lips. "Or at least another 5,256,000 minutes..." He smirks. "Now, hurry to work so you can hurry to me." He playfully pats my butt as if I was running into a football game.

I pick up my bag and start toward the door. I tell him I love him.

"Love you more," he says.

2

ADAM MORGAN

My fingers tap against the keyboard a few more times just as the sun is leaving its final stretch of light on this side of the world for the day. A breeze rustles the trees, shaking them of their fall-colored leaves, while laps of lake water gently lick the shore. I save the work I've done for the day and close my laptop—three thousand words will have to do. I toss my black-rimmed reading glasses onto the desk and run my hands through my ash-brown hair, pushing it off my forehead. I rub my temples a bit to alleviate a lingering tension headache and let out a deep sigh. As I stretch my arms out and roll my neck, a black squirrel darting across the yard catches my eye. It's not as if I haven't seen a black squirrel before, but it's a rare sight, and demands to be watched and noticed. I stare out of the large window behind my desk as the creature bounces from place to place, searching for food, complete in its sense of purpose and direction.

The lake house is an hour away from our home outside D.C. and it might as well be on a new planet. It's a verdant land that our forefathers would actually recognize, unlike the concrete and horn-blasted monstrosity that plays the part of our nation's capital. The house is far enough from the city to ensure no unexpected visitors but close enough for me to travel to whenever I need to be alone—or not alone, for that matter.

A secluded cabin on Lake Manassas surrounded by woods in Prince William County, Virginia, was just what my writing career needed, or at least that's how I sold the idea to Sarah. I had struggled to get the words out up until just over a year ago when we purchased this second home. It opened another world for me, a world in which I could write, a world full of obtainable desires, a world I could live in without feeling the constant pressure that I wasn't good enough. The natural beauty of the environment around me could be reflected into my work, and in this world I felt reborn.

Hardwood features so heavily in the make-up of our lake house that it feels like you've climbed inside a tree, rather than a human dwelling. The wide-open living area has large bay windows overlooking the lake and a massive fireplace adorned with various colored stones. A huge bearskin rug completes the sitting area and serves as a central point that separates it from the kitchen.

Forest-green marbled granite covers both the kitchen island and the countertops, and above and below are pine cabinets that have been stained to a rich almost caramel colored wood. Just off the sitting area, less than ten feet from the fireplace, over by the bay windows, sits my desk. This allows me the perfect view of all that nature has to offer in this neck of the woods and gives me the freedom of not feeling trapped in some small office.

It didn't take much to convince Sarah that we should purchase this home away from home. I think she could sense that I was drifting away—mentally, emotionally... or maybe she just wanted to show me that she could buy it. To remind me, once again, of her fiscal hold over me, wielding it as a show of power. Whatever the reason may be, I still got the house, so who fucking cares.

It was supposed to be our home away from home but turns out it's just my home. I've lost count of the number of times Sarah promised she'd come with me for a weekend but later canceled. This weekend was no exception, even on our tenth anniversary. I had hoped she'd make it down just for the day, but she phoned earlier telling me she had to go into the office once again. She also told me she loved me. She always tells me she loves me. I hold my wrist out, admiring my new watch. It's beyond expensive. Despite the cost, it was still a thoughtful gift. That's Sarah for you. She is thoughtful, even if she's never around.

I've always felt like Sarah was taking on the world, while I was just struggling to live in it. That's the woman she wanted to be, a powerhouse, a one-woman show where I just happen to be cast as an extra. It wasn't always like that. We met while I was in my third year of undergrad at Duke and she in her first. She was studying political science, while I was studying literature. Back then, we both dreamed of greatness. Sarah wanted to be a successful lawyer, and I wanted to go down as one of the truly great writers of our generation. Fifteen years later, one of us is still waiting.

Well, I suppose success flickered for me, for a moment, and went away just as quickly, and has yet to come back again. That's the funny thing about dreams. You always eventually wake up from them. My first book was a success, not from a mainstream or commercial standpoint, but from a literary perspective. One critic even called me, "The next David Foster Wallace," which I liked. The book has a nice cult following to this day, and I thought I'd duplicate that success, but books two and three have flopped by all standards, literary included. I'm surprised my agent has kept me on, and I'm sure if the book I'm working on isn't a success, I'll be getting the ax soon enough.

I've tasted a small sampling of triumph, but I haven't exactly lived out my dreams. Sarah's dream was to be a criminal defense attorney, one of the best. She's not one of the best: she is the best —like I always knew she would be. I just never thought I'd resent her so much for it.

But like I said, it wasn't always like this, and when I say this, I mean me running off to our second home any chance I get and her practically taking up residency at her office. After all, you don't become the best criminal defense attorney by loving your husband.

One would think that living in solitude and wallowing in my own self-pity would make me one of the great writers, like a modern-day Thoreau or Hemingway. But to date I have all the alcohol usage of Hemingway, just none of the success to go along with it.

Sarah has her work, and I have mine, and there was a time when we had each other, but that time has passed.

We had met at a party, a complete stroke of luck as it was out of the norm for Sarah to attend one, she would go on to tell me later that night. She'd much rather have her face in a book than be surrounded by sticky, hormonal bodies in a basement of a college house—but there she was, standing in a corner, casually sipping cheap beer out of a Solo cup, looking more out of place than a nun in a brothel. She held a partial smile trying to mask her discomfort, but her body language gave her uneasiness away. She was leaning against a wall, one leg crossed over the other, the Solo cup hovering near her lips, glancing around the party, one arm crossed over her chest tucked underneath her other arm. She was trying to make herself as small as possible, blending into the background, going unnoticed. But to me, she was the only person in that room.

Her shoulder-length blond hair was practically glowing under the black lights, a staple of any college party in the mid-2000s. Her green eyes that were speckled with flakes of yellow held all the mystery in the world. Her slender body was covered in a form-fitting white tee and flared blue jeans. An inch of her midriff was peeking out, and I couldn't keep my eyes off it. A sliver of her exposed, milky-white skin aroused me more than my ex's fully nude body had. I watched her. I studied her. Before I had ever uttered a word to her, I had memorized every curve, every line, and every freckle that I was privy to in that dingy basement. I pictured what she looked like underneath her clothes, and I would later find out that what I had envisioned was wrong. Her body exceeded the limitations of my own imagination. She was perfect, something I could neither conceive, nor comprehend.

It wasn't until an hour later when her eyes finally caught mine that I worked up the courage to go and talk to her. I towered over her petite body, but right from the beginning she always felt bigger than me, and I knew as soon as she realized it, she would be an unstoppable force.

At first, she was a little standoffish, giving one-word answers. I asked her name. She told me it was Sarah. I asked her who she was here with. She pointed to an inebriated, brunette grinding on a guy on the dance floor. I asked her if she wanted to dance. She said no. I told her she was beautiful. She shrugged her shoulders. I told her my name was Adam. She took a sip of her beer. I asked her what she was studying. She tapped her beer signaling she needed a refill and started to walk away. I grabbed her cup and poured my full cup of beer into hers. She smiled up at me taking the cup back and returning to her position against the wall.

"Smooth," she said as she took a sip.

I leaned against the wall next to her, and we stood in silence for what seemed like hours. Right from the beginning with Sarah—it always felt like forever. She casually sipped her beer, while she scanned the party and kept an eye on her drunk friend. I pretended to study the room with her, but my only focus was on her. At minute nineteen, Sarah's friend told her she was leaving with the guy she had been grinding on all night. Her words slurred, her eyes glazed over, and her hair fell in front of her face as she held on to the hand of the man she would soon spread herself apart for. Sarah didn't seem pleased, but she told her to have a good time and to call her in the morning. It was the most I had heard her speak all night. Sarah remained composed, casually sipping her beer.

At minute twenty, she finished her drink and dropped the cup onto the dirty basement floor, kicking it into a corner. She stood there a little longer, her eyes bouncing around the party and then to the side at me. She shifted a little uneasily, and I wasn't sure if she was moving toward me or away from me.

At minute twenty-one, I decided to find out, and I asked her if she wanted to get out of here. She said yes. When I got her safely back to her dorm room, I expected to give her a kiss on the cheek and tell her goodnight. Sarah didn't seem like the kind of girl to give into her impulses. As I went in for a small peck on her cheek, she pulled me inside, ripped off my clothes, and she puffed and gasped breaths of yes for the rest of that night.

Three years later, I asked her to marry me, and she said yes again. And although she has said yes to me countless times since then, I think that was the last time she truly meant it. If she hadn't been consumed with law school and then practicing law, I think we would have been—

The breeze sucks the front door closed with a slam. It startles me for just a split second, but I know it's her. Without even seeing her, I know her freckles are prominent from a day working the outside patio at the café. I know her brown doe eyes are lit up—filled with hope and joy. I know her long tousled hair sits underneath a hat she knitted herself earlier this fall. I know when she pulls that hat off, she'll still look effortlessly beautiful, messy hair and all. I know she'll be braless, wearing a form-fitting top and a dark thigh-length skirt. I know the waist of her shirt will be creased from where her apron sat all day. I know she'll smile when she sees me, and it'll take me less than sixty seconds to be inside her.

"Babe, I brought leftover baked goods from the café," she calls from the foyer.

I hear her wrestle her shoes, knee-length socks, and jacket off. I pull two glasses from the wet bar. I pour scotch into each glass, and just as she enters I have one drink outreached to her. With a little bounce in her step, she takes the glass from me, chugs it, and sets it back down on the wet bar. The heat from the stone fireplace warms her skin, and I notice the goosebumps on her arms flatten.

Before I can take a second sip, she's unbuttoning and unzipping my pants. She drops to her knees and looks up at me with a devilish grin.

~

I drop her legs on the bed and walk into the bathroom, closing the door behind me.

I can still hear her panting from the other side of the door, trying to regain control of her own breathing. She doesn't make a sound, and I assume she's still lying there. I hope it's in ecstasy and not pain. Sometimes, I take things too far—it's like I black out and when I come to, I realize the error of my ways. I can't help myself. Kelly just does that to me. When I'm with her, my animal instincts take over.

Sarah used to do that to me. But now around her, I'm barely a man let alone anything else.

At the vanity I look at myself in the mirror. A five-o'clock shadow has taken over my face, and my hair is out of place. My otherwise blue eyes are clouded with red. I can only stand looking at myself for a few seconds before I must look away. I'm not ashamed of who I am, but I'm not proud either. I splash some water on my face and then onto my chest, abs, and dick. I'm too tired to shower. I pat myself dry with a towel.

"Babe?" Kelly yells from the other room.

"Yeah, hon?" I answer as I start brushing my teeth.

"Your wife texted you."

I spit the toothpaste into the sink and rinse my mouth out, wiping my lips with my hand. Back in the bedroom, the lights are on now, and Kelly is sitting in bed, wearing a nightgown, while holding my phone. She smiles up at me.

"What did she say?" I slide a pair of Ralph Lauren pajama pants on.

"She wants to know what you're doing."

I take a seat on the bed next to her, pushing her long brown hair back. I gently kiss her neck and shoulder.

"Tell her I'm about to fuck the girl of my dreams again," I whisper. Kelly laughs and begins texting back.

"Your wish is my command." She giggles. I swipe the phone from her playfully and get out of bed. I quickly text back.

> *Since you couldn't make it to me, I'm coming back tonight to see you. No need to wait up. Love you.*

Before I can set the phone down, Sarah texts back.

> *I love you too. I got a chance to read the new pages you sent over lunch, and they're incredible. I'm so proud of you XOXO.*

I smile for a brief second, before a wave of guilt spans over me. I let out a sigh.

You're the best, babe. Let me take you out for dinner tomorrow night. Say yes.

My phone vibrates.

Yes.

Sometimes, I get a glimpse of who we used to be, and I think we can be that couple again. But I've fucked up too much for that to ever happen, and Sarah's career has always come first—before me, before a family, before everything. I don't foresee that ever changing.

I thought when we had kids, she'd slow down, but she told me five years ago she didn't want kids. I thought I'd be able to change her mind. I couldn't.

I set my phone down on the dresser and plug it into the charger. I look over at Kelly who is giving me bedroom eyes. She can never get enough of me, and I can't get enough of her. But I know that won't always be true. There was a time that Sarah and I couldn't get enough of each other either. That time passed long ago. Occasionally, those feelings resurface, but they're short-lived and usually induced by alcohol or time apart. Don't get me wrong, I love Sarah. If I didn't, I would have left her long ago. It's that love that I hold on to—not the money, the security or the houses. Kelly gives me the love that Sarah can no longer. They both complete me. It's sick I know, but it's true. I need them both.

"Are you ever going to tell your wife about us?"

"Are you ever going to tell your husband about us?" I retort.

She huffs and folds her arms across her chest. "It's not the same." Her words are quiet.

I leave and return with two full glasses of scotch, handing one to her and taking a seat. I put one arm around her and pull her close telling her I know. She lets out a soft, silent sob and as quickly as the cry left her body, she pulls it back in, regaining her composure. She takes a large gulp of the scotch and doesn't even flinch at the burn. She leans into me. We sit there in silence, drinking our glasses of scotch, trapped in loveless marriages where we come second to the people we love. When Kelly and I are together, we come first. I refill our glasses twice more, and then we have sex again. This time, I don't fuck her—I make love to her.

3

SARAH MORGAN

I'm poring over case files, the papers shifting and falling like the snow of a freshly plunged avalanche. I had planned to go into the office for just a few hours to prep for the week, but here I am sipping at my twelve-hour old coffee with oil circles floating on top to remind me of its age. My corner office is on the fourteenth floor, which is as high as one can get in D.C. without erecting a phallus taller than Mr. Washington's. It has floor-to-ceiling windows and is one of the biggest in the firm, and no one would contest as to why I was given it.

With several high-profile cases and the most case wins out of any attorney here, I more than earned my place as a named partner at Williamson & Morgan. The tips of my fingers rub my forehead, slowly massaging my temples as if to conjure myself back into a state of peace and normalcy. I slide my reading glasses off and drop them onto my desk with a resounding crash to punctuate my frustration. The clock on my phone reads 8:04pm. An exasperated huff exits my mouth to let the non-existent audience in my office know how taxed I am.

I send a quick text to Adam:

Sorry, I really wanted to be with you today. I miss you.

I drop the phone back on the desk. Grabbing the fork from on top of the Styrofoam container, I stab it into the Chinese food that has been sitting out for a few hours. I take a couple of quick bites, then slide the whole thing in the garbage can. My hair is pulled into a bun at the nape of my neck, every strand perfectly in place, even though I've been working for the past thirteen hours. I adjust my high-end black blouse and brush off my tailored skirt. I straighten my desk, which is in complete disarray and not typically how I live my life. With court dates and depositions looming over me, a little mess is going to have to do. I look out the windows of my office, admiring the lights of the city, the cars moving in unison, the people out and about enjoying their last few hours of the weekend.

"Anne, are you still here?" I call out.

The door of my office opens, and my sweet-looking assistant pops her head in. She's a petite woman with shoulder-length brown hair, and although she doesn't turn heads, she's pretty in a modest way. Her eyes while faint light up and she smiles at me, ready and eager to please. While I am the only other person in the office right now, it is not uncommon for Anne to scramble into work once she starts to see me sending work emails.

"Yes, Mrs. Morgan."

I drop my hands on my desk and give her a sympathetic smile. "Anne, how many times do I have to tell you? Just because I work ridiculously long hours doesn't mean you need to, and what's with the Mrs. Morgan?"

"Sorry, Mrs.—" She begins and stops as I put my hand up and stand. I approach Anne. The office has plush carpeting, which I picked out myself as it feels incredibly soft beneath my bare feet. I made sure to decorate so it had a homey feel, with a plush couch and recliner, a coffee table, pillows, a bookcase stuffed with books for both work and pleasure, and beautiful artwork on the walls. This office is my home away from home, as I've spent more time here the past eight years than I have at my actual home. I even got a treadmill for it, which sits in the corner facing the Washington Monument.

I reach Anne and put a hand on her shoulder. "Anne, you have worked for me for five years. We eat lunch together every Friday. We occasionally grab drinks after work. You travel with me for business. You've been to my house on countless occasions. You're my friend first and my employee second. Please for the love of God, never call me Mrs. Morgan again."

Anne shakes her head and smiles. She slides past me and slumps into the couch taking a load off. "Ugh, I'm sorry. I've been pulling double duty for Bob since his last assistant quit. He demands that I call him Mr. Miller. It's just become a force of habit." She rubs her brow.

I take a seat next to Anne. I put my bare feet up on the coffee table, let out a sigh, and pull my hair loose from its tight bun. Anne kicks her heels off and puts her feet up on the table too. We share a look of solidarity and understanding. Although she and I are different in nearly every way, we are one and the same. Two women trying to make it in a man's world. We work twice as hard as our male counterparts to make it just an inch ahead of them.

"That's because Mr. Miller is an asshole. I'll make sure he has a new assistant by the end of the week, and if the next one doesn't work out, I'll make sure he doesn't work out here either," I say with a laugh, although I'm completely serious. Bob is a decent attorney, but he has a huge ego and no respect for anyone else, except those that have more money or more power than him.

"Thanks, Sarah. You're too good to me."

"No—you're too good to me."

"You know who's not too good for anyone?" Anne asks.

"Who?"

"Bob."

We both laugh, and it feels good. I've had my head buried in case files forever. I miss this. I miss just hanging out without the weight of the world on my shoulders or someone's life and future in my hands.

"Oh, I wanted to show you these." Anne pulls out her phone. She opens her photo app and flicks her finger across the screen a few times.

I take the phone from her and look at each photo—a man crossing the street, a woman walking up the steps of the Lincoln Memorial, a falcon swooping low over a lake, a child looking up at the Washington Monument. "These are beautiful, Anne. You have such a good eye," I say admiring each picture.

"Thank you, just a little hobby of mine."

"It should be more than a hobby. You're very talented."

She blushes, and her lips press firmly together as I hand her back her phone.

My phone vibrates. I stand up and walk to my desk, quickly texting Adam back. I miss him. I miss us. We exchange a few more texts, and when I learn he'll be coming back late, it's decided. "Let's go out for some drinks," I say.

"Are you sure? You have to deliver the closing statement tomorrow morning." I can see the hope in her eyes from a friend's standpoint who wants the best for me and the uneasiness from an employee's stance who also wants the best for me.

"Yes, I'm entirely sure." I grin.

Anne claps her hands together. "I'll call us an Uber." She gets up, slides her heels back on, and walks towards my office door with a little bounce in her step.

4

ADAM MORGAN

T he slam of a car door wakes me from my slumber. It's pitch black inside and outside, and I don't have the slightest clue how my night ended with Kelly, but I assume it was with more rough sex since my cock feels like it's been dragged along a slab of pavement. I glance at the clock on the nightstand and in large red illuminating digits it reads 12:15am.

"Fuck," I whisper.

I should have been home with Sarah by now. I rub my hands over my forehead and down my face, trying to massage the nerves back to life. How the hell did I get this bad? I can't see more than a few inches in front of my face, but I can feel Kelly next to me. I can always feel her next to me. I scooch closer to her, running my hand along her cheek. She's dead asleep. I whisper her name trying to stir her, but the scotch has a stronger pull on her than it did me.

"Kelly," I whisper a little louder, but she doesn't move. The continuous vibration and ding of her phone distract me from her, but I've decided that if she's this tired, then I want her to sleep. I give her a gentle kiss on her cheek and swivel myself off my side of the bed without a sound. I tiptoe to her side of the bed and take her phone off the nightstand. I step out of the room meaning only to silence it, so it doesn't disturb her—but the text messages catch my eye. I look back into the dark room and then at the phone. I type 4357 into the passcode. The most recent text is from a girl named Jesse.

It reads '*I'm sorry.*'

I scroll past Jesse's most recent text to those before it. They're all from Scott, her husband. I read them in order, starting from the earliest at 10:17pm.

I wish you would come home to me.

Why does it have to be like this?

Babe... will you please answer me?

I love you so fucking much. Why can't you get that?

I didn't mean any of it. You have to believe me. It won't happen again. I promise.

Please tell me where you're at.

If you would just answer. I would leave you alone tonight.

Fuck you, you fucking dumb ass bitch.

You fucking lied to me. You're not still at work. I just called the cafe.

When I find you, you'll be begging me for last night's ordeal rather than what I have in store for you, you worthless bitch.

My muscles clench up in anger, but I keep scrolling anyway. This is her business, and she's never wanted me to be involved, but I would kill this piece of shit at this moment if I had the chance.

Too late. You're a fucking memory now.

That's the final text message from Scott at 11:45pm. Jesus Christ. What a fucking psycho. I want to pick her up out of that bed and hold her close and reassure that we're not all pieces of shit like her husband. I'm half tempted to text him back but riling him up is the last thing Kelly needs. Instead, I creep back in the bedroom, set an alarm on her phone for 8:00am, and place it on the nightstand. I lean down and plant a kiss on her cheek. I slide my hand up her thigh into her core. It's wetter than it's ever been, and I think at first, she's going to wake up for me immediately. But she doesn't stir, and when she doesn't, I take my hand away. I want to be there for her in every type of way—physically, mentally, and emotionally. I wipe my wet hand against my pants and quietly walk out of the room.

Outside, I don't turn on any lights and I allow my eyes to adjust as best they can in the dark. The coals from the fireplace help me find my way around the living room, and the bearskin rug lets me know when I'm outside the open-concept living room. The embers provide a soft glow as I creep my feet along the hardwood floor. I cross the kitchen keeping my balance with the granite countertops. The dull light of a pale moon provides a dismal backdrop to the front glass façade of the house. I find a pad of paper and a pen and write:

Kelly,
   It's you. It hasn't always been you, but it will always be you.

You're the words to a story I've been trying to write my whole life,
and tonight I determined the ending.

Love you, Love me, Adam

P.S. The maid will be here at 9am. Please make sure you're gone
before then.

I leave the note on the counter and walk to the entrance, picking up my items, and gently shutting the door behind me. I look down at my phone before getting into my black Range Rover. It's 12:30am. Shit, I'm half tempted to stay with Kelly, but I promised Sarah I would come home tonight, and although I won't get in until nearly 2am, at least, I'll wake up next to her.

More than an hour later, I pull up to our home nestled in the Kalorama neighborhood of D.C. The large brick Tudor house with six bedrooms and three-and-a-half baths is much too large for just Sarah and me, and a bit too ostentatious for my blood. But Sarah fell in love with it the moment she laid her eyes on it. It was the expansive fenced backyard and stunning oversized terrace that made her swoon. I thought for sure when she picked out such a large house it was because she had changed her mind about starting a family. We turned two of the bedrooms into offices, one for her and one for me. A third bedroom was converted into a library-study, a fourth into a gym and the fifth into a guest room. She hadn't changed her mind.

I pull into the courtyard next to Sarah's matching white Range Rover. Entering the house, I pass through the grand foyer with marble flooring, past the sweeping staircase and into the gourmet kitchen. I place my messenger bag on the counter and switch on a light. I get a bottle of water from the fridge and go to the master suite on the second floor. All the lights are off in our bedroom, except for a lamp on Sarah's side of the bed.

I push open the door and find her sleeping heavily on her stomach, completely relaxed. She's wearing a thin black tank top and black lace thong panties, not her typical nighttime attire. I expected to see her in a nightgown. Is she teasing me? Does she want me? Or did she just pass out from one too many vodka sodas, her drink of choice. Her silk-like blond hair is damp and is pulled back into a low ponytail—every strand neatly in place. Even when she's asleep, she's perfectly pulled together. My eyes follow the curve of her back and the smoothness of her toned ass, down her sculpted legs. Over the years, she may have neglected me, but she never ignored that body of hers. She stirs a little but doesn't wake.

By my side of the bed I shuffle off my pants and shirt. My eyes never leave her. She makes me so goddamn miserable, but so blissful at the same time. I fucking hate her as much as I love her. Does she know? Does she care? What am I to her?

I drop my watch on the nightstand a little too hard, and it makes a clunking sound, loud enough to wake her. Her eyes shoot open quickly and then ease when she realizes that it's just me. I expect her to roll over and go back to sleep, but she doesn't. Her eyes tighten, and her lips curve into a small smile. She glances at the alarm clock on my nightstand. 1:45am. She looks back at me but says nothing of my late arrival home. Her eyes beckon me.

"I know. I'm sorry I'm late." I slide into bed beside her.

"Don't be," she whispers patting the spot next to her.

I scoot closer, planting a kiss on her cheek. She makes a cooing sound.

"I've missed you," I say.

She looks up at me as I pull her close, holding her tightly. "I've missed you too."

I kiss her forehead. She pushes closer into me, entangling her legs in mine and resting her head on my bare chest. She runs her fingers up and down my abs.

"How was work?"

"Long," she says.

The silence stretches, and I wonder what it is that she's thinking. Is she mulling over case files in her head? Is she thinking about me? About us? Can she see the cracks in our marriage? Does she want to fix them or keep pretending like they don't exist? Like I don't exist. Like we don't exist.

"Let's have a baby." Her eyes brighten, and she looks up at me, waiting for my reaction. I can't help it. My face lights up, and I grin back at her.

"Are you serious? Are you sure you're really ready? After everything that... well... happened. I thought you'd never want to have kids." I examine her face for any indication that would betray the words coming out of her mouth. I had always hoped she'd want to have children, but I had accepted that that day might never come, given what happened to her...

"Yes." She nods, and I think she means it. I let out a laugh mixed with a cry, and I kiss her. I can't contain my excitement. My hands are all over her and her hands all over me. My lips move down her neck. I pull her black tank top off and kiss every square inch of her breasts and torso. I look up at her, and she smiles as I remove her panties. I kiss and lick and suck until she comes, and then I find my way inside her. She pants and moans beneath me. Her eyes locked on mine, big and full of hope.

"I love you, Sarah."

"I love you too, Adam."

And then I explode inside her. *I'm going to be a father*, I think. A single tear rolls from my eye as I collapse on top of her, breathless and hopeful. I can't do this to her. I have to end it with Kelly. Sarah is my wife, my family, my whole heart. She's done nothing but love me—even when it's at a distance, she has loved me. I roll off but stay lying next to her. I rub her stomach gently. Sarah is the mother of my unborn child. She deserves more, and I'm going to give that to her.

"Thank you," I whisper.

She kisses my forehead and wraps her arms around me hugging me tightly. "I want this for us. I want what you want." She closes her eyes and slowly falls back asleep, cradled in my arms.

5

SARAH MORGAN

A dam sleeps deeply next to me. I smile and run my hand along his face, wondering if I'm doing the right thing. But that's the thing about right and wrong—it's subjective. *He deserves this*, I remind myself as I run my hand over my belly, hoping our efforts took.

I had the epiphany a week ago, and last night when I was having drinks with Anne, it was solidified. I want more out of this life than a title and my name on a building. I want love. I want a family. I want meaning. I slide out of bed covering myself with a white silk robe and tying it loosely at the waist. I glance at my phone finding an unread text from Anne.

Did you make it home okay?

I quickly text back:

Yes. See you soon.

Anne texts:

Sorry for last night.

I recall the moment where it got a bit weird between Anne and me, and I quickly brush it aside.

It's okay. We all do dumb stuff when we're drunk.

A couple of hours later, Anne is greeting me with a cup of coffee and a smile at the office. She's perky... a bit too perky considering how intoxicated she got last night.

"Happy Monday!" She grins.

"Yes, Monday indeed. Is Bob in his office?"

"Unfortunately," she sneers.

"I'll take care of our little Bob situation." I pick up my coffee.

She gives me a nod and takes my bag from me, while I charge toward Bob's office. Bob is two offices down. His is nice but nowhere near as nice as mine. He started here around the same time I did, but unlike him, I made partner, and I know he has a chip on his shoulder about it. I assume that's why he's been trying to steal Anne from me. When we started, he didn't even look at me as competition. Now, he does. I made sure of that. I let myself in without a knock, and I find Bob sitting at his desk eating an egg sandwich without a care in the world. He's average looking with a somewhat sinister tinge to him thanks to his dark eyes and hair, tall height, and sharp jawline.

"Morning, Bob." I take a seat in front of his desk.

He nods straightening himself and setting his sandwich down. "What do I owe the pleasure, Sarah?" There's a twinkle in his mahogany eyes.

"Listen, Bob. You're going to stop asking Anne to run your errands or make copies for you or grab you food at all times of the day. Anne is my assistant and just because you go through assistants like pairs of underwear doesn't mean you get to sniff after mine. Got it, Bob?" I narrow my eyes and crumple my lips.

"Anne is paid for by the firm. She's fair game." He takes another wet bite out of his egg sandwich. He chews and smiles, pleased with himself.

"Actually, you're wrong about that. Part of her salary is paid for by the firm, the other part is paid for by me."

"Ha, that's ridiculous. Why would you do that?" He laughs.

"Because I treat people like actual people."

"What a load." He shakes his head and continues to chew his oversized mouthful.

"Bob, I'll tell you what. There's a partners meeting coming up. If your little assistant stealing games don't stop, I'll recommend that you be let go. We don't need any deadweight around here." I stand, towering over him.

"You're the one that's dead weight." He narrows his eyes.

"Good one, Bob. Look I'm not in the mood for your petty power-play bullshit so just don't mess with me on this and do as you're told for once. Understood?" I take a drink of my coffee.

Bob scoffs at me but doesn't say a word. He tosses the remainder of his egg sandwich in the trash and pounds his fist on his desk. I see myself out of his office and return to my own. Anne is fielding phone calls at her desk. I give her a wink and a nod, and she smiles back. An enormous bouquet of red roses is sitting in a vase on the coffee table. I lean down taking a big whiff. I can't help but smile. I look at the card attached to them. It reads:

Sarah, it's always been you. Love, Adam

"Those are beautiful." Anne stands in the doorway, admiring the flowers.

I set the card down and turn to her. "Thanks, they're from Adam."

"Well, I sure hope they'd be from your husband. Who else would get you flowers? What's the occasion?"

"Oh, nothing. We're just trying for a baby." I give a coy smile.

"What! Oh my God!" Anne practically screams bouncing into the office and hugging me.

"A baby... don't you mean a knick-knack?" a voice from outside my office says. I recognize it immediately. Matthew stands in the doorway, dressed in a J.Crew knit sweater and chino pants. He looks like a skinnier Brad Pitt, replete with dirty blond hair that is messy in a way that can only be achieved via a two-hundred-dollar haircut. He has dull blue eyes that draw you in slowly as opposed to striking you all at once, so you can savor the spell they create.

Matthew sashays across the room to me with all the poise of a runway model. He turns whatever room he is in into a stage. This is how he commands a room. This is why he is paid a king's ransom as a lobbyist for a pharmaceutical company that changes from time to time based on who's paying him the most. Matthew and I have been friends since our days in law school at Yale, but it's been over a year since I last saw him.

"Oh my God!" Without missing a beat, we are wrapped up in each other's arms. "What are you doing here?"

"Just got in yesterday," he says backing up while still holding my hands in the air. "Let me see you." I give him half a twirl. "Still killing it," he compliments.

I look to Anne who is standing a few feet from us, one hand holding her elbow as if she was completely out of place. "You remember my assistant?"

"Of course," Matthew walks to Anne and holds out a hand. "It's Anna, right?"

She nods and shakes his hand.

"No, Matthew. It's Anne, not Anna," I correct. Anne needs to learn to speak up for herself.

"I'm so sorry, Anne. It's great to see you again." He waltzes in and takes a seat in my chair. "Still got the biggest office in the building, I see." He looks around admiring my hard work.

"Would you expect anything less?" I raise an eyebrow.

"No way. Not from Sarah Morgan. But you plan to throw it all away for a knick-knack. Shame." He shakes his head in dismay.

"A knick-knack?" Anne asks taking a couple more steps toward Matthew. She gets as far as my desk before she stops.

"You don't want to know. Don't even get him started," I say with a laugh.

Matthew crosses one leg over the other and leans forward. "I just have this theory that animals and babies are the knick-knacks of our lives. Nice to look at and fun to collect, but they serve no real purpose."

"That's awful," Anne says with disgust.

"But is it?" he asks. "Why add burdens that slow you down? If anything, I am an altruist, looking out for Sarah's best interest."

"I told you, you didn't want to know. I love everything about Matthew except that." I take a seat on my desk next to Matthew. I pat his knee. "It's his only flaw." I laugh.

"And that I'm gay," he adds with a chuckle.

"That's not a flaw."

"It is for you." He winks and proceeds to tickle my side.

"Well, I think it's great that you and Adam are trying for a baby." Anne smiles.

"Is it? Am I crazy?" I look at Anne and Matthew for clarity.

"Yes," Matthew says.

"No way! Why would you say that?" Anne questions.

"I don't know. I've never wanted kids before. My childhood was less than ideal." Matthew nods along to my words. "But it just hit me when I was sitting at this café last week. I saw this woman pushing her baby in a stroller, and I had this pang of jealousy like a need for a child of my own. And now, I think it might be too late," I confess.

"It's never too late. There are fertility programs and adoption." She gives an encouraging smile.

"Let's hope it's too late," Matthew snarks.

I narrow my eyes at him, telling him to stop, while Anne gives him a stern look.

"I'm thirty-three years old. Like, do I even have the energy to be a mom anymore?"

"Are you kidding me? You're like the damn Energizer bunny, Sarah. You keep going and going. You're in here before 7am and leave after 6pm nearly every day—sometimes later. That lucky kid isn't going to have enough energy to keep up with you."

"That is the only thing I can agree with Anne on. You do have a crazy amount of energy," Matthew says. I smile at them both.

I've done so much in my career and have achieved things that most people never will. I've defended crooked politicians, murderers, and money launderers. I run corporate law firm teams, and I've helped build this company from the ground up. But for some reason, despite all I've accomplished, the one thing that scares me is being a mother, something that should come naturally. "Thanks, Anne," I say with sincerity. "No thanks to you, Matthew," I jab.

He dramatically grabs his chest, pretending to be heartbroken.

Anne asks, "What does Adam think of all this?"

"I've never seen him happier."

"Why am I not surprised?" Matthew rolls his eyes.

"What's that supposed to mean?" I push myself off the desk.

"Well, his career has flatlined. So, a kid will make him feel like his life has meaning again. It's the only reason the human race isn't extinct, because people with no purpose breed," he says nonchalantly.

Anne's mouth drops open.

I'm entirely used to Matthew's off-the-wall opinions. I swear he says things just to get a rise out of people, but I've learned to never give him that rise. "What brings you to D.C.?" I ask, ignoring his previous statement.

"Six-month contract here. You'll be seeing a lot of me." He winks.

"Aren't we lucky?" Anne says sarcastically. She'll get used to him.

"Sweetheart, you are." Matthew walks to the bookshelf and starts pulling out random volumes.

Anne tells me she's going to make sure everything is ready for court later this morning. This high-profile case has consumed me for the past year, and I'm hoping that once it's over, I'll be able to focus on Adam. She leaves my office closing the door behind her.

"Finally," Matthew says.

"Stop." I pick up some papers from my desk and shuffle them around.

"I'm just kidding, and I'm totally busting her balls." He takes a seat across from me at my desk.

"I know. I know exactly how you are." I smirk.

"I always test people. If they can't handle me at my worst, they don't deserve me at my best," he says raising his chin.

"But there is no best with you, Matthew."

"That's the secret they find out once it's too late." He laughs. "Now that I'm in town for a while will you have time for me?" He raises an eyebrow.

"You don't even have to ask."

ADAM MORGAN

S arah is gone when I open my eyes. For the first time in a long time, I wake up feeling good—like everything is going to be okay. Sarah finally wants what I want: a family. We're on the same page. All this time, I've been several chapters ahead of her, and now she's caught up. I hope she'll take a step back from the firm and focus on starting a family. I have a feeling what we did last night took, and in nine months we'll be welcoming a baby Morgan to the world. This is what I was meant to be, a father.

I slide out of bed and put on a pair of boxers, balled up beside the nightstand. With a bit of pep in my step, I brush my teeth, rearrange my bedhead, and throw a couple handfuls of water in my face. Today is going to be a good day. It's 11:30am, and I slept in a bit longer than I intended, but it doesn't matter, because today is the first day of the rest of my life.

As I go down the stairs, it hits me like a smack in the face... Kelly. Shit, I shouldn't have done that. I shouldn't have written that note. I should have ended it last night. I run back up the stairs to retrieve my cell phone. Just as I grab it, the doorbell rings. I quickly put on a pair of pants and a T-shirt and slip my phone into my pocket. The doorbell rings again.

"Jesus Christ. I'm coming!"

There are several loud knocks.

"Hold on!" I make my way down the hallway, down the stairs, and to the front door. I swing it open and find two men standing there in matching attire: tan Dickies uniforms, complete with utility belts and wide-brim hats. The looks on their faces are similar, stern and frustrated... or is that disgust or discontent? I can't really tell. I rub my eyes. The one on the left, a tall white male, with a hard jaw and piercing green eyes speaks first.

"I'm Sheriff Ryan Stevens. Are you Adam Morgan?" he asks.

I nod.

The one on the right speaks next, an even taller black man with broad shoulders, and a visage that looks chiseled from stone. "I'm Deputy Marcus Hudson. We need to ask you some questions about your whereabouts yesterday evening."

"What's this about?" I grip the front door with one hand and exchange glances with both the sheriff and his deputy. There are two squad cars parked on the street.

"We just need you to answer a few questions for us," Sheriff Stevens reiterates with a little more sternness and impatience.

I take a step back, still gripping the door. "Well, what's going on?" Confusion spreads across my face as I furrow my brow. I try to remain cool, calm and collected but that's easier said than done when I have no idea why two members of law enforcement are suddenly at my door.

"Maybe this would be easier if we did this back at the station," Sheriff Stevens suggests to me.

"How would that be easier? What the fuck is going on? Is Sarah okay? Did something happen to her?" My first thought goes to Sarah, always. She's a high-profile lawyer with a number of enemies due to the nature of her job. She's had death threats in the past. She's been harassed, and once she was physically assaulted. I know she's been working on a big case, although I'm not sure of the details. Because I never really asked her about it. I should have.

"Mr. Morgan. Try and remain calm," Sheriff Stevens says.

"Fuck this. I'm calling my wife." I pull my phone from my pocket and try to throw the door closed. Sheriff Stevens stops it with his foot, and he and Deputy Hudson push inside.

"Get the hell out of my house!"

The two men in uniform charge forward and grab me. They throw both my arms behind my back. My cell phone drops to the floor just before I complete my call. I struggle. I know whenever you see people struggling against the cops, you always think as a spectator, *What an idiot. Don't fight the police. You'll never win that battle.* But when you find yourself in that situation, when you have no idea what's going on, whether the ones you love are okay, or why this is happening... You fight like hell.

I throw Sheriff Stevens to the ground and get my arm free. The sheriff mumbles something like "You dick" under his breath and stands back up, charging at me. Deputy Hudson still has one of my hands behind my back.

"All right, I've had enough of this bullshit." Deputy Hudson brings his knee into my face. I drop instantly to the ground. Blood sprays from my nose into a puddle beneath me on the floor. Deputy Hudson drives his knee into my back, while the sheriff handcuffs me.

"You just had to do that, didn't you?" Sheriff Stevens says with a chuckle and a look of disappointment.

"I miss getting a little dirty," Deputy Hudson says with a grin, I assume, as I can't see his face.

Deputy Hudson stands up, brushing himself off. They pull

me to my knees. "Are you ready to come down to the station now, you piece of shit?"

I spit blood at his feet. "Fuck you... you're gonna regret that." I glare at him.

"I doubt that," he says. "Now, you have the right to remain silent..."

~

Two hours later I find myself alone in a small interrogation room with a stale cup of coffee on the table in front of me. A large one-way mirror is on the wall to my left. I drop my head into my hands. My foot taps the floor with fervor as my patience has worn thin.

"I want my phone call," I scream within the empty room. "I want my fucking phone call!"

The door opens, and Sheriff Stevens and Deputy Hudson enter carrying Styrofoam cups of coffee.

Sheriff Stevens sets a bottle of water in front of me. "Thirsty?"

I pick up the water, chug it, and crunch up the empty bottle. I toss it into a trash can by the door. They take their time settling into their chairs across from me. They give each other a glance as they casually sip their coffee. They're trying to look calm, but their clenched jaws and strained eyes give away the fact that they're pissed off.

"I want my phone call." I still have no idea why I'm here. These assholes roughed me up a bit and threw me into the back of a squad car. I haven't been charged with anything, and I've been sitting in this room for over an hour. I don't know if Sarah is okay. I don't know how I'm involved in any of this.

"Mr. Morgan—can I call you Adam?" Sheriff Stevens asks, as if we're on a first-name basis, as if he's trying to be personable with me. These fucking backwoods pieces of shit. I'm tired of this, and I just want to know what the hell is going on, so I nod with no enthusiasm.

"Good. Well, you can call me Ryan and this guy," he pats the deputy on the back, "you can call him Marcus. Now, we're here to ask you a few questions, and hopefully, you'll decide to cooperate with our investigation—unlike earlier. Do you understand?"

I take a deep breath and rub my forehead with my hands, trying to soothe the headache I have coming on. "Yeah."

"Excellent. Now, can you tell us where you were last night?" Sheriff Stevens asks.

My eyes dart around the room. "I was at my lake house over on Lake Manassas until around midnight. Then, I drove home."

They nod. Deputy Hudson pulls a notepad and a pen from his shirt pocket and begins jotting down notes. "Were you alone at the lake house?"

"No."

"Who were you with?"

"What's this got to do with anything? I want my lawyer right now. I'm not answering anything else until I know what's going on and why the hell I'm here." I stand up, kicking back my chair and shaking the table. The cups of coffee spill and two other deputies immediately charge into the interrogation room, restraining me.

Deputy Hudson stands quickly flinging his chair back. He charges at me, grabbing me by the neck. His eyes bulge, and his lips purse as he comes within two inches of my face. "Listen up, you little shit! Kelly Summers was stabbed to death in your bed. Perhaps you want to start telling us what really happened, because, with the amount of evidence stacked against you, your days are fucking numbered." He pushes me against the wall as Sheriff Stevens pulls him off telling him to cool it.

"I'm not going to fucking cool it. Kelly was a good girl. She was family, and this white-collar piece of shit comes into our town and kills her. Fuck this guy," Deputy Hudson spits. Drops of sweat accumulate at his hairline.

"Wha— what are you talking about? Kelly? She was fine when I left," I sputter, choking on my own words. "How? How did this happen?" I collapse. The room spins and spins. The deputies let me fall to the ground as they take a step back.

Who would hurt Kelly? The text messages from her husband. I recall them, each more menacing than the last and full of threats. It had to have been him. "Her husband. It had to have been her husband. Check her phone. Check her texts," I plead —trying to put all the pieces together, trying to make sense of it.

"Don't you fucking talk about her husband!" Deputy Hudson points his finger right in my face.

Sheriff Stevens pushes him away from me. He turns back toward me. "We're looking at all angles, but like the deputy eloquently said, this isn't looking good for you."

"I would never hurt Kelly. I-I-I couldn't. I loved her." I drop my head into my hands.

"That's great," Sheriff Stevens says with a hint of sarcasm. "Why don't you follow one of these deputies and go call your wife?"

7

SARAH MORGAN

I stand and take a quick, small breath. I look back at Matthew and Anne. They're sitting front row, and they both give me an encouraging smile. I nod slightly at them, adjust the lapels on my jacket, and walk toward the jury box. Before I begin, I make eye contact with each juror.

"Senator McCallan has worked in public service for over twenty-five years. In twenty-five years not once," I hold up a single finger on my right hand to highlight my point, "has his character or professionalism come into question. We paraded character witnesses before you, proving that very sentiment. Not once has he taken a payout. Not once has he disparaged another person, used his power for his own benefit, or caved on his principles."

I put my hand on my defendant's shoulder. "He is one of the rare shining beacons of public servitude in a swamp of lies, corruption, and under-the-table deals. It is this same exemplary service that has led him to the situation he is in today, for he is guilty of one thing... not backing down." I pass him a quick reassuring look and walk back to the jury box.

"Senator McCallan is now leading the sub-committee on

renewable energy, an effort praised by both pundits and the American people, but not by—you guessed it—big oil." I point to the two men on the public benches wearing beautiful bespoke suits, topped off by garish but equally expensive jeweled bolo ties. I pass through the swinging door between the prosecution and defendant tables and stand in the aisle next to them. "This was the one man they feared in this position. The one man they knew they couldn't brush under the carpet with a quick payout. The one man they wouldn't be able to go dig dirt up on and blackmail into silence."

I walk back toward the jury, pausing at the prosecution table, "So, what did they do? They created their own." I delicately point to the lead witness. The woman who this all started from. This part I'll need to be careful with.

"We should not be mad at this woman for her false accusations. We should not be mad at this woman for trying to drag Senator McCallan down into the mud," I pass her a sympathizing look, trying to convey that I truly mean this part, "because she is just a pawn in the game, not the puppet master. We have proven her ties to high-ranking employees at PetroNext, we found the 'secret' wire transfers to her 'brand new' bank account, and, ladies and gentlemen of the jury, if this isn't just a good ol' fashioned payout-for-a-smear play, then I don't know what is. We sympathize with her, truly we do. But you should also see this for what it is. Fake. Pure fiction. False accusations trumped up in desperation to bring down the one man they didn't know how to bribe and twist the way they wanted. My client is guilty of many things, fighting for the American people, staying true to his word, being a man of noble character. But raping this young woman? For that, he is unequivocally not guilty, and I urge you to find him as such. Thank you."

8

ADAM MORGAN

Sheriff Stevens escorts me to a pay phone hung on the wall in the center of a long corridor. Deputy Hudson is only a few steps behind the sheriff, watching my every move.

"Make it quick," Sheriff Stevens commands as he stops in the doorway.

I pick up the phone and hold it to my ear, closing my eyes for a moment and taking a deep breath. How can I tell her what's happened? How could I have done this to her?

I open my eyes and dial Sarah's cell phone number.

The phone rings and rings and then her voice is there. But it's her voicemail. I consider leaving a message but decide I can't tell her I cheated on her and I'm now a suspect for my mistress's murder over voicemail. I turn my back toward Sheriff Stevens and Deputy Hudson. They're chatting while keeping an eye on me.

"Hurry up, Mr. Morgan," Deputy Hudson says.

I wave my hand at him dismissively. I redial Sarah. She doesn't pick up. *Damn it*. I pull the receiver hook down, and this time I dial a different number.

"Hello," Eleanor says with apprehension.

"Mom... I'm in trouble. I need your help."

9

SARAH MORGAN

I take a sip of my Bollinger champagne, which I seriously earned after that case. For nearly a year, I worked nights and weekends and traveled back and forth to Texas. Anne is nibbling at naan bread, and Matthew is happily drinking his vodka martini.

"I must say, Sarah. I am impressed. I have not seen you in action since mock trials at Yale." Matthew holds up his glass. "To Sarah's sharp tongue." Anne and I hold up our champagne flutes. We all clink and drink.

"Watching her in action is literally my favorite part of the job. It's like watching the climax of a *Law & Order* episode," Anne says with a laugh and a hiccup. She doesn't drink much, so one or two glasses usually gets her going. She pats the corners of her mouth with a napkin and goes back to eating her bread to soak up some of the excess alcohol.

"But are you really going to go through with the knick-knack and give up the thrill of law?" Matthew scrunches his eyes while taking a bite of rice.

"I'm not going to give up law. I can do both." I raise an eyebrow to him.

"You sure about that?" His eyebrow matches mine.

"Yes." I drink the rest of my champagne and refill my glass.

He lets out a huff. "Fine. Fine. Fine. It appears I'll be Uncle Matthew after all. Someone is going to need to teach that fetus to be fabulous." He brings his vodka martini to his lips. "Should I order shots to celebrate?"

"You're bad," Anne teases.

"Oh, he's..." My phone rings interrupting me. I pull it out, and on the screen, in all caps, it says ELEANOR. Immediately, there's a lump in the back of my throat, and I swallow hard to force it down. I don't want to deal with her now, and I almost don't answer it, but something in my gut urges me to take the call.

"Sarah Morgan," I say in an overly professional tone in an attempt to convey my importance to her.

"Sarah, Adam's been trying to call you. Why didn't you answer my son's calls?" There is irritation and frustration in Eleanor's voice. What else is new?

"I was in court."

"Oh yes, I forgot you worked."

I roll my eyes. "What do you mean you forgot? Adam hasn't written a book in four years. Who do you think...?" I decide to not even finish the sentence as there's no point. She has always hated the fact that I work. I've never been sure if it's resentment or her credence in traditional and outdated gender roles.

"It's neither here nor there. Adam needs you. He's at the Prince William County Sheriff's Station."

Anne mouths, "Are you okay?" I nod.

Matthew sips at a fresh martini the waitress just delivered.

"Wait, what? In Virginia? What happened? Is he okay?" My thoughts blend into one another as if they had just been thrown into a Vitamix.

48

"I'm not sure. But it's serious, and you need to g
trying to catch a flight tonight or tomorrow."

Anne sets her fork down listening intently. Matthew
closer.

"Okay. I'll go right now." My voice becomes panicked.

The phone line cuts out. I freeze not knowing what to do.
What could have happened? I just saw him this morning. But in
my experience, everything can change in a moment.

"Sarah. What's going on?" Anne asks pulling me from my
frozen state.

"That was Adam's mom. He... needs me. I-I have to go." I
stand up putting my black suit jacket on.

"I'll come with you." Matthew stands.

I nod, but I'm on autopilot. I don't know what I'm doing. I'm
just doing it. I slip my phone into my Hermes tote bag. Before I
take off, I place three hundred-dollar bills on the table for lunch.

"I can get this." Anne tries to hand me back the money.

"No. Just finish up and go back to the office. I'm sure it's
nothing. I'm sure everything's fine, and I'll be back in a couple of
hours." In my gut, I know it's not okay. Things may never be the
same again.

"Okay. I'll cancel your meetings for the day and please don't
worry about anything at the office. Just take care of whatever is
going on and keep me updated."

I bite my lip and nod. Matthew and I rush out of the
restaurant.

It's an hour later that I find myself face to face with a man by
the name of Sheriff Ryan Stevens. He matches the rough
description of millions of men on this planet. Sandy brown hair
kept high and tight in typical, ex-military-turned-police fashion
adorns his head, sitting just north of his intense green eyes.
These eyes have seen a lifetime of experience already and show
as much fatigue as the rest of his face. The detail that I notice

...ough, is how he carries himself. This is a man in
...is a man who cares about his work; and this is a man
...e crossed. Despite the lethargy and years of abuse to his
... by his line of work, his spirit is matched by none, even
...puties half his age.

I'm seated across from him in a small, disorganized office.
Matthew is waiting for me in reception. I wanted him in here
with me, but not until I knew what was going on. I still am
unclear, and I have yet to see Adam, but I've been assured that
he is all right and that I will be able to speak with him after I've
talked to the sheriff regarding the incident my husband was
involved in.

"Mrs. Morgan, thank you for your patience," Sheriff Stevens
says.

"Sarah is fine."

"Ryan is fine as well." There's a bit of snark in his voice, but
there's kindness in his eyes. Whether that kindness is for me or
not, I don't know.

"What is going on?" I cross one leg over the other, leaning
back in my chair.

"I need to ask you a few questions before you see Adam."

"Okay."

"Was Adam with you last night?"

I take a moment to think of the night before. I came home
late from going out with Anne. But Adam came home later than
me. He said he had been at the lake house writing, which is the
norm. He goes there to write frequently and stays there for days
at a time. It was one of the main reasons we had gotten the lake
house. He was having trouble for the longest time putting words
on paper, and when he came to me with the idea of buying a
vacation home close enough for him to work at, but far enough
out of the city for us to vacation to, I was on board right away. It
was the perfect solution. Although I've rarely been there. Anne's

spent more time there than I have. She spent a week t̄
past summer as a part of her Christmas bonus, one wee.
time off at my lake house. It was nice she had the opportun.
use it for what we had intended it for—vacation. Work kept r.
too busy to take frequent weekend trips, but it turned Adam's
writing around. He's been churning out pages like never before.

"Yes, at some point," I finally land on.

"And what point was that?"

I pause trying to think over my answer carefully.

"Well, I had fallen asleep. But I woke up around 2am and he
was there. He could have been home for much longer."

Sheriff Stevens nods and jots down a few words on a pad of
paper in front of him. He glances up at me and then writes down
a couple more words. He chews on the end of his pen and
glances at me again—this time, running his eyes over my body.
"And that's at your home in D.C., correct?"

"Yes."

"What happened after he got home?"

"We talked." I let out a small cough. "And we had sex." I
know something terrible has happened. This is an interrogation,
and there's no sense in holding any information back. Adam
couldn't have done anything wrong, so honesty is the only thing
that is going to make this all go away, whatever this is.

"Is that usual for you two?"

"A husband and a wife having sex, Sheriff Stevens?"

"No, you and Adam?"

"What does this have to do with anything?" I'm irritated, and
I'm done playing games with this small-minded sheriff. I tear
apart men like him every day. I may be here as Adam's wife, but I
am a defense attorney.

The sheriff taps his pen against the desk. He's waiting for me
to speak as he has no intention of answering my question. He's
trying to get an understanding of Adam's and my relationship,

What could he think Adam has done? Sure, we don't
.ne perfect marriage, but who does? And why is it any of
.usiness?

"We're trying for a baby," I say not actually answering his
question, but side-stepping it. If he doesn't answer my questions,
I won't answer his.

"Congratulations." There's a hint of sarcasm in his voice.

"Are we done?"

"No, Mrs. Morgan. Do you know a Kelly Summers?"

"No." I let out a deep breath. *Maybe she's our cleaning lady?
No, that's not her name.* I shake my head adding to my resounding
no.

He nods and underlines something on his notepad. He
selects a file folder from a stack of papers and pulls out an 8x10
photo, placing it in front of me. It's a picture of a beautiful girl
with long brown hair and sparkling blue eyes. She's smiling.
She's younger—probably late twenties. She is a stark contrast to
Sheriff Stevens, where he is serious, worn down, on a mission;
she is carefree, letting life take her as it wants.

"This is Kelly Summers. Are you sure you don't know her?"

I pull the photo a little closer and lean in really taking it in.
Her beauty is truly captivating. Her freckles spread lightly along
her nose, her lips are full, and her cheekbones are prominent.

"I don't know her." I push the photo back toward him. He
nods, taking the picture and putting it back in the folder.

"Are you and Adam having marital problems?" He taps his
fingers on the desk.

"You know what, Sheriff Stevens? This is getting ridiculous. I
don't know what Adam and I have to do with this Kelly woman,
and I've had enough. I want to see my husband right now." I'm
half standing when Sheriff Stevens slams his hand on the desk.

"Sit down!"

"Or what? You'll arrest me? Take me to my husband." I stare him down. Although he is large, he is so small to me.

He flips open the folder and throws a dozen crime scene photos on the desk. Right away, I notice that they've all been taken in our lake house. A woman is lying in our bed, covered in blood. Her eyes are expressionless. Her torso and chest are mutilated, skin gouged and scraped. I drop my purse, and my hands immediately cover my mouth as I let out a gasp and a whimper.

I drop to the side of the desk regurgitating a bit of my lunch into my mouth. The acid burns as I try to force it back down, but this only makes my eyes well up with tears even more.

And then it hits me. Now I know why I'm here.

I feel a pat on my back. It's Sheriff Stevens. He's trying to calm me down.

"I'm sorry." He hands me a Kleenex and keeps his hand on my back. I stand facing him, though my legs are a bit wobbly beneath me. I wipe my mouth and pat at my eyes, trying to compose myself. This isn't like me. I don't break down. I'm strong. He asks me if I'm okay and I nod. Where I once was just trying to figure out why I was here, I now need to go into lawyer mode, because this "kind and simple" sheriff routine is really the work of a seasoned pro, watching, calculating.

There's a knock on the door. Sheriff Stevens keeps a hand on my shoulder—still trying to play nice. I close my eyes and take a deep breath. I regain control of my breathing and attempt to compose myself.

The door opens, and I turn to find a tall black man in similar clothing as Sheriff Stevens. His eyes are cold, bloodshot, and they do not meet mine. He says, "He wants his lawyer."

Sheriff Stevens nods. "Marcus, this is Sarah, Adam's wife. This is Deputy Hudson." I shake his hand.

His eyes bounce off me. There's a rage in them. "Should I let him call his lawyer?"

Before Sheriff Stevens can speak, I interrupt. "There's no need."

"Why?" they both ask in unison giving each other a puzzled look.

"I'm his lawyer."

10

ADAM MORGAN

I've seen the crime photos. I know what they think I did. My poor Kelly. How could this have happened? I was right there with her the whole night, but I didn't do this. I tried to explain repeatedly about her abusive husband, and they kept saying they were looking at all angles, but it seems they've already picked their fucking angle.

I hope my mom was able to get ahold of Sarah, though I don't know how I'm even going to face her. Things were just looking up for us. I was going to end it with Kelly once and for all. I was going to be a good husband again, the one that Sarah deserves. But most importantly I was going to be a father—oh God. The baby? What if she's pregnant? What if the baby grows up without a father? I can't let that happen; I have to get out of this. I need to be there for my child.

Deputy Hudson questioned me for the past hour and a half. Another officer stood guard, which was for the best—because I thought for sure Deputy Hudson was going to kill me or at least try. I don't know how he knows Kelly, but I'm sure he does. He finally left me alone and scurried out when I refused to answer any more questions. I demanded my lawyer. I should have asked for one right away.

This is bad. This is really bad. They found Kelly in my home, stabbed to death. My fingerprints are going to be all over the place, all over her. We had rough sex and the note I left... Now that I think about it, it doesn't look good. It doesn't look good at all. But the texts from her husband are undeniable. There's something there. They'll have to investigate him because there's no way they could ever believe that I would do this. I couldn't. I wouldn't. Kelly and I had a great time, and I loved her. She was there when I needed someone. I would never hurt her, but her husband would and has.

I stand up and pound on the one-way mirror, tears stream down my crumpled face.

"Get me my fucking lawyer!" I pick up a chair and throw it at the mirror. It bounces off and hits the ground.

11

SARAH MORGAN

Sheriff Stevens escorts me into a small room with a one-way mirror through which we can observe Adam. He's visibly shaken, sitting at the table tapping his fingers, fighting back the tears, and contemplating.

"Have a seat." Sheriff Stevens gestures to a chair.

I composed myself in the bathroom prior. I'm no longer here as Adam's wife. I'm his lawyer. I'm Sarah Morgan, top criminal defense attorney. I must remind myself of that every minute or so. I have to be the strong and proficient woman I am. I know Adam didn't do this. I honestly can't believe that he would even be capable of hitting someone, let alone killing a person. But I also thought he would never cheat on me and, as the sheriff's investigation shows, he has been—for at least a year, with this Kelly woman. I shake my head in disgust thinking about it. I can't believe it. I don't believe it yet. Not until Adam admits it to me. He couldn't have done any of this.

I pull a notepad and a pen from my purse and look to Sheriff Stevens. "Just tell me the facts of the case."

"Are you sure you want to hear this?"

"Yes, don't spare any details."

He gives me a sympathetic look and nods. I'm sure by now, he knows exactly who I am. When I walked out of that bathroom, Sheriff Stevens had a new respect for me. I'm sure he Googled me and found that I was not just some lowly housewife. He looked at me with compassion and admiration. Maybe he thinks I'm crazy to stand behind Adam. But Adam is my husband.

"The victim's name is Kelly Summers. Age twenty-seven. She was found this morning at approximately 9:15am by a cleaning woman by the name of Sonia. Kelly was found dead in bed at Adam and..." he coughs. "I guess your bed at a lake house in Prince William County. She had been stabbed thirty-seven times in the neck, chest, and torso. Due to how gruesome this murder was, it would appear it was a crime of passion. There are no defensive wounds, which tells us that she was asleep when it occurred. Her eyes were open when she was found, which tells us that she had awoken during the stabbing.

"A toxicology report is being done, and we believe she had drugs in her system, which would explain why she didn't wake right away. A preliminary autopsy found semen in her mouth, vagina, and anus. There is bruising on her right shoulder, but that appears to have been caused at least a day or two before. She has a couple of small tears in her anus and vagina, which would insinuate rape or rough sex. They found skin under her fingernails," he finishes. He looks away, then back at me.

I finish jotting down the notes and look at him, "Is that everything?"

"That's all we have as of now." Our eyes meet, and I can see that he feels sorry for me. I can see how uncomfortable he is. I can see him questioning why in the hell I am defending Adam. The look I give back is a look of strength and vulnerability. I don't know why I'm doing this. A loud bang on the glass pulls my attention away from Sheriff Stevens.

Adam is pounding on the other side of the one-way mirror. He seizes a chair and throws it. It bounces off and hits the ground with a thud. He screams and then collapses to the floor in a puddle of anguish.

I turn back to Sheriff Stevens. My mouth drops open and my eyes widen. I've never seen Adam react like that. I've never seen him do more than raise his voice. I've never seen him this enraged. Maybe he could be violent.

He comes across less like a confused man in the wrong situation, and more like a wild animal backed into a corner, capable of anything to claw its way out. I see a fire in Adam's eyes that I didn't know existed. To be honest, before this moment, if someone had asked me if I thought Adam was capable of murder, I would have quickly said no. Deep down, I thought he was a bit of a pussy. But now I see that I was wrong. Lurking beneath the surface is something else, something more.

"I need to see my client."

Sheriff Stevens nods. "Just so you know, we just got a warrant to search both homes and pull DNA. We're also looking at conducting a polygraph test if Adam is cooperative. But I'll give you some time to speak to him."

"Okay." I stand up and collect my things. Before I pull the door open, I turn back to the sheriff. He is inches from me, and I can feel the warmth of his breath. "Thank you, Sheriff Stevens."

He gives me a nod and tells me that he'll be outside the room and that he'll send someone in for the DNA testing in twenty minutes. I close my eyes and take a deep breath, reassuring myself that I can do this.

12

ADAM MORGAN

The door opens, and I pull myself off the floor and stand up. As soon as I see her, I almost collapse again. She's beautiful. Dressed in a black pencil skirt that hugs her hips in all the right ways, a white form-fitting blouse and a tailored jacket. Every strand of her blond hair is in place, wrapped in a bun at the nape of her neck. As per usual, her pouty lips and green eyes draw me in, and it's her eyes that almost cause me to lose it. They're slightly red, and there's a small smear of black mascara. She's been crying. I've never seen her cry. What the fuck did I do?

"Sarah. I'm so sor—"

She holds up her hand stopping me. She gestures me to take a seat in the most formal of ways. I pick up my chair from the floor and place it upright. There's no sense in arguing. I didn't kill Kelly, but I did cause this. I caused all of this. I take a seat, folding my hands in front of me and hanging my head.

Sarah takes a small breath and approaches the table, her black heels clicking along the floor. Everything she does is with purpose. She is trying to hold it all together. She sets her bag down on the table and pulls out her chair slowly. With complete composure, she takes a seat. She runs one hand over her hair and takes another small breath. Her eyes are the same eyes I've always looked at, but she's looking at me as if she doesn't know me. Her gaze dances around me. She's assessing me, questioning me. She's treating me like I'm... a client.

"Sarah." There's a little aggression in my voice. I don't mean it, but I don't like the way she's looking at me. How can she even question that I would do something like this? How can she act like she doesn't know who I am? I'm her husband.

She pulls out a notepad and a pen. She sets them on the table, neatly, parallel to one another. She places her hands on her lap and looks directly at me. "Adam." She pauses. She's choosing her words with care, and I don't know why she can't just talk to me.

"Sarah. I didn't do this. I didn't kill her, I swear it. I couldn't do it. I was sleeping with her, but I would never hurt her—you have to believe me," I plead while fighting back tears.

She doesn't flinch. She doesn't react. "Okay." She jots down a couple of words. Her eyes well up. She swallows hard. She's so strong, and I'm the one breaking her. I'm supposed to be the one protecting her. Her chest rises and falls.

"Sarah, I love you. I love you so fucking much. I just want this to be over. I want things to go back to the way they were. I want to start a family with you. I want to be with you and only you. I'm an idiot, and I should never have cheated. I know that, and I promise I will spend the rest of my life making it up to you —just as soon as this is all over. I swear to fucking God." I grab her hand wanting her to show me some sort of emotion, wanting her to love me, wanting her to yell at me or hit me or something. I need her to be mad at me. I need her to cry. I need her to tell me she loves me. I need her to hold me. I need her to tell me everything is going to be okay.

She pauses. Her hand is warm, but her eyes are cold. She's

hurting, and I don't blame her. She pulls her hand away. "Adam, I need you to understand, I am here as your lawyer, not your wife."

I stare at her in disbelief. "Why are you defending me? After what I did to you?"

"Because when I said 'til death do us part' I meant it and I'm the only person that has any chance in hell of getting you off." There's ice in her voice and rightfully so.

I drop eye contact. I can't look at her. How could I do this? How could I get us to this point? "I'm sorry." I let out a soft sob.

She puts pen to paper and gives me a stern look. "I need you to tell me everything... every single detail. Do not leave anything out. Do you understand?"

I nod. I don't know how I'm going to do this. I should just tell her that I'll get a different lawyer, but she's right—she's the best, and she's my only shot at getting out of this. From what Deputy Hudson told me, the evidence is stacked against me. He said I'll for sure fry, and he'll be happy to see me pay for this crime. They'll find my semen in Kelly. They'll find my fingerprints and DNA all over her. They'll discover texts and phone calls and meet-ups that go back over a year.

"When did you two first meet?"

"About a year and a half ago."

"And how did you meet?"

I close my eyes and take a deep breath, remembering that warm summer day—the day Kelly entered my life.

13

ADAM MORGAN

It was the beginning of summer, and we had just purchased the lake house a few weeks before. Sarah was supposed to come down for the weekend to help me get the finishing touches on the house, but work kept her in the city like it had the previous two weekends. It was late morning when a caffeine headache kicked in. I had just finished unpacking my office and found there was no coffee in the house, so I decided to go for a walk. I hadn't met anyone in town yet, and it seemed everyone pretty much kept to themselves in typical elitist, D.C. suburban transplant fashion. I picked up my laptop and my bag and walked the ten minutes into town.

The town is ablaze with the dichotomy of the area—a mix of rustic Virginia charm and all the trappings of your standard one-percenter needs. Large oak and juniper trees engulf the town's perimeter, a sea of green paused only by the economic center. That day, the old cracked asphalt streets looked almost wet in the morning heat.

The contrasts are poetic in their sadness. A small quaint church sits only a block away from a franchise commercial banking spot. Little mom and pop businesses, laundry service, diners, gift shops, stand shoulder to shoulder with chain pizza joints, Starbucks, and designer clothing stores. The modernization looks less like progress, and more like a virus that has infected the town.

I finally found a small café called Seth's Coffee. It had just the small-town unique charm I was looking for. Hardwood flooring that creaked loudly as you walked across it. Mismatched furniture, ranging from hardwood chairs and carved driftwood tables to steel diner chairs with bright red plastic-covered vinyl seating. None of the dishes were a part of a set, and the menu was written over the counter on an old blackboard that looked like it had been commandeered from a nearby schoolhouse. Colorful chalk covered the random spots on the wall, which shared the space with photographs, paintings, and sculptures all from local artists, price tags included.

Nothing matched or paired together, and in that wild miasma of clashing, everything worked, and it was utterly beautiful. Or at least I thought it was until that beauty and charm were put to shame when I saw her, Kelly. She caught my eye immediately. It was the light of the uncovered hanging light bulbs playing off the sparkle of her blue eyes and her carefree attitude that grabbed me like two strong hands around my throat, and it wouldn't let go.

She was working the patio, so I decided to take a seat out there. Every fiber of my being just wanted to know her, who she was, what she liked, what made her... her. I didn't just want to be in her presence, I needed it.

I pulled out my laptop and began typing. What I wrote was a description of her. I watched her every movement, bouncing around from table to table, taking care of the needs of every patron. I waited for my turn. She was captivating, every part of her. Maybe it was the loneliness that made her much more appealing or perhaps it was that she seemed nothing like Sarah.

Sarah is a calculating, a type-A personality through and through. Sarah is always put together, no matter where she is or how she is dressed, whether in pajamas or in a $2,000 business suit on her way into work. But then there was Kelly, imperfectly perfect. Her freckles splattered across her face. Her long brown hair flowing around her shoulders in the warm summer breeze. She occasionally tried to tame it, but as soon as she waited on tables, she, for the most part, would let it do its thing, while she did hers. Her apron was haphazardly tied around her tiny waist. Her breasts were full and uncaged under her white tee. Her nipples were prominent and slightly visible, but she didn't care. She carried herself most unapologetically, smiling and laughing around the patio area.

Finally, she was standing right in front of me. I hadn't met her, but I felt like I already knew her. That's what watching someone for some time will do. Her face lit up with the sun shining down on her from behind. Her short skirt grazed the side of the table as she swayed her hips.

"Hey, what can I get for you?" Her voice was light and airy.

I stared into her eyes, and it was then I noticed that the same sadness I had in me, she had in her. I've always believed the eyes cannot lie. They hold the truths we are unable or unwilling to speak. Her eyes full, large, and bursting with pain. But pain from what? Her smile faded a bit as she waited for me to speak. She stared back into my eyes, and I like to think she recognized the hurt and loneliness in mine.

"I can give you a few more minutes," she said. Her voice had lost some of its lightness in those few seconds.

"No, no." I smiled at her, letting her know from this point on things were going to be all right. Maybe she didn't know what that smile meant to me, but I knew I would soon make her understand what it meant. She smiled back.

"I'll have a cup of coffee... black."

"You got it!" The lightness in her voice had returned.

"I'm Adam." I held out my hand to shake hers. She looked down at it and then reached hers out to shake mine with only the slightest bit of hesitation. I noticed the band on her ring finger, and she noticed mine. We stared at each other's hands for seconds, our eyes met, and there was a sense of understanding between us.

"I'm Kelly." Her smile spread even wider, and then she was off to fetch me my coffee. I stayed there all morning. It was an hour later that she asked me what I was working on. I told her in detail about my writing. It was two hours later that I learned about her life, her upbringing, her hopes, her dreams. It was three hours later that she took her break. She sat with me and chatted, and it was then that she told me about him, Scott, her husband.

Her description of him was laced with dark undertones. I mean she was sitting there with another man—me—opening up. Clearly, something wasn't right. But she spoke and spoke about how they had met. She nearly described it as a fairy tale. Girl meets boy. Boy and girl fall in love. Boy and girl marry young. Boy and girl live happily ever after... but then girl opens up to a mysterious man in a café. Something wasn't adding up. It was the cracks in her voice that gave it away. Scott had hurt her. She didn't need to tell me that for me to know.

Four hours later, I was packing up my laptop. I had drunk several cups of coffee and eaten a light lunch. Kelly had returned to my table to chat several other times. Our conversations had turned from our personal lives to the small town, the weather, the work I was doing on the lake house. The connection between us that felt strong that morning, had weakened by afternoon. Kelly seemed to have put her guard up, and I was ready to walk away. It was silly of me to get wrapped up in this idea of Kelly and me saving each other. Saving me from a dull marriage and an inattentive wife, and me saving her from Scott, a man who had hurt her in some way.

I started walking out of the café, and she stopped me by calling my name. I turned around. There she stood untying her apron, folding it up, and putting it in her purse. She slid on a pair of sunglasses, threw her bag on her shoulder, and took a few steps toward me. "I think I have to come see this house you've been talking my ear off about." Her voice was low. The patio had cleared out and was now empty.

"I think you do too," I said with a smile.

Kelly signaled me to start walking with a slight nod, and I did. She followed a few steps behind the whole way. We crossed paths with no one in the town, and when I closed the door to the lake house, she jumped into my arms. We ripped at each other's clothes and fucked right there on the floor of the living room, on the bearskin rug, in front of the unlit fireplace. We fucked three times that afternoon. She couldn't get enough of me, and I couldn't get enough of her. Like heroin, she was addicting right from the first taste, the first high—and I never came down from that high—until today.

14

SARAH MORGAN

I don't flinch when he tells me the details of how they met and fucked within four hours. I'm not here as his wife. I'm not here to judge him. I'm here to defend him. I'll react when I can—when it doesn't affect the case. Right now, I must listen. I simply take notes. I make eye contact with him sporadically, and I find he has a difficult time meeting my eyes. I'm not surprised. He's been lying to me for the past sixteen months. He's been fucking another woman. If he could lie to me for this long maybe he could kill. No, I have to stop thinking like that. It won't do him any good.

"You met Kelly Summers sixteen months ago at her place of employment, Seth's Coffee?"

He nods.

"And you fucked... I'm sorry had sex with her the first day you met?"

"Yes." He pauses. "I'm sorry, Sarah." He tries to reach for my hand, but I pull away.

"This isn't the time." I straighten my papers, aligning all the edges perfectly. It's what I do when I don't know what to do. I tidy. I clean things up.

68

He leans back in his chair and slides his hands down his face, pulling at his skin that seems to have paled from lack of sleep, grief, and stress. His eyes are bloodshot, and a five-o'clock shadow has taken up residence on his face. Despite what he has done and his appearance, he is still handsome to me. I can see why Kelly couldn't resist him. I couldn't resist him either.

"Did your relationship with Kelly continue regularly?"

"Yes, we saw each other several times a week, and she spent many nights at the lake house." He lets out a deep breath.

"And you mentioned her husband, Scott. What do you know about him?"

Adam sits up straight. A sense of hope and anger appears in his eyes. I can tell before he even starts speaking, he hates this man and he wholeheartedly believes it was this man that killed Kelly.

"He's not a good person. I know he had to have something to do with this. He was abusive. He threatened her. He hurt her, and I think he knew about us—" he says in a fury.

I cut him off. "Why do you think he knew about you and Kelly? Did you ever have any interactions with him?"

"Because of the texts from that night. He threatened her. He said he knew she was lying. He said he would hurt her."

I jot down a few notes about Scott.

"If he threatened Kelly, that could help us with reasonable doubt and could give us a person to point the finger at. An abusive husband is very fitting. I've seen it a hundred times in my cases. If he had the means and the opportunity, it's an easy win," I say.

Adam's eyes light up. "Really?"

"Yes, but let's not get ahead of ourselves. That's one avenue we can pursue... now, did you ever meet Scott?"

"No—but I didn't have to to know what type of man he was." Adam clenches his jaw and tightens his eyes.

"And what type of man is that?" I bite at the end of my pen.

"A bad one."

"And what does that make you?" My eyes narrow.

Adam's expression goes from pure anger to one of guilt.

"I'm sorry. I shouldn't have said that." I pause for a moment glancing down at my notes and then back at him. "This is a total conflict of interest. I may be the best chance you have of getting out of this, but I don't know if I can remove the pain and anger I'm feeling from this case."

"Please," he says. His eyes beg me to help.

I chew on the end of my pen cap. I know we had our issues, every marriage does—but to lie to me for the past sixteen months. Yes, I was inattentive, and yes, I wasn't exactly the loving wife, but that doesn't mean I didn't love him and that doesn't mean I never stopped loving him. Even now, at this moment I love him. I hate him, but I love him. Everything I was doing, I was doing for us. I was doing it for our future. Every night I spent at the office was for us so we could have the life we've always dreamed of. If his writing career wouldn't have tapered off right when it started, maybe I wouldn't have had to work so hard for the both of us.

The problems in our marriage were just as much his fault as they were mine. I did everything I could. I bought him a fucking house to help with his writing career, and instead, he used it to wine and dine and fuck another woman. Stop. I can't think like this. I don't know if I can separate myself from this. I just need time to think. I have to take a step back.

I begin gathering my things and push my chair back. Adam asks what I'm doing. Tears are forming in his eyes as panic sets in. He thinks I'm giving up on us, on him. I'm not. I don't say anything. I hold back every emotion—anger, betrayal, sadness, worry, fear, all of it. I push it down, so far down.

The door behind me swings open as I take a step back. I'm

thrown to the ground. My head clips the edge of the table and blood trickles down my face. I let out a scream. A six-foot man in a deputy's uniform lunges over the table, tackling Adam to the floor. I wince as I touch the cut on my forehead and examine the blood on my fingertips. The officer with buzzed cut blond hair and wide shoulders pummels Adam's face as he straddles him on the ground. Adam is trying to scream for help but struggles as the fists keep cutting him off and adding more blood to his mouth.

I get to my feet, stumble over to the officer and try to pull him off Adam. I punch him in the side of the head and ear. It doesn't even phase him. Adam's face is covered in blood, and his right eye is already swollen shut. He's trying to stop the punches with his arms, but he's no match for this man who is full of rage. I hit the officer again, and this time he stops for a second, looking back at me. His eyes are arctic blue and cracked with fissures of blood. He pushes me back without saying a word.

Just as I fall into the wall, Sheriff Stevens and Deputy Hudson storm in. They rip the man off Adam, who is nearly incapacitated on the floor. They're screaming at him to stop.

"Deputy Summers, stop this right now!" Sheriff Stevens commands as he pins him into a corner. Deputy Hudson holds the officer back too. A couple more officers swarm in, holding back this enraged man. The veins in his forehead and neck are prominent. His piercing eyes are bloodshot with rage. Sweat is dripping from his forehead. He's breathing with such intensity, I think he may collapse. I've never seen that much anger in a person. He lets out an exasperated growl. His lips purse in a tight inhalation, right before giving way. His nostrils flare so wide they could split apart. His face crumples, and he lets out a howl. This man breaks right in front of us. Tears pour from his eyes. Snot drips from his nose. His body loses all the tension it had been holding and turns practically into a puddle. The sheriff, deputy, and officers stop holding him back, and Deputy Hudson now helps hold him up.

"Scott, buddy, it's going to be okay. I would have done the same. I actually tried to do the same." Deputy Hudson pats his friend on the shoulder.

I lean against the wall. *Oh my God. That's Kelly's husband. He's a cop.*

Adam is writhing in pain on the floor, barely awake. Deputy Hudson and the officers are coercing Scott out of the room. Sheriff Stevens looks at Adam and shakes his head. He shouts for someone to call an ambulance. Then his eyes bounce to me, and it's the first time he's noticed I'm here and that I'm hurt. He runs to me, wrapping one arm around me and inspecting the cut on my forehead.

"Sarah, I'm sorry. Are you okay?" Sheriff Stevens says, clearly embarrassed for what has taken place in his police station. There's also a tenderness there. He cares that I'm hurt. He touches the cut, and I wince in pain. "Sorry," he says again.

"It's okay. I'm fine."

"Let's get you cleaned up and looked at." He tries to escort me out. I push away from him and kneel beside Adam. Another officer is trying to wipe up the blood with paper towels.

I push the blood-soaked hair off his forehead. "Are you okay?"

"Yeah," he says. I get paper towels and try to wipe some of the blood away from his eyes so he can see me, so he can see that I'm here for him. I run my hand along his cheek, reassuring him that I'm going to take care of this, that I'm going to be there for him.

I turn back to Sheriff Stevens. He closes his open mouth.

"This is unacceptable!"

"I know. I know. I'll take care of this. Officer Summers is on administrative leave. He shouldn't have been here. He wasn't supposed to be here."

"Then why was he here?"

Sheriff Stevens doesn't answer. He doesn't have an answer. He just shakes his head. Two paramedics enter carrying a bag and a gurney, and they quickly begin helping Adam. I'm shooed away as they kneel on each side of him, asking him questions to verify whether or not he's okay.

I take a couple of steps back, and Sheriff Stevens places his hand on my shoulder. "They'll take care of him. Let's get you cleaned up." It's more of a suggestion than a command.

I nod and follow him out as the paramedics place Adam on a gurney.

～

I'm sitting in Sheriff Steven's office. He returns with a small first aid kit. He leans against his desk in front of me and wipes the dried blood away from the cut on my face. He's told me more than once how sorry he is, and I think he truly means it. But I'm not sure whether he's sorry for what Scott did or sorry for the situation that I'm in, or both.

"I don't think you'll need stitches, but it's a pretty good cut," he says interrupting the silence that fills the room.

I don't say anything. He continues inspecting my injury, but I think he's just using this time to investigate me. His eyes keep locking with mine, but it's me that looks away every time. I'm not sure what he's trying to figure out. Maybe why I would be with a man like Adam? Maybe why I would stand by him after all that's happened? He applies some Neosporin and then covers the wound up with a couple of butterfly bandages. He closes the first aid kit and then takes a long look at me. I can tell he wants to say something. I give him a look that I hope conveys that he can ask me whatever he wants. I need to know what he is thinking. I need to know what he is trying to figure out. I can't read him, and it scares me. I can read everyone. But him—I can't.

"Can I ask you something?"

"Yes." I press the bandages down ensuring they're in place.

He walks to his side of the desk and takes a seat. He pauses, and for a second, I don't think he's going to ask me whatever it is he's wondering. I take a small breath and try to relax. I shift a bit in my chair and cross one leg over the other. Sheriff Stevens taps his fingers on his desk, contemplating. He sits forward in his chair and leans on his hands. "Do you think he did it?"

"What kind of question is that?" I scrunch my face up in disgust.

"It's just a question." His eyes lock with mine.

"It's inappropriate." There's disdain in my voice.

"It is." He nods. He doesn't care whether or not his question is inappropriate and it's then that I realize why he doesn't care. He's let his guard down. I think I get what he's trying to say by what he's not saying. He's not sure whether Adam did it or not either. Sure, all the evidence points to Adam—but he's wondering, could this case really be that easy? Is Adam that dumb to kill a woman in his own bed and leave her for the cleaning lady to find? Things are never what they seem.

I don't think Sheriff Stevens wants to just pin this on Adam and call it a day, even though it would be quite easy to do. I think he wants to help me find out who really did this. It's completely unorthodox, but at the end of the day, my focus is on defending Adam whether he did it or not; and Sheriff Stevens's focus is finding the person who did this. He doesn't care about closing this case quickly; he cares about closing it correctly.

"I don't believe Adam did this," I finally say, and I hope that I said it with enough confidence.

Sheriff Stevens nods and leans back in his chair again. "This is a bit unconventional, but I'd like to take you to the crime scene, and I want you to tell me what you see."

"I'd like that," I say without hesitation.

"Good."

"Just let me in there. I don't give a damn about your Podunk protocol." Matthew pushes his way through the door past the receptionist and a police officer. I turn around and immediately when he sees the bandage on my face, he knows nothing is what it should be.

"I apologize. My colleague, Matthew, came with me today."

"What did they do to you?" Matthew practically runs to me. He examines my head and shoots a sinister look at Sheriff Stevens. "She's a lawyer. She'll sue you—and I know people so powerful, they'll bring this whole town to its knees." He constricts his eyes and then returns his attention to me. His face softening as he looks me over.

"I'm fine. I will fill you in." I give him a reassuring look. Matthew has always been protective of me.

15

ADAM MORGAN

I awake in a hospital, my left hand cuffed to the bed railing. My head is pounding, but not nearly enough from the beating I remember receiving. There's an IV hooked up to me. *Ah, that's it. A nice drip of painkillers flowing right into my bloodstream is why I don't feel the full ramifications of the thrashing I took.* There are no windows in this room, so I have no idea what time of day it is or how long I've been out for. This is precisely what I expected it to be—a small hospital room, with sterile white walls and white floors. The heart rate monitor beside me beats at an even pace, reassuring me that I'm still alive. I feel my face with my fingertips noticing ridges, bumps, and things definitely out of place. I can't see out of my left eye, and I bring my fingers to it feeling the swollen bumpiness of my eyelid.

I'm about to call for a nurse when I remember something, something from when I was lying on the floor of the interrogation room writhing in pain, dipping in and out of consciousness. I remember Deputy Hudson's voice, the words that left his mouth. He called the officer that attacked me Scott. *Kelly's Scott. He's Kelly's husband.*

Things just got a whole hell of a lot more complicated. How

did I not know he was a cop? How did Kelly never tell me? No wonder she was scared. No wonder she felt like she couldn't get away. Look at him. He was massive. I'm not a small man, and I didn't stand a chance against his gorilla fists. Imagine what Kelly had to go through. Just imagine. Poor Kelly. I know Scott did this. He could have easily pulled this off, and with him being a cop, he would have known how to. That's just it. He's a cop. He couldn't have made any mistakes, right? I'm completely screwed.

A nurse enters nonchalantly. She's thumbing through a clipboard of papers. She glances at me, notices that I'm awake, and it startles her. "Oh heavens, you're awake!"

I try to sit up, and she runs to me, telling me to stop. She readjusts the machines hooked up to me and then scurries out.

A few minutes later, Sheriff Stevens enters. He kicks his feet a bit as he walks in. I can tell he's not happy, but that unhappiness isn't with me. "How you holding up?"

"Fine, I guess."

"Listen, Adam. I'm sorry that went down the way it did. It wasn't right, and I want you to know that Officer Summers has been suspended." He runs a hand through his hair as he speaks.

"He should be in jail!"

"I know you think that, but you have to understand that he just lost his wife. Nothing excuses his behavior, but you have to at least get where he's coming from."

The beeps on the heart rate monitor speed up intensely as I try to keep the rage inside me in check, but I can't. "That motherfucker killed her, I know it!" I sit up halfway. Instantly, drops of sweat form at my hairline. My breath quickens as my heart pounds, and my hands shake.

"Now, wait here a minute, Mr. Morgan. What makes you think that Scott had anything to do with the death of Kelly Summers? That was his wife, and she was found in your bed in your home." He doesn't say it to challenge me. He's inquisitive.

He's entertaining what I'm saying, and I don't know if it's because some small part of him believes me or if he's just trying to rile me up.

"He knew about us. About the affair. He was texting her the night she died. He was threatening her. He was abusive. Whatever you think he is, he's not."

Sheriff Stevens pulls a chair beside my bed and sits. He takes a deep breath and looks me up and down. He's evaluating me, trying to understand me. He wants to know the truth—maybe not my truth, but the truth.

"There have never been any allegations of abuse made against Scott Summers by Kelly Summers nor any other person in this town," he says matter-of-factly.

"Kelly was too scared to come forward. She just wanted to run. Now, I know why. I understand now."

"What do you understand?"

"Scott's a cop... She knew there was no chance of her getting away from him or him paying for his crimes."

"I've never liked Scott," the sheriff admits.

"What?" I'm making sure I heard him right. Why is he telling me this? Why is he here? Is this a game? Or is he actually trying to help me? I don't know what's happening or why it's happening to me.

"You heard me. I shouldn't tell you that, I know that. But to me, something has always been off about Scott. He has too much of an all-American boy persona in this town, and I've learned that everyone has skeletons in their closet and that the people who appear to be good are usually the worst of them all." He leans back in his chair.

I don't know what to say to that. I don't break the silence until I realize that I had forgotten about Sarah. She was hurt, or at least I think she was. I think the blood I saw on her face was her own, but it could have been mine. "How is Sarah? Is she okay? Was she hurt?"

"Sarah is fine—just a small cut on her forehead, but that girl's a fighter. Not even a six-foot man could take that woman down," he says with a smile.

I nod, knowing that's true. "Where is she? I want to see her."

"I told her to go home and take care of herself. She'll be back in the morning. I hope that's okay."

"Of course."

"Now, I'm going to look into Scott because it's the right thing to do. I'm not convinced that you're the one that did this, but I'm also not convinced you're innocent either." He stands up.

"Okay," I say because there is nothing else I can say. He knows what I think, and I'm not going to sit here and try to convince him that I didn't do it. I know at the end of the day it's the evidence that matters; at least that's what I've learned from Sarah. I trust her to find that evidence, and I think I almost trust Sheriff Stevens to help her find it.

"There's an officer stationed outside your room. I'll bring Sarah back tomorrow to see you." He hesitates for a bit. "I'll get to the bottom of this. You have my word." He walks out before I can respond.

16

SARAH MORGAN

Matthew drove me straight home. He tried to dissuade me from taking on the case. He said I was making a mistake. I told him it wasn't any of his business.

I was too tired to go to the office, too frustrated to try to explain to Anne or anyone else what was going on in my life. I don't think I can even face anyone. I'm feeling far too much— angry, scared, sad, fearful, and a mix of other things I can't even describe.

This is going to get out soon. The press is going to eat this up. With my status in D.C. and the fact that Adam is a published novelist, it's only a matter of time until it gets out. What will I say to Anne? To my colleagues? To my clients? I can't worry about that. My focus must be on Adam and this case.

I've been in and out of sleep all day. When I'm fully awake, I mull over everything, meaning the facts of the case I have. There's Adam who is undoubtedly the most obvious suspect. He has means, motive, and opportunity—which is all the D.A. needs to put together a case against him and convict. But there's also Scott, and the interaction I had with him supports what Adam said. He has a temper, and he apparently cannot control it. Plus, the text messages Adam mentioned are pretty damning. He also has means and motive, but the question is, does he have the opportunity? I take a pad from my nightstand and jot down a couple of notes. I write *opportunity* and circle it.

Could there be anyone else? Kelly was the victim, but she was having an affair. What else was she doing? What else was she into? Is there anyone else that would want her dead? I write down *Seth's Coffee*. I must talk to her co-workers, her customers, and anyone else that may have been in contact with her.

My phone rings. I don't recognize the number, and I hesitate to pick it up. It's 9pm, but it could be Adam calling from the hospital. I should have gone back and checked on him, but Sheriff Stevens assured me that he was fine and that I needed to go home and rest.

I pick up the phone. "Hello."

"Hey, Sarah, it's Sheriff Stevens. I'm just calling to check in on you and let you know that Adam is doing just fine. I just left the hospital, and he's awake."

"What did the doctor say?" I'm not worried about how I'm doing. I'm concerned about Adam.

"They said he has a broken cheekbone, a minor concussion, and some bruising. But he'll heal up. I submitted the paperwork to our insurance company, so you don't need to worry about the cost."

"I don't care about the cost. I just care that he's okay."

"Well, he is. Sorry to bother you," he says, and he's about to hang up.

"Wait." There's a bit of panic in my voice. I don't want him to hang up. I for some reason want to talk to him, but I don't know why—maybe it's because he understands what I'm going through. Perhaps it's because he showed me kindness and understanding when no one else at the department did. Maybe it's because I can't seem to read him or maybe it's because I want his help—actually, I need his help.

"Yeah?" he asks waiting patiently for my response. He seems to be hanging on my every word. I think he wants to talk to me too.

"Thank you, sheriff—"

He stops me. "Ryan, call me Ryan."

"Ryan. I'm sorry I've been short and ill-tempered with you. I know this is in no way your fault and I know you're trying to help. I'm just trying to hold it together, and I don't mean to take it out on you."

I hear him let out a sigh—whether it's a sigh of relief or a sigh of frustration, I don't know. "Sarah. I don't know you that well—but... If Adam did this, I'm just here to find out the truth and enact the proper justice. If Adam didn't do this, the same is still true. I'm here for you in a professional manner and a friendly manner. I guess what I'm trying to say is I'm here for you regardless of what we uncover together, I'm just looking for the truth."

I think I'm starting to understand Sheriff Stevens and where he's coming from. And although it's highly inappropriate and not something I'd even entertain, I'm flattered. I'd like to tell him off and tell him how wrong what he said is, but I need him. I need his help, and I can't just blow that off, but I'll keep this strictly professional.

"I appreciate that, Sheriff Stevens."

He doesn't correct the name I call him by this time. He understands exactly what I'm saying. He understands that this, whatever this is between us can't happen.

"Goodnight, Mrs. Morgan. I'll see you tomorrow at 11am as planned."

"Goodnight." I end the call. As I'm about to place the phone on the nightstand, it buzzes signaling a text. It's from Matthew.

I'm sorry for what I said. You're right. It's not my business, but I'm here for you if you need me. I've got a busy next couple of days, but I'll come to see you as soon as I can.

I hold my finger down on the text and select the heart reaction. I set the phone down, and I close my eyes, hoping I'll sleep tonight, but knowing that I won't.

17

ADAM MORGAN

After Sheriff Stevens left, I thought about calling Sarah—but I couldn't, not yet, at least. I know she's physically okay, but I can't imagine what I'm doing to her mentally and emotionally. Sarah is the strongest person I know, but a person can only take so much. I feel like telling her to drop the case and hire someone else because she doesn't deserve this. She shouldn't have to clean up my mess.

Sure, I know in my heart I didn't kill Kelly—but I did have an affair, and without that affair, none of this would have ever happened. At least, I don't think it would have. Maybe Scott would have still killed Kelly, but it wouldn't have happened in our house, and I wouldn't be involved.

Scott has to have been the one. I don't care what kind of show he put on today or that he beat the ever-living shit out of me, it was him. I know it was. I just hope Sarah and Sheriff Stevens can prove that it was him.

I close my eyes and try to sleep, but my mind keeps replaying not only the events of today but the events of the last sixteen months. I think about all the times I had with Kelly. I try not to, but I do. I love my wife, but I loved Kelly too. A few tears escape my eyes, and I let them roll down the sides of my face onto the pillow. What have I done? What the fuck did I do?

18

ADAM MORGAN
TWO WEEKS EARLIER

I had just finished a full day of writing, and by that, I mean a
full day of sitting in front of a blank computer screen, while
sipping scotch. My eyes were strained from staring at the white
Word document. But thanks to the scotch, I was numb to
everything else.

I had planned on driving back home since Kelly had
canceled on me for a third time that week. But I was in no state
to drive and I'd decided to stay and get a fresh start in the
morning. I shut down my laptop and walked into the living
room, swirling my crystal glass of booze. I lit the fire and flipped
on some classical music. I was about to select a book from the
bookshelf to escape for the evening when I heard a knock at the
door. I thought it might be Sarah with a surprise visit and at that
moment, I was glad Kelly had canceled.

But on the other side of the door I found Kelly, broken and
beaten. Tears streaming down her face, colliding with the dried
blood from her nose and lip. Her right eye was black and blue,
and her hair was a knotted mess. I gasped at the sight of her, and
she nearly collapsed into my arms. I pulled her inside and

walked her into the living room, wrapping a blanket around her cold body.

"Who did this, Kelly?" I nearly screamed in anger as I ran to the kitchen for an ice pack and a rag. She cried harder.

"Do I need to call the police?" I placed the ice pack to her eye. I wiped the blood away from her nose and lip with the rag.

"No... No, don't," she pleaded. I continued to dab and wipe the blood away. We sat there until her cries fell silent and I knew she was ready to talk. I brought her a glass of scotch and refilled mine. It was going to be a long night. I sat beside her, holding her, trying to reassure her that everything was going to be all right.

"He's never going to stop," she finally said, slicing through the silence.

"Who?"

"Scott... my husband."

I pulled her in a little closer. I knew she was married. But I had assumed her marriage was like mine, loveless, boring, inattentive, and extinguished... not like this. I thought I had it bad—but Kelly had it worse, far worse. I may be bored, but she was in danger.

"Have you gone to the cops?" I took a gulp of scotch.

"I can't." She shook her head.

"Why?"

"I just can't." She sounded exasperated. She finished off her drink, and I didn't push it any further. Her look told me to stop.

"What can I do?" I asked. I got up and refilled both our drinks. I set them on the coffee table and retook my place on the couch. Pulling her into my lap, I stroked her hair and the side of her face. I had been seeing Kelly for the past year. I cared about this woman. I loved this woman. I wanted to save this woman. This couldn't be how our lives played out. This couldn't be it.

"You can't do anything. He'll never stop." Her eyes were glazed over, and there was no hope in them. She truly believed what she was saying.

I couldn't let her give up. "I can help you get away."

"I can't run. He'll always find me."

"We'll run away together... you and I," I said, and I think I meant it.

"Sometimes, I think the only way I'll ever get away from him is in death."

"Don't say that. Why would you say that?"

"There are things you don't know about me." She looked at me intently. Then she looked away as if she regretted what she had just said.

"What don't I know about you? I love you, Kelly. That's all I need to know. I love you, and I want to help you. Tell me how I can help you."

"I don't think you can help me. Scott has a hold on me."

"What is it? Tell me." I squeezed her hand tightly.

She took a deep breath and sat up. She picked up her drink and downed the whole thing in one gulp. She turned to me, and she let everything out, everything Scott had been holding over her.

"I was married before, and although we loved each other, we weren't always good to each other. And my name... isn't really Kelly Summers. It's Jenna Way. I had to change it after what happened, after I was accused of killing my first husband. I didn't kill him." She paused. I gave her hand a small squeeze. She looked at me and continued. "We had had a fight earlier that day, which was the norm for us. Our relationship was full of passion, both good and bad. When I came home later that night, he was dead. He had been stabbed to death. I was the primary suspect. I didn't do it, I swear. I loved my husband, but I was charged with his murder. When some of the evidence was misplaced during the trial, the charges against me were dismissed. He helped me be free, but he owns me now, so really, I'm not free. I'm still paying for a crime I didn't commit. I'm still serving my sentence. Just not in a jail cell, but with Scott. I know it won't end well for me, and I know the only way I will be free is if he is out of the picture." She hung her head.

I tried to remain calm while I digested what she had confessed to. I didn't know what to say. I didn't know what to ask her and I didn't even know if I should say anything at all. That wasn't what I was expecting to hear. Kelly had a darkness inside her that I couldn't even comprehend. I thought I knew this woman. But I didn't even know her real name. Who was she? Did she kill her husband?

When I didn't respond right away, she seemed to get nervous. Her eyes bounced around the room and then on me. She fidgeted with her leg and repositioned herself. "I'm not a bad person." She took a deep breath, then got up, and I thought she was going to leave, but despite what she'd told me, I didn't want her to leave. I wanted to understand.

"Wait," I said. She stopped as I got up from the couch. I stood inches away from her. Her eyes lit up a bit from my presence and the possibility that I wouldn't let her just walk out the door with nowhere to go. I inched closer to her and tucked her hair behind her ear.

"I know you as Kelly, not as Jenna."

"I know. I'm sorry," she interrupted. I placed a finger on her lips to silence her, and I told her I needed to get this out. She obliged.

"I fell in love with Kelly, not with Jenna. Who you were doesn't matter to me. What you've done doesn't change the way I feel about you. This past year has been one of the best of my life, and that's because of you. What you go through, I go through. What you need, I need. I promise you this, Kelly, Scott will never hurt you again." I planted a light kiss on her forehead. She looked up at me and hope had returned to her eyes. She leaned in for a kiss, and I kissed her back. She winced a bit thanks to her split-open lip but didn't pull away. Sometimes, the pleasure is worth the pain.

19

SARAH MORGAN

T he elevator doors shut, and I close my eyes for a moment gathering all the strength I have deep inside me. I have down the look of being in control and pulled together. An expensive skirt with a tight blouse, a pair of black Louboutin heels and a custom-tailored jacket. My hair is pulled back in a high ponytail, and I had my makeup professionally done at my local salon this morning. They were able to cover up the bruising on my forehead, but the cut is still bandaged. I need to look the part. I need to look strong.

The doors open, and Anne is waiting by them with a cup of coffee and a sympathetic yet encouraging smile. "What happened? Are you okay?" Her eyes go directly to the Band-Aid on my head.

"It's fine. Let's walk and talk." I take the cup of coffee and pass her swiftly. She catches up, eager to please and understand.

I fill Anne in on what's going on, as I need her to get a head start on using the firm's resources for background checks on Kelly and Scott. I need to know everything. As we go through the office, I notice quiet murmurs from colleagues. No one knows the full story yet as there hasn't been anything in the news, but that hasn't stopped the rumors from circling. I'm not one to cancel meetings, miss court dates, or disappear from the office, so I'm not surprised that people are talking.

Anne closes my office door behind us, and I take a seat on the couch.

"Are you sure you're okay?"

"Yes. Please don't ask me that again," I say curtly.

"Sorry. Those background reports on Kelly and Scott Summers should be in by the end of the day." She kneels beside the coffee table and begins organizing papers into files.

"What is everyone saying?"

"Mental breakdown. Husband is having an affair."

"They got one thing right." I roll my eyes. "Has Bob been sniffing around?"

"Not yet. He got back from his weekend getaway Monday morning, so he's still playing catch-up."

"Good."

"Do you think he did it?" Anne asks quickly.

"I don't... know."

She gives me a fearful look, and I know she immediately regrets asking. "I'm sorry."

"It's fine, Anne. Really. I just can't believe this happened. One moment, you and I are having an amazing time out. Then I'm home and then I'm told my husband is a murderer."

"I can't believe it either. Wait! You said he came home late that night and you guys... you know, tried for a baby. Isn't that his alibi?"

"The preliminary report revealed that Kelly had to have been murdered between 11:30pm and 12:15am. I couldn't verify that he was home until around 2am when I woke up," I say.

"And we were out in D.C. until..." Anne ponders.

"After midnight, although it may have been a bit later."

"Yeah, that's right." Anne sits there thinking. I can see that she wants to be of more help.

"Anne, please don't worry about this. This isn't your problem. You've already helped me in more ways than you can even imagine." I smile at her.

She starts to get a little teary. She stands up and tries to fan her eyes with her hands. Anne walks over, taking a seat beside me on the couch and gives me a hug. "Don't tell me not to worry about you. You're my best friend, Sarah. I would do anything for you. Please know that I'm here," she whispers into my ear. I hug her a little tighter, and she hugs me back.

"Thank you, Anne. You are so special to me." I glance at the clock on the wall behind her and realize that I need to be going. I pull away, and we share a look that says regardless of what happens, we're going to be there for each other and that we're going to be okay.

"I have to go meet with Sheriff Stevens." I stand up and begin to collect my things. I can feel the pressure change in the air: my office door is now open, meaning I must have a new guest in the room with me. I slowly turn to see who it is and somehow, I already know.

First, it was the smell, the dead giveaway of the Chanel No.5, so classic, so expected. This is matched with the monochrome outfit adorning her well-maintained figure. Not a shred of personality in her outward appearance, which itself tells you everything you need to know about her. Her features are hard and are kept in place by routine visits to a plastic surgeon, but the kind who does a superb enough job that only a well-trained eye can even tell that the skin isn't 100 percent natural. The entire entrance is punctuated by the final click of a black Manolo Blahnik heel (never Louboutin's, "red is ostentatious"), announcing that she is here and ready for her proper allotment of attention, which by normal tally is all of it.

"Hello, Sarah," Eleanor greets me, and without an invite, she's already closing the distance between us. "It's lovely to see you." She opens her arms for a hug when she reaches me and although we do embrace one another, we barely touch.

"You got in quick, Eleanor," I say. A little too quick. I was hoping it would be another day or two before she graced me with her presence.

"Of course. This is my son we're talking about, after all." She holds her head high and carries her classic black Chanel purse close to her as she takes a seat in front of my desk. Glancing around, she says, "Your office is cute." The remark is condescending at best. I sit down in my desk chair.

From the doorway Anne raises her eyebrows at me and backs out of the office. Eleanor clearly had no intention of acknowledging her presence.

"Now, tell me what's going on with Adam." She crosses one leg over the other and places the palms of her hands on her knee.

Eleanor is not going to like hearing this. To her, Adam is a perfect specimen. He's all she has left of her deceased husband. Adam's father was a hedge fund manager, and five years ago he passed away unexpectedly from a heart attack. They say it was due to bad eating habits and the stress of the job, but I like to think Eleanor played a role. She is truly a demanding woman. However, for the sake of this case, I'll put our differences aside and continue to swallow each jab, insult, and condescending remark.

"Adam is a suspect in a murder case—"

"Impossible," Eleanor interjects. "My boy would never!"

There's no point in arguing with her. Parents are typically delusional when it comes to their children. Even Ted Bundy and Jeffrey Dahmer had loving parents who were unaware of the evil that dwelled within their offspring.

"He's suspected of murdering his mistress." I hold eye contact with Eleanor, hoping she'll understand what I'm saying, hoping she'll see that Adam isn't as flawless as she thought he was. Maybe she can think clearly about this.

She squints for a moment, then she relaxes. "He cheated on you?" she asks. The connection is obvious, but I'm sure she just wants me to say it out loud.

I nod.

She turns her head away from me, her chin raised. I would say she turns her nose up, but it's permanently turned up. Eleanor sighs. "Well, I'd like to see him. I'll need to get all the facts from Adam." She looks back at me.

I nod again. "He's being held at the hospital in Prince William County."

"What? Why?"

"He was involved in an altercation at the sheriff's station last night," I say. I don't go into any more detail.

"My poor son. Why didn't you tell me this from the beginning?"

Anne pops her head in. "Sarah, you've got to go if you're going to meet Sheriff Stevens in time."

"Sheriff Stevens? Why aren't you going to see Adam?" Eleanor questions.

I stand from my seat, and she stands from hers, flipping her bag over her shoulder dramatically.

"I'm going to look at the crime scene, but I'm visiting Adam after." I finish gathering my belongings.

"I'll go with you." It's not a suggestion. It's a demand.

"You can't. It's a crime scene. Why don't you just go get settled, get something to eat, and I'll text you later." I toss my tote bag over my shoulder. "Anne can help you."

"I don't need any help," Eleanor says defiantly.

"Okay, but I've got to go. I'll check in with you later, Eleanor."

95

I quickly walk toward my office door. I say to Anne as I pass, "I'm not sure I'll make it back here today, but if I don't, I'll call you."

"Oh, yes. You go. I'll take care of everything," Anne says.

"I'll be seeing you, Sarah," Eleanor calls from behind and then all I hear are the clicks and the clacks of her heels.

~

An hour later, I'm pulling up to the lake house. Sheriff Stevens's vehicle is parked in the driveway, and he's leaned up against the side of it, dressed in his sheriff's uniform up top and blue jeans. He's wearing a pair of aviators and carrying a folder, and when he sees my vehicle, he smiles. I park behind him and get out of the car.

"Good morning, Mrs. Morgan." It's all formalities today. I still wonder why he's being nice. Does he think Adam is innocent? Does he feel sorry for me? Or does he have some other motive for this nice guy act?

"Good morning, Sheriff Stevens." He shakes my hand, and I notice he is sweaty despite the cool weather. What is he nervous about? Does he know something?

"We're just going to take a look around, and you tell me if you notice anything out of the norm," he says leading the way. I follow, a bit apprehensive. I wouldn't notice anything out of place even if it were. I rarely came here. This was essentially Adam's home. I don't say a word though. I'm sure there's stuff the police missed, and I bet I can at least help with that.

Sheriff Stevens turns back to me and hands over the folder he was carrying.

"Almost forgot, here are the results of the autopsy as well as DNA. We're still pulling phone records and running additional tests on some of the evidence we collected here."

I nod, opening the folder as I walk. I trip on the first step of the wraparound porch because I'm face deep in the autopsy report. Sheriff Stevens catches me and pulls me up onto the porch. We lock eyes, inches apart from one another. My breath is a bit ragged. His breathing is steady. He asks me if I'm all right and I tell him yes. I step back from his embrace and straighten my skirt, while he bends down picking up the papers.

"Do you want to take a seat and read that over before we go inside?" He points to the bench on the porch. I nod, knowing I should look over the report before trying to assess the crime scene. I take a seat and begin flipping through the papers.

"Kelly Summers had Rohypnol in her system?"

"Yes." Sheriff Stevens paces back and forth on the porch. He's not one to sit still.

"Odd. What about Adam?" I ask looking up at him. "Did he have the same drug in his system?"

"No," he says without hesitation.

"Did you test for it?"

"I believe so, but I'll double-check with the lab."

I flip through a few more pages and then stop when one catches my eye. I scan the text quickly and let out a breath of frustration.

"She was pregnant?" I look up at Sheriff Stevens. He shuffles his feet a bit and instantly he is visibly upset. He seems to collect himself almost quickly enough not to notice that this news bothered him. I supposed it would bother anyone. A woman and her unborn child stabbed to death. He finally nods.

"About four weeks along. The D.A. is now looking at a double homicide, and given the brutality of the crime as well, they'll push for the death penalty." He thinks he's breaking the news to me, but any competent attorney would put that together quickly.

"Was Adam the father?"

Sheriff Stevens breaks eye contact. He doesn't want to tell me, but he already has.

"Yes." It looks as though he's going to say something else, but he doesn't. He sucks back in the words and begins to pace again. He wants to be anywhere else in the world right now. I can't fucking believe Adam got this woman pregnant. Did he know? Was he hiding it from me? Did she want money out of him or was she going to tell me? One minute, I'm confident Adam would never do this and the next, I'm not so sure. What the hell was he thinking?

Sheriff Stevens stops pacing and puts one hand on the porch post, leaning up against it. I can feel his eyes on me. "Listen, I'm going to go grab a quick coffee, and give you time to digest and finish reading over those. Would you like one?"

I don't look up. I keep reading. "Yes, black, please." My attention is solely focused on the task at hand.

"Okay. I'll be back in a minute. Please don't go in there without me."

"In my own house?" I say with a bit of sass.

He lets out a sigh and goes down the porch steps. I look up from the paper and watch him walk away. I hadn't really noticed how good he looked before. Tall, broad shoulders, a freshly starched shirt. Despite his shortcomings and worn-down visage, he really does have a commanding attraction to him.

"I won't go in my house without you."

He turns back with a slight grin, trying to force the uncomfortableness out of this conversation. "Good, I wouldn't want to have to arrest you too. It seems to run in the family." He chuckles and then shakes his head as he catches the awkwardness of his attempt at humor. I continue flipping through the pages, rolling my eyes at him.

Sheriff Stevens is gone no more than twenty minutes, and by the time he returns, I've gotten through all the information.

Kelly Summers died as a result of her stab wounds. She had Rohypnol and a BAC level of .16, twice the legal driving limit. She had bruises on her back, shoulder, and hip that were caused at least twenty-four hours before she was murdered. The skin underneath her fingernails is a match with Adam. Semen was found in her vagina, anus, and mouth—and according to the DNA results, the semen is a match with Adam as well. However, there were two additional sets of DNA found in her vagina that do not match Adam.

Sheriff Stevens walks up and hands me a cup of coffee. He casually sips at his own while he takes a seat on the bench inches from me. He's taking in the view from the porch, glancing around at squirrels running to and fro and the mass of fall-colored leaves, just barely holding on.

"What'd ya learn?" He takes another drink of his coffee.

I close the folder and place it beside me, sipping at my own drink. "There were two other sets of DNA found in her. Have you run any tests on those?"

"We'll get Scott's back later this afternoon, and I'm going to assume he'll be a match with one of them, but that just proves he had sex with his wife."

"What about the other set of DNA?"

"We're hoping the phone records give us more insight into that. Maybe she was seeing someone else. Maybe she was raped, and that's the real murderer. We're not sure."

"Seeing someone else?"

"That third set of DNA caught us by surprise too." He turns to me raising one of his eyebrows.

"What's your theory?" I lean back into my seat.

He leans back too, getting a little more comfortable. "Well... before finding the third set of DNA I thought we just might have our man. But now Adam as the murderer doesn't sit well for me. I'll be honest, Adam didn't make sense before the DNA results."

"Why?"

"It's too easy."

"What do you mean it's too easy?"

"It's just too easy. Adam, a well-educated and well-established author, kills his mistress in his own house. It doesn't make any sense. Unless, of course, it was by accident. But I don't see how someone could stab another person thirty-seven times by accident."

"I don't think Adam did this." I give him a look of sincerity. "Although, deep down I can't be sure," I sigh.

Sheriff Stevens creases his brow. "What do you mean you can't be sure?"

"Like you said, what if it was by accident and Adam tried to cover it up by making it look like a murder? Or what if he blacked out and did it and doesn't remember doing it?"

"That's possible," he says rubbing his chin.

"I need to see him and get all the details from that evening. All the commotion with Scott cut our preliminary chat short. And all I know right now is Adam is the only one that had the means, motive, and opportunity to do this. His motive could have been that Kelly was threatening to tell me or maybe she wanted to leave him or abort the baby."

A police car rolls up the driveway, its tires crunching dead leaves and dry dirt. It pulls up beside Sheriff Stevens onto the grass, marking its territory. Deputy Marcus Hudson steps out of the car. He looks like a G.I. Joe action figure in his uniform and a pair of aviators.

"What are you doing here, Deputy Hudson?" Sheriff Stevens calls out to him. He stands from the bench and walks to the stairs of the porch. Deputy Hudson takes a few steps toward him and crosses his arms in front of his chest as if he were actually here to protect and serve. Although, who here needs that protection is unclear.

"Just checking to see if you need any assistance." Deputy Hudson looks around nonchalantly and then returns his attention to Sheriff Stevens.

"I don't," Sheriff Stevens says dismissively.

"Mind if I wait out here then?" He leans against the hood of his vehicle.

"Knock yourself out." Sheriff Stevens turns back toward me, while Deputy Hudson removes his aviators and narrows his eyes... seemingly directed at me.

"Are you ready to go inside?" Sheriff Stevens asks. I nod, and he helps me up from the bench.

We walk through the front door, ducking under the crime scene tape. Inside, the house is still. Many things are strewn about, which I'm sure is from the police search.

In the kitchen I set down my coffee cup and the folder. I glance around trying to spot anything out of place. The kitchen appears to be well kept, despite random cupboards and drawers left partially open.

In the living room the bearskin rug is kicked up. The decorative couch pillows and throw blankets are on the floor, but other than that everything else is in place, including the built-in bookshelf. Every book is pushed in and facing the correct direction. I look at the wet bar and notice the uncapped scotch decanter.

I point to it. "Was that tested?"

Sheriff Stevens walks a couple of steps from the kitchen into the open-concept living room.

"Not that I'm aware. What should it be tested for?" He takes a few more steps and stands beside me.

"Well if Rohypnol was found in Kelly's body—maybe, this is how it got there." I put the cap back on the decanter. Sheriff Stevens rubs his chin.

"Good point," he says. "When we're done here. I'll have

Deputy Hudson do another once-through." He pulls out a pen and a small notepad from his pocket and jots down a few things.

I nod and walk to the bedroom. The bed is unmade. The once white sheets are stained red and brown, soaked through to the mattress and there's a puddle of dried blood on the floor beside it. The smell of iron and decay hits me like a smack in the face. I cover my nose, trying to breathe through my mouth. I take a few more steps into the bedroom, standing right before the bed.

Sheriff Stevens stands behind me. I can feel his breath on my neck. "Are you okay?"

I nod. It's not convincing, because I'm not okay. None of this is okay. How could Adam do this to me? What the fuck was he thinking? Did he plan on leaving me? Would he have left me if she was still alive? The anger takes ahold of me and comes out in the form of tears. I don't cry when I'm sad. I cry when I'm angry. I turn toward Sheriff Stevens. He sees the tears and immediately wraps his arms around me, pulling me in for a comforting embrace. He rubs my back with one hand, while the other strokes the back of my head. We stand there for a few minutes. He makes me feel less angry. He makes me feel like everything is going to be all right at this moment. He makes me feel like things can get better. I'm grateful that I forgot my place, even if only for a moment.

"Let's go." He escorts me out of the bedroom.

Once in the living room, I glance around again, and my eyes stop at Adam's writing desk. It's disorganized, the drawers are pulled out, and his chair is flipped over. I run my hands over the cherry wood. I remember the day I surprised Adam with it. It was right after he got his first book deal. I was incredibly proud of him and I had never seen him happier. The memory makes me smile, makes me remember the us we were before all of this. And then I remember what I liked about this desk, what swayed me to pick this one out. My hand grazes over the top of it, sliding to the panel on the right side—I push against it. It clicks in, and then a concealment compartment opens. Inside is a handgun and a manila envelope. I don't flinch at the gun. I knew it was there. Adam had purchased it shortly after we bought the lake house. It was meant for protection—a job it failed to do. It's the manila envelope that makes me feel uneasy.

"Well, shit. Can't say we would have found that," Sheriff Stevens remarks from beside me.

I reach for the envelope.

"Wait." He stops me. He pulls out a pair of gloves and hands them over. Once I've put them on, he nods, granting me permission. I reach for the envelope and slowly open it, pulling out a 5x7 photo. It's a picture of Adam and Kelly with the lake house behind them and the water in front. He's wearing boxers. She's wearing a thong, but she's topless. The closeness of his body covers her chest. Her legs are wrapped around him. His hands are cupping her butt. Her hands are around his neck. Their lips are connected in a passionate kiss. They look happy.

Sheriff Stevens lets out an awkward cough. He pulls out an evidence bag and carefully slides the gun into it. I start to slip the photo back into the envelope, but instinctively, I stop. Someone took this photo, and it looks like Adam and Kelly weren't even aware they were being photographed at that moment.

I turn the picture over and written on the back in Sharpie marker are the words, *"END IT OR I WILL."* I look at Sheriff Stevens. My eyes grow wide.

He groans. "Things just got a whole hell of a lot more complicated," he says shaking his head.

"Someone knew about Kelly and Adam. This is a threat. This is proof that Adam didn't do it." My voice is full of enthusiasm. "This is a huge break. It's reasonable doubt."

"Let's not get ahead of ourselves, but I will admit this bodes well for Adam."

I slide the picture back into the envelope. Sheriff Stevens bags it up. "We'll get it tested for fingerprints."

"What about handwriting analysis?"

"We'll need handwriting to analyze it against," he says raising an eyebrow.

"Of course." I'm getting ahead of myself. I need to slow down and really think this all through. *But wait—if this was hidden... Adam had to have known about this. Adam must have put it here.*

"You ready?" Sheriff Stevens walks toward the front door. I nod and take the folder from the counter on my way out.

Outside Deputy Hudson is still leaned up against his car.

Sheriff Stevens closes the house up and turns back, giving me a sympathetic look. I lower my chin a little. It was hard seeing Adam happy with Kelly. He was supposed to be happy with me, not another woman. Sheriff Stevens puts his hands on my shoulders and rubs the sides of my arms. It's completely inappropriate, but it feels nice, almost comforting.

"You did great. I'll get someone here to pull a sample of that scotch to test, and I'll get the lab started on the photo—"

"Hey! What's going on with you two? Is there a second affair going on that we should all know about?" Deputy Hudson yells from the car. A large smile is plastered across his face as he smacks his chewing gum loudly in an obnoxious manner to punctuate the brazenness of his commentary.

I'm snapped back into reality and a wave of questions cascades over me. Professionalism replaces empathy, and our former roles reappear. Defense attorney. In-the-way sheriff's department.

"Nothing, Deputy Hudson. Mind you that your presence here was neither required nor requested and is highly suspect at best. So, please carry on with your important patrol of the perimeter of your own vehicle." Sheriff Stevens rocked back on his heels.

"What about the murder weapon?" I ask ignoring Deputy Hudson. Back to the facts.

"We never found it. We've searched both homes and the surrounding woods, but nothing." The sheriff drops his hands to his side and shifts awkwardly, not knowing how to end this.

"Do they know what it is?"

"They deduced it may be a small kitchen knife, a pocket knife, or even a letter opener. They're running additional tests to try to narrow it down. But chances are we'll never find it anyway."

I give a slight nod and then shift a bit. I need to talk to Adam. Does he know that Kelly was pregnant? Did he know all along?

"Well, I should probably get going. I need to stop by the hospital to check on Adam." I step away from Sheriff Stevens and walk toward my vehicle, glancing only for a second at Deputy Hudson.

He smiles and nods at me. "I'll be seeing you," he says in a friendly manner, but it seems more like a threat.

My smile back is small and curt, enough to remain professional.

"Sarah," Sheriff Stevens calls out. I stop and turn, facing him. He walks down the porch steps to his car and stops. "Adam is being moved back to the jail for processing." He pulls open his car door. "You can follow me there if you'd like."

20

ADAM MORGAN

I'm lying in my bunk dressed in standard inmate's attire: orange cotton pants and top. The doctor released me this morning. It appears they don't take too kindly to a patient suspected of murdering a young local woman. They got me bandaged up quick, and after one night of observation, they sent me here. *Here* being a tiny room with a twin-sized bunk, a toilet, and a sink, surrounded by cinder block and steel bars. I shouldn't be here. I don't belong here.

A guard taps his baton on the bars of my cell, telling me I can come out to the common room. He unlocks the door, and I follow him down a hall to a room with some tables and chairs and a television in the corner. There're only a few other inmates here, this being a small town and all, and this not being a well-equipped prison. Two of them are playing cards at a table, and the third one is reading a book at another table alone. The two at the table look up at me as I enter and whisper to one another. The third guy never looks up. *Must be a good book. It's probably not one of mine.*

I take a seat at the table nearest the television and settle in, hoping to escape through the means of some bad daytime television show. But no such luck as a special news report comes on. A news reporter is standing in front of my lake house speaking into a microphone, "A brutal murder has shaken the small town of Brentsville. Kelly Summers, a twenty-seven-year-old local woman, and wife to local Sheriff's Deputy Scott Summers was found viciously murdered early yesterday morning by cleaning lady, Sonia Gutierrez. Reports say she was brutally stabbed to death. Police are not releasing the name of the primary suspect as the investigation is ongoing. If you have any information regarding the death of Kelly Summers, please contact the local authorities."

I hang my head in shame and embarrassment. Not releasing the name of the suspect? Are they fucking kidding me? *You're standing in front of my house. How could this have happened?* The primary suspect should be Scott, not me. I don't care what the evidence says, I didn't do this. I would never do this. Why won't anyone believe me?

"Morgan," a guard calls from behind. "You have a visitor."

I stand up and drag my feet to the door, following behind. He opens the door, and inside, I find Sarah sitting at the table in the small room. Her side of the table is covered in notebooks and papers. The guard closes the door behind me.

"Sarah, I'm so happy to see you. This is a nightmare." I want to hug her. I want to kiss her.

She looks up at me and gives me a small smile. I get the hint and take the seat across from her. She's jotting down notes and flipping through pages. "I heard you were released from the hospital."

"Yep." I know she wasn't looking for more response than that.

"We need to talk about the night Kelly was murdered." She flips her notepad to a blank page and puts her pen to the paper. Her eyes return to me, and she finally catches sight of the aftermath of my beating from Scott. My right eye is closed completely. My skin is newly colored with purple, black, yellow, and red. My left cheek is swollen and filled with stitches. My lips are split in several spots, and my teeth are stained as if I had just consumed a bottle of wine, thanks to the blood that pooled in my mouth.

Her eyes give a flicker of sympathy as a part of her must have thought for a moment, *My poor husband*, but this quickly disappears and instead her eyes focus and pierce me.

What is she thinking now? Why is she even helping me? "What do you want to know?" I lean back in the chair.

"Everything." She narrows her eyes. I know from an attorney's perspective, she really wants to know everything, but as my wife, she shouldn't have to hear any of this. But maybe she wants to know. She wants to know how truly disgusting and dishonorable I am. "Are you sure?" *Because I'm not sure this is a good idea anymore.*

She slaps her pen down and glares at me. "Adam. I told you yesterday. You need to be completely honest with me. What you did in terms of your infidelity doesn't matter, nor what you did to me."

"Okay. I just don't want to hurt you." I reach my hand out for hers.

She pulls away. "You already have." She picks up her pen and writes the date and time on the piece of paper. "What time did Kelly Summers arrive at the lake house?"

"Sometime after 5pm."

"Take me through what happened after she arrived."

I tell her everything—how we drank scotch, fucked multiple times, how rough I was with her, how much I enjoyed it, how much Kelly enjoyed it, how she was begging for more without even uttering a word, how I left her in the middle of the night to come home, the note I wrote, everything.

Sarah doesn't make any gesture, sound, or remark to let me know how displeased she is with me. To let me know how much she hates me. And then I wonder, *Does she even care? Does she care that I was cheating on her? Or is she trying to be strong? Is she trying to be professional?* I can't tell. I can't read her. She's my wife, and at this moment, I don't even know her. The look she gives me is cold and distant. Her movements are almost robotic. Her eyes are clear and calculating.

"Wait a minute." She circles a note on her paper and pulls me from my thoughts. "What time did you two fall asleep?"

"I don't know." I try to think back and recall the time, but I don't even remember going to sleep or even being tired. The last thing I remember is having sex with Kelly.

"You have no idea what time you went to sleep?" she questions again.

"We must have just passed out after sex." I don't have a better answer. I really don't know.

"There's a period of time you don't remember from that night?" She gives me a quizzical look.

"I guess." I shrug.

"You guess? You're being accused of murder, and you guess? Are you kidding me, Adam?" She drops her pen on her paper and massages her temples with the tips of her fingers.

"Well, what the hell do you want me to say?"

"I don't know. But it doesn't look good that you can't remember part of that night. The prosecution will easily turn that statement you just made into—well, if you can't remember, maybe you don't remember killing her. You need to remember. You need to be sure." Her frustration is showing, which isn't the norm for Sarah. She's always so calm and collected. I need to be sure of everything that happened that evening, but if this goes to trial, I'll have time to prepare.

"I do remember hearing a car door slam. It's what woke me up."

"Are you sure?" she asks with a bit of skepticism. "You're positive it wasn't a tree branch falling or an acorn hitting the roof? There are all sorts of sounds in the woods."

"Yes, I am... at least I think I am." I rub my forehead as if the misplaced memories from that night will suddenly become clear.

Sarah lets out a huff and scribbles some notes down on her notepad. "What about the photo?"

"What photo?" I look at her and then I look past her trying to recall. *Shit.* It hits me. My eyes widen. *How could I have forgotten about it?* In everything that's happened, I forgot something so important, something that could help prove my innocence.

"When did you receive it?"

"A few weeks before. It was in our mailbox at the lake house. Someone put it there, because there was no postage or anything," I explain. Sarah jots down more notes. "Someone is trying to frame me, can't you see?" I stare into her eyes.

She takes a deep breath. Her eyes lock with mine. "I'm trying to help, Adam—but you have to tell me everything. You have to remember everything. You're lucky I found that envelope. It's a huge break, but we have to figure out who took that photo, who threatened you." She breaks eye contact and flips through her notes.

She's right. I'm not helping. I need to look at everything, like the way I examine one of my books when I'm editing it. Where are the plot holes? Which characters aren't fleshed out? Who is really driving the story? And why? What's the crux of the story and what should I be looking for?

"They found three sets of DNA in her," she says with exasperation, changing the subject.

At first, I don't understand what she's saying. My eyes are wide again, and my mouth is partially open.

"One of them is yours. One of them is Scott's. And the third is unknown."

"What are you saying?"

"I'm saying you weren't the only man she was cheating on her husband with. I'm saying you weren't special. I'm saying she was a whore." Sarah looks just as surprised as I do after the words leave her mouth.

"Jesus, Sarah!"

"I'm sorry. I'm just. I'm still... processing all of this." She looks away from me, almost like she's ashamed for her outburst. I tell her it's fine, even though I don't think it is. None of this is fine. Kelly is dead. She was sleeping with another man. How could she?

"Maybe she was raped by that third man?" I offer.

"Maybe."

"Maybe that third guy killed her too." I'm trying to make sense of all this, but none of this makes sense. *How could Kelly be seeing someone else? Why would she be? Was I not enough? Did she not love me like I loved her?*

"Maybe. But I thought you were convinced it was Scott?" She jots down a few more notes.

"I thought I was too. I mean, I am. It had to have been him. He was abusive. You saw what he could do. He beat the hell out of me, and he hurt you, and I know what he was doing to Kelly." I'm trying to convince Sarah just as much as I'm trying to convince myself. It has to be Scott. This third guy—maybe he was a one-night stand or maybe she was assaulted. I just can't believe there was someone else. Kelly wouldn't do that to me. She loved me. I loved her. We had something special.

"Well, that all may be true. But there's no evidence to point to Scott. He may have been abusive, but that doesn't mean he killed her. Plus, there were no reports of domestic abuse between Kelly and Scott."

"She wouldn't go to the police. He was the police. She was terrified."

"I get that, but without evidence, it won't hold up in court. The texts he sent her will help your case, but if he has an alibi, it won't really matter. Husbands and wives fight. Right now, we have you at the scene of the crime, you were the last one to see her alive, and your DNA is all over her. Plus, there's this...." Sarah slides a piece of paper out of a folder and places it in front of me. It's in my handwriting. It's the note I wrote to Kelly the night of her death. These were my last words to her. She never got to read them. She was already dead when I wrote them.

I read the note to myself again.

Kelly,

It's you. It hasn't always been you, but it will always be you. You're the words to a story I've been trying to write my whole life, and tonight I determined the ending.

Love you, Love me, Adam

P.S. The maid will be here at 9am. Please make sure you're gone before then.

"What was that ending you had decided?" Sarah's eyes are glossy.

I stutter trying to find the words but knowing I don't want to reveal these words to her. But I have to tell her the truth. It's the only way she can help me. "I had decided to leave you and be with her."

Sarah's expression doesn't change. She looks at me and then drops her eyes to her notepad. Her lip quivers ever so slightly, and her eyes tighten. She takes a few notes.

"But I changed my mind. When you told me you wanted to

have a baby and start a family with me, I decided I was going to end it with Kelly and I was going to be completely dedicated to you and our family." I reach for her hand. She doesn't reach out for mine. She shuffles around some papers.

"And you decided that two hours after writing a note to Kelly pledging your love to her."

I nod. *I'm an idiot. How did I get myself into this mess?*

"A jury could read this letter one of two ways—the way you just stated or a more ominous way. The ending could have been her death, and your little P.S. at the end could be you trying to make it seem like Kelly was still alive when you wrote this note. I believe what you said because only an idiot would try to cover up a murder with a letter."

"Well, I'm not lying about that," I confirm.

"You said you had changed your mind about leaving me for Kelly after I told you I wanted to have a baby?"

"Yes. Absolutely. All I've ever wanted was to start a family with you. I love you so much, Sarah. I'm sorry for what I've done and I wish I could take it all back, but I can't. Just know that I'm going to spend the rest of my life making it up to you. You're my wife. You're my everything. You're my forever."

"Kelly was pregnant," Sarah blurts out.

My mouth drops open.

"She was four weeks along." There's not an ounce of emotion in her voice. It's as if she were reading from a list. "According to the DNA results, you were the father."

Those words stab me in my gut and rip out my heart. I mouth, *What?* but the words don't come out. I stand up from my chair too quickly. The chair falls backward, hitting the ground with a thud. I drop my head into my hands and pull at my hair. I let out a loud howl. I cry for my unborn child. I know how this looks. Pregnant dead mistress. I try to compose myself, regain control of my emotions. Deep breaths, in and out.

"Did you know she was pregnant?" She looks up at me.

"You think I knew? How could you think I knew about this?" I pace back and forth, throwing my hands up. "How the fuck could you think that?" I ask again, this time with more bite and anger.

"How could I think you loved me, or you were faithful to me? How could I think when you said 'I do' that you meant it? How could I think that you and I were going to spend the rest of our lives together? How could I think that you weren't fucking and impregnating some other women behind my back? How the hell could I think any of that, Adam?"

By the time she's done screaming, she's half standing, and for a second, I think she's going to lunge at me—but she doesn't. She straightens her jacket and sits down on her chair. She smooths out her hair with the palm of her hand and calms herself.

I take my seat in front of her. She's right. I have no right to be angry at her for thinking that I knew Kelly was pregnant. I don't know how Sarah and I are going to get through this, and if we do, I'm not convinced we're going to get through it together. "Now what?" I ask.

"I'm going to look into Scott. I'm going to try to find out who sent the photo to you and who the third set of DNA belongs to. I need you to get your story straight."

"It's not a story."

"You know what I mean," she huffs.

I put my hand out to take hers and this time she lets me. I tell her I'm sorry again, but there are not enough apologies in the world to fix this, to fix what I've done. She squeezes my hand and then packs up her stuff.

I tell her I love her.

"Your mother is in town. She stopped by my office this

114

morning," she responds. There's no "I love you back," and I don't blame her.

"Really? How is she?"

"She's... your mother."

As Sarah turns to leave, she stops and looks back at me. "If charged, the D.A. will push for the maximum penalty allotted for a double homicide in the state of Virginia." Her voice shakes.

"And what's that?"

"Execution."

21

SARAH MORGAN

Anne walks into my office wearing a black pencil dress with her hair pulled up in a slicked-back ponytail. Every day she looks a little bit more like me. She's carrying two grande Americanos from Starbucks, one in each hand, and a file folder is tucked under her left arm. She closes the door behind her and shuffles quickly to my desk, setting down both coffees. She takes a seat across from me and places the folder on her lap.

I was supposed to come in yesterday after meeting with Adam, but I couldn't. I needed to be alone. I needed to process everything. I haven't told Anne about what happened at the jail or about the results of the autopsy or the DNA or the fact that Adam was the father of Kelly's unborn child or about the threatening note and photo Adam received. I'm sure she's anxious to hear what I have to say.

"How's mother-in-law-zilla?" Anne asks trying to lighten the mood right away.

I shake my head. "Don't even get me started." I take a sip of coffee. "I'm sorry I didn't stop in or call yesterday. Things just got crazy and overwhelming, and I didn't know how to handle it. Thank you for covering."

"What happened?" Concern and empathy spread across her face. She leans forward giving me her full attention.

"They found three sets of DNA inside her."

"Three?" she asks not in a way to question what I said but to confirm her shock. She holds up three fingers as she says it.

I nod and take a sip of my coffee. "Three. One is Adam's, one is Scott's, and one is unknown."

"She was sleeping with three men?"

"It would appear so."

"Jesus... girl gets around. Well, maybe that third set of DNA is the one responsible for her death...?" Anne suggests.

"That's exactly what Adam said."

"Who is this third man? Has anyone seen her with anyone else other than Scott or Adam?"

"As of now, no one saw her with a third man." I take another sip of my coffee and tap a pen on my desk. "Someone also sent Adam a photo with a threatening note. It was a photo of him and Kelly together, and the note said, 'End it or else I will.' Someone knew about them..." I bring the tip of my pen to my mouth and chew on it for a moment.

Anne's eyes are wide. Her mouth opens and then closes. She doesn't know what to say. I don't even know what to say. She swallows hard and then brings the coffee to her lips, taking another sip. "Are they testing anyone else?" Anne crosses one leg over the other. She places the folder from her lap onto the desk.

"Who would they test? They can't just go around testing any random man just because they don't know who the third set of DNA belongs to. They have to have cause."

"I know that. I'm saying is there anyone else that seems suspicious? Anyone else that may have had an affair with her, someone she worked with or was friends with or maybe an old boyfriend?"

"According to Sheriff Stevens, no one seemed suspicious at

her work, but then again, you never know with his police work. No past boyfriends that he or Scott knew of and she didn't really have any friends—well except my husband, I guess," I say trying for dark humor. The attempt flops. Anne gives me a sad look, and I deliver a small smile, trying to convey that I am in fact okay, even if I don't know if I really am.

"What do you mean, 'you never know about his police work?' Does he seem off?" Anne always picks up on the littlest things I say. It's why she's so great as my assistant.

"I don't know. He just seems a bit overly friendly."

"Overly friendly?"

"I don't know how to explain it. He just seems like he's more interested in this case than he should be."

"Do you think he knew Kelly or something like that?" Anne leans back in her chair. This has piqued her interest.

"No. Well, yeah. Her husband is on the police force, and it's a small town. He had to have known her. But I think he's flirting with me. He told me he would be there for me regardless if Adam were convicted and... and it's just the way he looks at me too." *Maybe I need that right now. I think I do. Sheriff Stevens might just be the person I need right now, more than I know.*

"That's really weird." Anne juts her nose.

"Is it though? Should I be worried? I should be, shouldn't I?"

"Well, he is the sheriff of the town, and you are the woman of a husband who supposedly murdered a resident there. And you're also the defense attorney for said husband. He might see you more as a victim, like the wife of a murderer rather than the defense attorney and he could just feel bad for what you're going through and the circumstances surrounding the case," Anne suggests.

"He doesn't seem to think Adam did it either. Don't you think it's odd that he told me that as the defense attorney on the case?"

"Yes, as the defense attorney. But not as the wife. He's probably just not able to draw the lines between what's appropriate and what's not given what's going on. This is an extremely odd predicament you're all in."

"I know, and sometimes, I wonder if I'm doing the right thing," I confess.

"Right thing?"

"Standing by my husband when he didn't stand by me."

"You're doing the right thing because you're a good person. Just because your husband was wrong, doesn't mean you have to be. You've stayed true to you and at the end of the day that's what matters. Whether he spends the rest of his life in jail or not, Adam is going to regret what he did to you. I can promise you that."

I press my lips together, raise my eyebrows and give a slight nod.

"Oh, by the way, the background checks on Kelly and Scott came in. Now I'm not you when it comes to investigative work, but I did find something that seems very odd. I just wasn't able to figure out exactly what was going on." Anne hands over the file.

I begin flipping through the pages. "What was the odd part you found?"

"For starters, Kelly Summers isn't her real name. It's Jenna Way."

"Jenna Way? Why the change of name?" I flip through the papers trying to find the answer to my own question. It's in my nature. If I ask a question, I have to find the answer. I typically don't trust others to give me the correct information. I mean, Adam didn't for all this time. He gave me half to nearly none of the pertinent information of what he was doing before Kelly was murdered and even now when his life is on the line, I know he's not telling me everything.

"Well, she was married before Scott. And her previous husband was murdered."

I'm still flipping through the papers. "What? How? By who?"

"He was stabbed to death by Kelly or should I say Jenna, and the odd thing is, she got off." Anne raises her eyebrow.

"That's really odd. None of it makes any sense. How did she get off?" I thumb through the papers.

"Evidence went missing during the trial, and the charges were dismissed. But guess who one of the arresting officers on the scene was?"

"Who?"

"None other than Scott Summers."

22

ADAM MORGAN

The guard opens the door, and I step into the small room. Immediately my body is wrapped in Mother's arms. She smells of her usual perfume and she's wearing all black as if she's dressed for my funeral. The guard informs us that visiting hours are over in ten minutes and then closes the door behind him.

"Sweetheart," she says kissing my cheeks. "What did they do to you?" She examines my face—poking and prodding to ensure it's healing properly. She's not a doctor, but she's seen enough of them to think she knows what she's doing.

"It's nothing, Mom." I pull her back in for a hug, so she'll stop staring and trying to put my face back together. I guide her back into her seat and I take the one across from her. She reaches for my hands, holding them, just gazing at me. Her mouth opens, then closes, then opens again, searching for the words to say.

"What, Mom?"

She says nothing. Continues staring.

"You're trying to decide if I did it?"

"No." Her response is resolute.

"No?" I cock my head.

"You're my son. I know you didn't do this and I'm going to get you out of here." She squeezes my hands.

"Mom, I was sleeping with Kelly. They found her body in my bed. My DNA was all over her." I shake my head. Saying it out loud makes me realize how truly fucked I am.

"Having an affair isn't a crime," my mother snaps back.

"Mom! Fuck the affair, look at the evidence they have!"

"It doesn't matter. I'm going to get you the best defense attorney." She nods as she speaks.

"I already have one."

"Who?"

"Sarah!" Mother has never treated her fairly. No matter what Sarah did she could never live up to my mother's expectations of success because their visions of success never aligned.

"Sarah? She's the one that got you into this mess."

I pull my hands away. "What? How?"

"Well, if she would have been more focused on loving you than her career, you wouldn't have been diddle-dipping elsewhere in the first place. Plus, she deprived you of fatherhood and stopped me from being a grandmother." Mom crosses her arms in front of her chest.

"None of that is true, Mom." I let out a huff and roll my eyes. "She just wasn't ready yet. You know why and you know what she went through." I narrow my eyes. *How can she say things like that about my wife? Sarah has been through enough, and she doesn't need this from my mother.*

"Yeah, yeah, yeah. Everyone has a pity story, Adam."

"Enough, Mom!" My voice raises more than I've ever raised it to my mother. She doesn't flinch. She doesn't even bat an eye. I could literally throw this table across the room and punch her right in the mouth, and she'd still look at me like I was the reason the sun rose every morning.

"Oh, sweetheart. Jail is already making you temperamental." She reaches across the table and caresses my cheek. "I'm going to bring you some of that peppermint tea you like. That used to help calm you down as a child." She smiles at me.

I take a deep breath. The door opens and, in the doorway, stands Sarah. My mom turns her neck to look.

"Eleanor. Adam," Sarah greets.

"Hello, Sarah." My mother's greeting is cold as usual.

"Adam isn't supposed to have visitors until after his arraignment. How did you get in here?" Sarah questions.

"I have my ways." Mom smirks.

"What are you doing here?" I ask. "Any good news?"

Sarah takes a couple of steps into the room and closes the door behind her. "I'm just here to tell you that they are officially charging you. You'll need to enter a plea tomorrow." She makes steady eye contact with my mother and me. "But I'll be back in the morning to cover it with you. I just... I just wanted to give you a heads-up."

"Officially charged?" I question.

Sarah nods.

"This is ridiculous, Sarah." My mother stands from her chair. "You need to fix this." She points at my wife.

"I'm working on it, Eleanor. The D.A. believes he can prove Adam's guilty beyond a reasonable doubt, so he's going for it."

"But I didn't do this!" My eyes get wet and my voice quakes.

"I know, sweetheart," Mom says. "And we are going to get you the best attorney money can buy, and it'll all be over soon."

Sarah shakes her head. "I'm going to go." She turns on her foot.

The guard pops open the door and stands there like a soldier at attention. "Visiting hours are over," he announces.

Mom rushes around the table and hugs me. "I will be back tomorrow, cubbie-bear," she whispers in my ear.

"Mom, don't call me that. I'm in jail." I push the words through gritted teeth trying not to let anyone hear me.

Sarah side-steps the guard to leave. My mother releases me and whips around. "Sarah, wait! I want to take you out for dinner. You know, discuss next steps," my mother insists.

Sarah stops and looks back at us. "I have a lot of work to do and—"

Mom holds her hand up. "Your excuses won't work with me. We're going."

23

SARAH MORGAN

We are seated across from each other at Pineapple & Pearls, Eleanor's choice. The restaurant has a fixed menu, and while I'm sure the selection will be divine, it is just another example of her being in control of the situation.

"Where do we start, Sarah?" she asks me.

"We? We don't start anywhere. You aren't a lawyer nor are you a law enforcement official, so there isn't a scenario where you get to rummage through evidence or crime scenes or anything else to help Adam. You just need to let me do my job." I deliver squarely to her. Hopefully, she will take the overt hint and drop the notion of teaming up to save her baby boy.

"And how do you expect me to do that?"

Of-fucking-course she doesn't drop it. "Do what, Eleanor?"

"Leave this all in your hands. I mean how can we even trust you to do the best job here?" She scans the drink menu as she speaks as if she and I are talking about the weather or some other mundane thing.

"Excuse me?"

She looks up at me. "I think you need to accept some fault in this too. And if that's the case then..."

"What?" *Where in the hell does she get off? On what planet does this, any of this, make sense?*

"I mean husbands don't typically cheat on loving wives."

"That's wildly inappropriate." I shake my head in disbelief.

She keeps going. "And Adam has always wanted to be a father... and I, a grandmother, and you have withheld that joy from us."

I hold my hand up. "I'm going to stop you right there, Eleanor..." I would love to reach across the table and claw her Botox face off.

"Now, I know you had a rough upbringing with your dad's passing and your mom's drug addiction—but that's not something you get to hold on to forever...." She pauses when the waitress arrives. "We'll have two Manhattans." She closes the drinks menu and hands it to the waitress.

I have half the nerve to storm out of here, but I know that won't do Adam any good.

"Actually, I'll have Tito's double vodka soda with a lime," I correct. The waitress nods. I give a small grin.

"Bring them both anyway. I'm going to need two," she says to the waitress. "Now, what was I saying?"

My hands are beneath the table clenched so tightly, my nails are digging into my palms. The moisture and warmth tell me I've punctured the skin.

"Oh, yes... I've lost people too. My husband died, but you don't see that stopping me from living my life." Eleanor nods as she speaks as if she's giving me some sort of motivational speech, but the only thing she's motivating me to do is to flip this table into her and walk out the door.

I relax my hands, looking down at them for a moment. There are small bloody puncture wounds on each palm. I clutch my napkin and take a deep breath. *I can get through this. I've endured worse.* The waitress sets down my vodka soda and two

Manhattans. I take mine and drink nearly the entire thing. Eleanor is still talking about how I should live my life and how Adam is not at fault.

"...and addiction clearly runs in your family, Sarah. You might just be addicted to your work. I'm just trying to help and I want to make sure Adam is getting the best defense possible." She takes a slow sip of her Manhattan, while holding eye contact with me.

"He has the best defense possible and it bodes well for Adam that his wife of ten years is not only standing behind him but is also defending him in the matter."

"It's the least you can do, Sarah. Now, are you sure you're equipped to handle this?" She attempts to raise an eyebrow, but her Botox infested face isn't able to comply.

"I'm positive."

"Well, I suppose your work addiction will provide a benefit for once." Eleanor smirks.

My eyes nearly roll out of their sockets. "I suppose it will."

"Ugh. I really wish you would have paid more attention to my son and upheld your wifely duties. Adam wouldn't be in this predicament otherwise. Such a shame." She shakes her head as she speaks.

She'll keep going on all evening unless I tell her what she wants to hear. I take a deep breath.

"You're right, Eleanor. I should have been a better wife to Adam. But I promise you this, I will be better now, and I'll make sure Adam gets the justice he deserves," I say with a stern nod.

The waitress sets down the first course.

Eleanor smiles back at me. "I knew you'd see it my way. Now, let's enjoy our meal."

24

ADAM MORGAN

Once again, I find myself lying in a metal bunk with a mattress I swear is as thick as a piece of cardboard. I've spent sixty of the last seventy-two hours lying in this bed thinking about how I got here. I'm still not sure how I went from having an affair to being the primary suspect for the murder of my mistress. How did I end up here?

Sarah feels nothing for me anymore, I know this, and I can't say that I blame her. Even if by some miracle she is able to get me off, we'll never have what we had before—if we had anything at all. I'm not so sure anymore. Was I just convenient, a warm body to come home to? No, I'm sure there was love before, but I look at her now... and I think I've hurt her to the point where there's no going back. She does still have feelings for me, but those feelings are overpowered by feelings of hatred, anger, sadness, regret. Will I survive this? I don't know. Will we survive this? Probably not.

Our meeting yesterday didn't end well, thanks in part to my mother's comments. After Sarah told me they were officially charging me, she and Mom left for dinner. I can't imagine that meal went well.

A guard smacks his baton against the bars of my cell. "You've got a visitor."

I stand up and drag my feet across the floor. I really don't care to speak to anyone, but visitors and time in the rec room are the only things that break up the hours while I'm here. I follow the officer until we're standing in front of the interrogation room. He opens the door, and there's a man with a blond buzz cut sitting in the chair. His back is to me. *New lawyer*, I think. Perhaps Sarah finally decided enough was enough, and my mom hired a new attorney. I pass him and when I sit down to take my seat across from him, it's then that I find out who he is. Scott Summers. I try to stand back up to leave.

"Relax, I'm just here to talk." He puts his hands up trying to show that he is not a threat to me. His voice is deep and husky. It's the first time that I've heard him speak. Last time we met, his fists did all the talking. I look back to the guard and then back at the chair deciding.

"It's up to you, Adam. I'm not going to force you to sit here," the guard says. We all exchange looks and then I decide to take a seat. If anything, maybe Scott will slip up, and I'll uncover something that'll help my case. What do I have to lose? My life? At this point, I wouldn't consider it much of a loss anyway.

"Thanks," Scott says.

"No funny business, Scott. I'm breaking a few rules by having you here, so don't screw me over. I'll be on the other side of this door. You've got twenty minutes." The guard steps out and closes the door behind him.

I lean back in my chair and wait for him to speak. I don't know why he's here and I don't know why he wants to talk to me. But he's here and he can be the first to speak.

"Like I said, I'm just here to talk. I just want to know what happened. I want to know what you know." He has dark circles under his eyes and an unkempt beard. His button-up plaid shirt is wrinkled and his hair is frayed. He clearly hasn't been taking care of himself.

"I've told everything to the police. It's all in my statements, and I know you have access to them. So why are you here?"

"I do, and I have read them, but I want to hear it from you," he says.

"What do you want to know exactly?"

"Did Kelly ever say anything about me? Did you know she was married?"

"Yes, I knew she was married, and I know what you did to her." My eyes narrow. I want to reach across this table for all the times he hurt her.

"What is it that you think I did to her?" He scrunches up his face and leans back.

"You were abusive to her. You hurt her. You bruised her and made her bleed. Do you think you're some big powerful man? Do you think hitting your wife makes you a tough guy?" I slam a fist on the table.

"What are you talking about? I never laid a hand on her. How could she say that?" He pounds his fist on the table, which doesn't do much for his case.

"I've seen her bruises. I've seen her with a black eye, a bloody nose, and a fat lip. Don't sit there and deny what you did. Are you scared that the police will find out what you've done and look to you as the primary suspect? Because I know it was you that killed her. I know it." I clench my jaw so tight my teeth ache.

"Are you fucking kidding me? I loved Kelly. There was one time about two weeks before she died that I accidentally caught her in the face with my elbow when I was hanging drywall in our home, but that's it. She left and said she was going to a neighbor's house to use their first aid kit because ours was missing. Are you telling me she went to your house and told you

I hit her on purpose?" He's pissed, but there's also sadness in his eyes. Either, he's an incredible actor, or he's telling the truth.

"She did come over crying and told me all about what you did and what you had been doing to her over the years. I've seen her bruises on more than one occasion. Why would she lie?"

"I don't fucking know. Maybe for sympathy. Maybe for attention. I don't know why she would do that. But I can tell you one thing, she used to come to me back when I was an officer in Appleton, Wisconsin and tell me all the same stuff about her first husband, that he was abusing her. I would never intentionally hurt her and now I'm starting to think, maybe he didn't either." He's glancing all over the place as if he's putting all the pieces together. But his furrowed brows and wide eyes show me that it's not making sense. None of it does. Why would she do that?

"She told me about her first husband. She told me you were holding it over her, that you'd say you could go back and get her convicted of his murder if you wanted. It's why she couldn't leave you."

"None of that is true. I never talked about him. I never brought that part of her life up. When we left Wisconsin, we left that chapter of our lives behind us." He looks me straight in the eye. He wants me to believe him, but I don't know whether or not he's telling the truth. How could I? I don't know him. All I know is what Kelly has told me about him.

"Why would she lie about that?" I ask.

"I really don't know. But I swear to you I never hurt her."

"What about the texts you sent her the night of her murder? You threatened her!"

"I know. I regret sending those," he says with a soft sob. "But I didn't kill her. I was with my partner, Marcus, all night."

"Convenient. Is that why you're here? To convince me that you're innocent in all of this?"

He rubs his face with his hands as if he's trying to wake himself up from a bad dream or something. "No, I came here to look you in the eye and for you to be man enough to admit what you've done."

"I didn't kill Kelly. I wouldn't. I loved her, and I know you don't want to hear that as her husband, but I did."

Scott shakes his head.

The door flings open and in the doorway is Sarah, her assistant Anne, and a man in a pinstripe suit. It takes me a moment to recognize him. It's Matthew, Sarah's best friend in law school. I haven't seen him in years—but Sarah stays in touch with him via text, calls, and emails. She's even visited him a few times in New York. Sarah looks at Scott and then at me and from her expression, I know she's pissed.

"What the hell are you doing speaking to my client?" she shouts, her attention directed at Scott.

He gets up from his chair. "I was just leaving," he says calmly.

"This is not fucking okay. Where is Sheriff Stevens?"

Scott tries to pass her, but she blocks the doorway with her small and slender stature. She juts her chin up at him.

"Like I said, I was just leaving," Scott says.

"I don't care. You have no right to speak to him!" She crosses her arms over her chest.

"I know. I'm sorry."

"Sarah, it's fine. We're done talking. Just let him go," I say.

"What were you two talking about? As his lawyer, I have a right to know."

"Come on, Scott." The guard ushers him out. Sarah doesn't step aside, and he has to practically shrink down to nothing to get past her. Her death glare returns to me. I'm targeted with matching glares from Anne and Matthew. Anne is like Sarah's puppet, doing and saying whatever she's told. Their relationship has always rubbed me the wrong way. Anne idolizes Sarah, and Sarah basks in that attention. Matthew has always been Sarah's sidekick, and it appears Robin has returned to Batman's side.

"Are you trying to lose this case?" Sarah taps her Louboutin stiletto rapidly on the tile floor. It's clearly a rhetorical question, and I simply shrug.

She shakes her head. "Are you going to tell me what that was all about?"

"It was nothing. He just wanted to talk about Kelly." I don't know why I'm not saying any more, maybe because what Scott said destroys my case. If Scott was never abusive, why would anyone believe that he killed her? And if he was with Deputy Hudson all night, he couldn't have murdered Kelly. Then again, an officer having his partner as an alibi doesn't sit well for me. It's all a bit too perfect.

Sarah and Anne take a seat in front of me. They start pulling out files from their bags. Matthew leans against the wall behind them as if standing guard.

"What brings you here, Matthew?" I ask.

"I'm in town a while for business... and I guess the timing isn't great, considering..." Matthew says looking around.

"Timing was never your strong suit," I say.

"Clearly not yours either," Matthew quips.

"Will you stop?" Sarah narrows her eyes at me. "Matthew is helping with your case, so show a little respect."

I nod and lower my head. Jail is already turning me into a hardened asshole, or maybe I've been one all along.

Sarah reads over her notes briefly and then looks to me. "Did you know Kelly Summers' real name was Jenna Way?"

"I did. She told me about her past two weeks before she was murdered."

"And you decided to leave that bit of information out?"

"It slipped my mind."

"You're a suspect for murder and the fact that the woman you were sleeping with killed her first husband slipped your mind?" There's anger in her voice. Once again, I don't blame her.

"She was never formally charged," I argue.

"Yes, she was. The case fell apart in the middle of the trial after evidence went missing—which, from the looks of it, Scott may have helped make disappear." She tightens her jaw.

Anne crosses her arms in front of her chest. Matthew shakes his head. I wish the two of them weren't here. I don't need the additional judgment. Mine and Sarah's judgment is more than enough.

"Kelly said she didn't do it," I confess.

"That's what all murderers say," Anne pipes up.

"Isn't that what you've been saying?" Matthew smirks at me.

Sarah turns around and shoots a look at Matthew. I can't see her face, but Matthew says, "Okay, okay, I'll stop," so I know she's sticking up for me. Matthew has always been protective of Sarah, and I can understand the cutting remarks, but I appreciate Sarah defending me.

"Your arraignment is in one hour," Anne interjects. She pulls a pair of pants, a button-down shirt, a tie, and dress shoes from her bag and slides them toward me.

"You'll need to enter your plea as you're being officially charged for the murder of Kelly Rose Summers and her unborn child," Sarah says. Her eyes meet mine. She tightens her face, but a tear breaks through, and before the dam opens, she wipes it away and takes a couple of small breaths—closing the dam for now... or maybe for good.

I nod as I knew this was coming. Sarah told me yesterday.

"If you plead not guilty, the D.A. will try for the death penalty. If you plead guilty, they're offering twenty-five years with no possibility of parole. What would you like to plea?"

"Well, not guilty of course. I didn't fucking do this." Anger grabs hold of my voice.

She nods. "All right. We'll be back in an hour for your arraignment."

They pack up their stuff and walk out, leaving me there alone with a pile of clothing.

25

SARAH MORGAN

Anne, Matthew, and I walk to a small coffee shop across the street as we have thirty minutes before Adam's arraignment. Matthew and I take our seats at a high-top table, while Anne orders us coffee.

"Adam looks awful. I've never seen him like that," Matthew says. "It's been a while but still."

"It suits him though," I say. I'm still mad at him for withholding information about Kelly, or should I say, *Jenna*. I would have scolded him yesterday if Eleanor hadn't been there. And now today, I find him talking to Scott Summers, Kelly's husband. He's a possible suspect, he's part of my defense strategy, and Adam is destroying it. Anne takes a seat at the table.

Matthew tightens his eyes, "Do you think it's a good idea for him to plead not guilty, especially with the death penalty on the line?"

"Based on the evidence, probably not. But it's not my job to sway my client. I'm simply supposed to present them with their options."

The barista sets down our cups of coffee.

"But he's your husband," Matthew argues.

"He's my client first."

Matthew nods, dropping it. I glance at him as I take a sip of my coffee. *What's his angle here?*

"Let's not forget that jerk cheated on her for over a year," Anne says with a bit of sass.

"And if it were up to Adam's mother, I'd be the one on trial. She thinks this is all my doing." I shake my head.

Matthew nearly drops his drink.

Anne's eyes shoot open. "She said that?"

"She said I need to take responsibility because a man doesn't cheat on a loving wife."

"What a bitch—" Anne immediately slaps her hand over her mouth as the words come out.

"I second that," Matthew laughs. "Is she going to be around for a while?"

"I assume for the whole trial. She's treating this thing like Adam's the new lead in *Hamilton* rather than the accused in a double-homicide case."

Anne and Matthew laugh.

"I'll try my best to keep her out of your hair," Anne says.

"Thank you. Now, we're going to have to start pulling witnesses. The greatest strength we'll have in this case is casting doubt on Adam. Kelly has a twisted past with a lot of loose ends. There's a number of people that may have wanted her dead, especially if she killed her first husband. That man had family and friends, and I'm sure none of them were happy that she got off scot-free... pun intended."

Anne lets out a chuckle as she pulls out her notepad and begins making a list.

"Plus, the threatening note and photograph. Someone took that photo. Someone wrote that note, and we need to figure out who," I say.

Matthew nods.

"Any witnesses you want me to contact?" Anne writes down more notes.

"Yes. Let's pull Sheriff Stevens, Scott Summers, Deputy Hudson, and let's find a relative of her husband, someone that has bad blood with her. We're also going to need to pull her phone records. I want to find out who that third set of DNA belongs to." I pause and quickly go over everything in my head, thinking about all possibilities. "Also, I'd like to talk to a few of her co-workers. Maybe there's someone there that knew more about her past or her indiscretions, someone that can give us more insight on Kelly. Right now, no one seems to really know who she is." I take another sip of my coffee.

"Got it, boss," Anne says.

"I can take care of the phone records. I know people in high places who are willing to go to low places... for me." Matthew winks.

I give him a small smile. "Thanks, Matthew. I appreciate it."

"No problem. I have to jet off to a meeting—just send me the phone numbers." He stands and pulls me in for a tight hug. "I'd do anything for you, Sarah." He kisses both of my cheeks, says goodbye, and heads out of the café.

I glance down at my watch and look at Anne. "We should probably head over."

26

ADAM MORGAN

I'm waiting outside the courtroom handcuffed and dressed in the clothes Sarah delivered. A guard is standing beside me, ensuring I don't run—as if I'd have anywhere to run to. I'm pleading not guilty because I know I didn't do this. But I also know that in some cases not committing the crime isn't enough to be innocent. And I think I might be one of those cases. The evidence is stacked against me. I know that. Sarah knows that. Everyone knows that. I'll need a miracle to get out of this.

My mother comes walking through the courthouse doors, dressed in all white as if she believes she's my guardian angel. She pulls her Chanel glasses from her face and slides them into her bag. She stops right in front of me, surveying my attire. "You look perfect, darling," she says, planting a kiss on each of my cheeks.

I shake my head.

My mother looks up and down at the guard standing beside me. "Are those necessary?" She points at the handcuffs around my wrists.

"He's entering a plea for double homicide today... so, yes."

"How could anyone think such a handsome and charming

man could be guilty of anything?" She pushes the hair off my forehead gently.

The guard rolls his eyes. "No touching please, ma'am."

Mom gives him a dirty look, then glances around the lobby. "Where's Sarah and her little assistant?"

"They just went to grab coffee."

"Giving into their own vices over my son's well-being? Doesn't seem like a very strong defense team."

"Mom, stop."

"I'm just saying." She flips her hand at me dismissively.

Sarah and Anne enter the courthouse, each carrying a cup of coffee and a tote bag. A coffee would be great right about now, but if I'm wishing for things—a glass of scotch would be much better. They're chatting as they approach me. I wonder where Matthew ran off to. He's always showing up randomly and then disappearing. Sarah is wearing one of her standard power skirt suits in the color heather gray. Anne is dressed in a similar style, but her outfit probably costs a tenth of what Sarah's does. Sarah's whole demeanor changes when she sees my mother.

"There you are, Sarah," Mom says. "I was wondering when you were going to get around to defending my son."

Sarah stops quickly about a foot away. Anne gives an awkward nod and stands beside her. "The arraignment hasn't started yet, Eleanor."

Sarah practically turns her body away from my mom, making it very clear she has no desire to speak to her. "Here's how this is going to go. You'll enter your plea, and I'm going to try to get you out on bail. The judge will either grant or deny bail, and then he'll set a trial date. Do you understand?"

"Yes. What are my chances of getting bail?"

"I'd say you should have a good chance. You have no criminal history and you've been cooperative thus far. But on the flip side, District Attorney Josh Peters may fight it, and I wouldn't be surprised if he did."

"Why?"

"Yes, why would anyone want to see my son behind bars?" Eleanor asks. Sarah ignores her and only focuses on me.

"This is a very violent crime, and he is seeking the death penalty, and because of that you might be deemed a flight risk." She takes a sip of her coffee, then looks back at me. Her face softens. She holds the cup up, offering it to me. I glance down at my handcuffed hands and shrug. She brings the cup to my lips and pours it into my mouth. It's lukewarm, but it's better than anything I've had in the jail. Sarah gives me a small smile as I pull away. Maybe she does still love me.

"Thank you."

She nods.

The information she just told me finally sinks in. "Wait, I'd have to spend the duration of the trial in jail if bail is denied?" I ask to confirm even though I know the answer to the question. I just want to talk to Sarah as husband and wife, not as lawyer and client.

"That's correct." I notice she has a bit of sweat on her forehead and her face is turning pale.

"That's ridiculous. You better take care of this, Sarah." Mom taps her heel on the floor.

"Are you okay?" I ask. She gags, hands her coffee to Anne, and runs to a nearby garbage can in the lobby and throws up. Anne rushes to her side and rubs her back, asking her if she needs anything or if she should reschedule. Sarah shakes her head and scurries off to the bathroom.

"She'll be right back," Anne says walking over to me.

"Is she okay? What's wrong with her?" I'm concerned not only for my wife but if she'll be able to handle this hearing.

"I don't think she can handle this case. We should shop around," Mom whispers into my ear.

"Stop, Mom."

"I'm sure she's fine," Anne says.

"Maybe you should go help her," Mom says to Anne, shooing her away. "Sarah's clearly not strong enough on her own."

27

SARAH MORGAN

I walk out of the bathroom stall and splash some water on my face. I take my makeup bag from my tote, re-powder my face, swish around some mouthwash, and reapply my lip gloss. I feel fine now, but I don't know what came over me—the stress of this case, poor nutrition, inadequate sleep, or fucking Eleanor. I have to pull it together. I pat down my hair and smooth away any flyaways.

Pulling out my phone, I text Anne—*I'm fine. Must have had something that didn't agree with me. I'll be back in a few minutes.*

I give myself a once-over in the mirror, straightening out my top and skirt and tightening my ponytail. I pick up my bag and walk out of the bathroom, running smack bang into District Attorney Josh Peters. The coffee he's holding spills all over the both of us, and we both apologize to one another.

"Sarah, I'm sorry," D.A. Peters says.

"No, I'm sorry, Josh."

"Wait right here." He dips into the men's bathroom. He comes out moments later with a wad of paper towels. He hands me half, and we both wipe and dab at the coffee. His white button-up shirt is stained, but it's hard to even see where the coffee was spilled on his black pants and jacket. I find myself glancing up at him as we blot ourselves. He's in his mid-thirties and overqualified for the job he's in. He could have gone into corporate law or defense, but his moral compass kept him in the public sector.

We finish getting as cleaned up as possible. D.A. Peters even wipes up the spilled coffee on the floor and then collects the soiled towels. He disappears into the bathroom and returns a moment later carrying just his briefcase.

"Listen, I know we're on opposite sides and what your situation is, and I just want to let you know that I'm sorry for what you're going through, but I'm still going to do my job." He stands firm with perfect posture, his presence giving no hint of the sympathy he is trying to exude with his words.

"I wouldn't expect anything less from you, D.A. Peters."

"Good. Are you ready?"

"Actually, I'd like to speak with you about the plea deal."

"Sure." He widens his stance and puts one of his hands on his hip. The open posture is supposed to signal an inviting tone as he waits to hear my offer. I have to give it to him, he has all the nuances down to a tee.

"Can we take the death penalty off the table and go for life in prison for a not guilty plea? You know just as well as I do, juries have a hard time coming up with a conviction when the death penalty is involved, and there's a third set of DNA. We don't even know who it belongs to." I hold my hands out, palms face up as if offering a physical item to him.

"The evidence is stacked against Adam with or without that DNA. You know that, Sarah." He re-crosses his arms and closes his stance as if to say, *deal time is over.*

"I know," I say feeling defeated. He's right. That DNA doesn't really matter if we don't know who it belongs to. Kelly was found dead in our home, and Adam was the last person to see her alive, plus his DNA is all over her."

"And Adam failed his lie detector test," D.A. Peters adds.

"Yeah, and so did Scott. You know as much as I do polygraphs are a bunch of pseudoscience bullshit." I narrow my eyes at him.

"Fine. I'll tell you what. If he pleads guilty, I'll reduce the sentence from twenty-five years to twenty years without parole. But that offer expires in five minutes."

"I'll go talk to my client. Thank you."

Adam is still standing handcuffed in front of the doors of the courtroom. Eleanor is deep in conversation with him. Nothing good can come of that. The guard is near him but inattentive, and Anne is sitting on a bench alone, looking around aimlessly.

"Hey," I say interrupting Eleanor and Adam.

Anne quickly gets up and joins us.

"Are you okay?" Anne and Adam both speak at the same time. I tell them I am.

"Maybe we should have someone else stand in for you." Eleanor looks me up and down.

"I said I'm fine and I renegotiated the plea deal."

"What is it?" Adam asks.

"D.A. Peters offered twenty years with no possibility of parole if you plead guilty. It's a good deal considering what you're looking at. I can't tell you what to plead, but I do have to present it to you."

He draws his eyebrows together and squeezes his eyes shut for a moment. He was hoping for a miracle, but twenty years is still a long time to spend behind bars. He'll be fifty-six when he gets out. But it's better than the alternative, which is death if a jury finds him guilty. With the current evidence, a jury would most likely have no problem passing out a guilty verdict.

"That's a terrible deal, Sarah. My son is innocent. Twenty

years? I'll be dead by the time he gets out." Eleanor stomps her heel.

I ignore her and look to Adam.

He looks to me. "What would you suggest?"

"As your lawyer, I'd say take the deal."

"What about as my wife?"

I take a moment to decide what to say. "As your wife, I'd say fight like hell."

"All right then. Tell him no deal." There's positivity in his voice. I don't know where that came from, there's nothing positive in this case. I nod at Adam, and he sends back a partial smile, a small glimmer of hope in his eyes.

D.A. Peters walks up to us and says hello to everyone. "What's it going to be?"

"My client will be pleading not guilty."

"You're making a mistake. My son is innocent." Eleanor folds her arms in front of her chest.

"Okay then." D.A. Peters nods, walks past us, and enters the courtroom. Adam, Anne, and I follow and sit on the left side of the room at a table. Eleanor takes a front row seat. I hope she keeps her mouth shut during this. Better yet, I hope she doesn't. Perhaps the judge can do me a solid and charge her with contempt of court. Anne pulls out a couple of files and places them in front of me.

"All rise! The court is now in session. The Honorable Judge Dionne presiding," the bailiff announces.

Judge Dionne, an old man with thinning white hair and glasses hanging at the tip of his nose enters and sits at his bench. He flips through a couple of pieces of paper and then redirects his attention to D.A. Peters and me. "In the matter of the People of the State of Virginia v. Adam Morgan. Counsel, please state your appearances," Judge Dionne says.

"District Attorney Josh Peters representing the People of the State of Virginia, Your Honor."

"Sarah Morgan representing Adam Morgan, Your Honor."

Judge Dionne raises an eyebrow when he hears Morgan and Morgan. He immediately puts two and two together. "Interesting. Defendant, please state your full name for the court."

"Adam Francis Morgan."

"D.A. Peters, will you please state the charges that have been made against the defendant in this case?" Judge Dionne asks.

"Yes, Your Honor. The state charges Adam Morgan with first-degree double homicide against Kelly Summers and her unborn child."

"It is my understanding that the defendant is planning to plead not guilty to the charges brought by the People. Before I take your plea, I must ensure that you understand your constitutional and statutory rights. You have a right to be represented by counsel at this arraignment, which I see you have already retained."

"Yes, Your Honor," Adam says.

"You have a right to a preliminary hearing within ten court days after the arraignment or entry of a plea. You have the right to a speedy trial..." Judge Dionne goes on and on. I've heard this spiel a thousand times before, but this is Adam's first time hearing it. He listens attentively, never breaking eye contact with the judge. I don't realize I've zoned out until the judge finishes with, "Do you understand these rights?"

"Yes, Your Honor."

"Mrs. Morgan, do you believe that you have had enough time to discuss this case with your client? Have you discussed his rights, defenses, and the possible consequences of his plea with him? Are you satisfied your client understands these things?" Judge Dionne asks.

"Yes, Your Honor."

"Mr. Morgan, are you prepared to enter your plea?"

"Yes, Your Honor."

"Mr. Morgan, you are charged with double homicide in the first degree. To that charge, what is your plea?"

Adam stands. "Not guilty, Your Honor," he says with all the confidence in the world.

"The court accepts the defendant's plea of not guilty. Court is scheduled to begin two weeks from today, Monday, November 2nd. Bail is set at $500,000."

"Your Honor, the state recommends that Adam Morgan be held without bail," D.A. Peters says.

"Your Honor, that's ridiculous." I stand.

"Adam Morgan is facing the death penalty. He has the means to flee. We believe he is a flight risk, Your Honor," D.A. Peters argues.

"This is his first criminal charge of any crime whatsoever. My client has been cooperative throughout this process," I argue.

"I've heard both sides. Bail is set at $500,000, and Adam Morgan will be put on house arrest for the duration of the trial," Judge Dionne rules.

"Thank you, Your Honor," I say.

"Court dismissed." Judge Dionne smacks his gavel.

"Well done." D.A. Peters shakes my hand. "But don't count on that kind of luck throughout the trial."

"It's not luck. It's talent," I say as he walks away.

"What happens now?" Adam looks at me.

"I'll get the money pulled together right away, and you should be fitted for an ankle bracelet and discharged this afternoon. You will need to remain at the lake house during the trial. Sheriff Stevens cleared it yesterday, so it's no longer an active crime scene. You'll only be able to leave the house for set court dates. If you violate the terms of bail by either missing a court date or leaving the lake house, you'll be thrown back in jail. Do you understand?"

"Yes." He holds up his hands for the guard to cuff him.

"I'm going to go to talk to Sheriff Stevens. I'll meet you at the lake house this afternoon. An officer will bring you home."

"Okay. Thank you, Sarah."

Anne packs up our stuff and follows me. As I pass Eleanor, she nods and gives me a pleased smile. It's the first time I've ever received one from her. I return a tight smile of my own.

Sheriff Stevens is waiting at the back of the courtroom, holding a couple of file folders stuffed with papers.

"Hey, Sarah," he says, doing his best James Dean impression from *Rebel Without A Cause*. He is leaning up against the wall, head slightly cocked, eyes slightly squinted.

"Sheriff Stevens, this is my assistant Anne. Anne, Sheriff Stevens." They shake hands and exchange greetings.

"The test results on that scotch came back. They did find Rohypnol in it, and we tested the blood draw we took from Adam the night of his arrest. There wasn't any Rohypnol in his system."

"That doesn't make any sense. If he was drinking the scotch too, he must have had Rohypnol in his system," I say.

"Maybe he wasn't drinking from the decanter," Sheriff Stevens suggests. "Sorry, I don't have better news for you."

"What about that third set of DNA? Did you guys get a match in the criminal database?"

"Unfortunately, not. We're still looking into it. We did get the phone records back." He hands me the file folders. "Her texts are printed out as well."

I hand the folders off to Anne who sticks them away in her tote bag. "Did you have a chance to read through them? Anything unusual?"

"The texts from the number that appear to be from the other man she was seeing are from an unregistered number."

"Like a burner phone?"

"Exactly. Whoever he is, he didn't want anyone to know he was in contact with Kelly. Maybe he's the one that did this or perhaps he's married himself," he offers.

"Can we find out anything about that number?"

"As of now, it's a dead end. Going through the texts more closely might give us some sort of clue as to who he is, but there's not many text messages between them anyway. However, since a formal charge has been entered in the court, this case is closed for us. I can get you any information you need that we already have, but I can't put any more man-hours into this case."

"What about Scott? Did you look into him?"

"We did. He has an alibi for the night of Kelly's murder."

"Who?"

"Deputy Marcus Hudson," Sheriff Stevens says.

"Were they both working that night?" I tap my foot in annoyance at the information coming my way.

"Nope, just two buddies hanging out at Scott's house."

"Right..." I say sarcastically. "What about the photo with the threatening note?"

"We pulled fingerprints and ran them through a criminal database. No match. So, all that means is the person who sent it isn't a criminal... yet." Sheriff Stevens raises an eyebrow.

Anne's tote bag falls to the floor with a loud thud, and nearly everything spills out of it. She quickly bends down and gathers her items. "Sorry," she says as Sheriff Stevens and I bend down to help.

Something isn't adding up. Something's fishy. Adam didn't have Rohypnol in his system, but it was in the decanter, and the police forget to even check for that. Deputy Hudson is Scott's alibi, and they were just hanging out at Scott's home all night with no other witnesses. Is this sloppy police work or is there something more sinister going on? I'll have to get to the bottom of it because I'm clearly not getting any help from the Prince William County Sheriff's Department.

We stand up, while Anne finishes packing her tote bag.

"Holler at me if you need anything. I'll be bringing Adam to the lake house this afternoon. Maybe I'll see you there," he says.

"Yeah, maybe."

He walks out the courtroom doors. I turn to Anne just as she gets her bag back up on her shoulder.

"We're on our own now?" she asks.

"Looks that way."

"Do you want me to hire a private investigator for the case then?"

"No, I think we can handle this. We have two weeks to prepare for preliminary trial. I need you to go back to the office and start going through those texts. Compare them to what Matthew sends over to make sure they match up. I'll be back in tomorrow morning. Please call me if you find anything."

"You got it." She nods and marches out the door.

I can't hire a private detective just yet. I have to put up the half mil for Adam's bail, and I can't use the firm's resources to hire a detective. It's too big of an expense, and it'll get flagged. I'm sure Eleanor would put up the money, but I don't even want to give her that small victory. She's already involved herself too much and she's going to end up compromising the case. I'll just have to handle it myself.

28

ADAM MORGAN

Sheriff Stevens escorts me from the car into the lake house. He's explaining how much room I have outside, which is about twenty yards from the house in all directions. My mom pulls up and parks her Cadillac rental. She was sure to follow closely behind the entire time, running red lights and only pausing at stop signs as if she were involved in a high-speed pursuit.

"This is quaint," Mom says looking at the lake house.

"Let's get you fitted for an ankle bracelet, and I'll get the transmitter set up inside," Sheriff Stevens says.

I lead the way. The sheriff sets up a black box and then tells me to have a seat on the sofa. He walks over and kneels beside me. Pushing up my pant leg, he fastens the bracelet around my ankle. Mom glances around the house and then at me. She frowns at the ankle bracelet.

"Do you have any wine, Adam?" she asks.

"Yeah, Mom. There's some in the kitchen." She makes herself at home, pouring herself a large glass of red wine and rummaging in the cupboards. She goes into the fridge and pulls out sausage and cheese and begins slicing them up.

"Now, it is waterproof. Showering with it ain't a problem. If you remove it, we'll know. If you leave the premises, we'll know. You got yourself a nice place here, so just settle in."

"All right," I say pushing my pant leg back down. He stands up and takes a couple of steps into the living room, glancing around. "Is there anything else I should know?" I ask.

"Nope. That's it—did Kelly ever talk about the other guy she was seeing?"

"I didn't even know there was another guy."

He makes a hmmph sound and walks to the built-in bookshelf. He reads the spines and randomly pulls out one here and there. I look into the kitchen and watch my mom fill her wine glass a second time.

"You never got the sense there was someone else?" he asks.

"No."

"She never slipped up and mentioned another man's name or anything like that?"

"No, like I said, I didn't know she was seeing someone else." There's an edge of annoyance in my voice.

"Here, some snacks for you, honey." Mom sets down a platter of cheese, sausage, and crackers. Sheriff Stevens pops a piece of sausage in his mouth, while Mom stands beside him holding her glass of wine.

"Will you be working on finding the real criminal responsible for this murder, Sheriff Stevens?" Mom takes a sip and raises an eyebrow.

The sheriff lets out an awkward cough.

The front door opens and closes with a bang. Sarah's heels tap across the hardwood floor. "Hey, you're still here?" she says to Sheriff Stevens.

"Yeah, I was just leaving actually." He turns from the bookshelf and takes a step toward the front door.

"He has a criminal to catch. Don't you, sheriff?" Mom questions.

Sarah just mumbles to herself, but she seems disappointed that he's leaving. Why does she want him to stay? Is she trying to get more information out of him for the case? Or is there something between them?

"I can stay a few more minutes if you'd like." Sheriff Stevens clears his throat.

"Great. Let me get you a coffee." Sarah heads to the kitchen.

"Is that such a good idea?" Mom takes a gulp of her wine. "We really don't need to be distracting him."

No one pays any mind to my mother's comments, including myself. Something isn't right. Why is she offering him coffee? Why does he feel comfortable in my house? Why did she come here? Was it to see me or to see Sheriff Stevens? Is she interested in him? Is he interested in her? I'm not really in a position to be indignant or pry, but something is very off here. However, the last thing I need is to push Sarah away more than I already have. This will have to wait.

Sarah moves around the kitchen making a pot of coffee and putting out two cups. She opens several cupboards as she's clearly unfamiliar with the house. Sheriff Stevens leans against the counter. I watch him watch her. His eyes are scanning her body up and down. If they haven't already fucked, he wants to. That much is clear.

I get up, walk to the kitchen, and stand right beside him. I puff out my chest and stand a bit taller. "Can I get a cup too?" I ask.

Sarah turns back and looks at me. She nods, but the look she gives says *Get it your fucking self*. She pulls out another mug. She's probably just being polite since Sheriff Stevens is here. She wants nothing to do with me. I'm sure she wishes I was rotting in my cell during the trial.

Sheriff Stevens and Sarah begin talking about the case. She asks about the witnesses that he's interviewed, and it sounds like he interviewed nearly everyone Kelly worked with as well as Scott.

"Did you know her first husband?" Sarah asks.

"I had heard something about it," Sheriff Stevens says.

"And what's that?" I pipe in.

He gives me a look, a *why are you talking to me* look. "That he was murdered—"

"Yeah, by her," Sarah says with a bit of bite in her voice.

"What?" Sheriff Stevens widens his eyes.

"It was in her file. The case against her fell apart during the trial after some key evidence went missing. Isn't that where you heard about it from?" Sarah asks. She pours three cups and hands one to me and one to Sheriff Stevens.

"If she did murder her first husband? And hypothetically, if Adam killed her? Is it even a crime? Like double jeopardy or something?" Mom calls from the living room. The wine is clearly going straight to her head.

"Yes, Eleanor. Killing someone is a crime." Sarah rolls her eyes.

Mom hiccups. "Someone's got to be asking the hard questions around here." She mollifies her hiccups with another mouthful of wine.

Sheriff Stevens takes a drink quickly and then slams his fist against the counter. "Shit. Ouch!" He winces.

"Yeah, it's hot coffee," I say with a laugh. This guy is a moron. He gives me a dirty look. Sarah quickly sets down a glass of cold water in front of him. He drinks the whole thing in one gulp and thanks her for it.

"Well, I better be going," he says. "I'll let myself out." He says goodbye and leaves rather quickly. Sarah and I stand on opposite sides of the kitchen, holding our cups of coffee, and looking at each other. She's trying to read me, and I'm trying to read her. Is something going on with Sheriff Stevens? Why did he leave suddenly? Did he pick up on the fact that I was figuring these two out? Are they having an affair? If they were, would I even have the right to be mad? Of course, I would. She's still my fucking wife, and she's my lawyer. Her only focus should be my case, not some hick sheriff. She sets her cup of coffee on the counter, her eyes looking off into the distance, not fixated on anything.

"I have to go," she says suddenly as if she was just snapped back to reality.

"Can't you stay?"

"No." She dumps her coffee cup in the sink and leaves the house without another word.

"Good riddance. I thought she'd never leave." Mom says as she refills her drink.

"She was here for five minutes." I shake my head and pour myself a glass of scotch. I take a seat on the couch. "Can you please try to put down your sword, Mom? Sarah is my wife, and she's defending me. You need to try to get along."

She sits down on the loveseat and cradles her wine with both hands. "I suppose I can try."

29

SARAH MORGAN

I park my car outside Seth's Coffee and watch as a few customers enter and leave. Someone there must have seen Kelly with a man other than Adam or her husband, Scott. Who does that third set of DNA belong to? It has to be someone that would have a reason for wanting to remain hidden. Why else would he use a burner phone? I get out of the car and pick up my tote bag. The café is only open for another hour, so I'll have to work quickly.

I enter the establishment and take in my surroundings, being sure not to miss anything or anyone. The café is small and filled with eclectic furniture and décor. Nothing quite matches, but somehow it does, and it works. Random wooden tables, chairs of many colors and made of different materials—plastic, wood, metal. There's an orange couch with a coffee table in front of it and two white leather chairs on either side of it, all situated in a cozy area.

A middle-aged man is sitting on the couch. His gaze bounces around the café, from his laptop to other customers to me and back again. A woman sits alone at a table reading a book. She doesn't look up, and her attention is solely on the book four inches from her face. There's soft classical music playing. A lone barista is leaning against the counter fiddling with her fingernails. She's a young black woman with full, ringlet hair and big brown eyes. I'd guess her around the same age as Kelly. Perhaps they were friends.

When she notices me, she straightens up and greets me. Her name tag says *Brenda*.

"Hi, I'll take a small black coffee." I pull out my wallet.

"Can I get a name for that?"

"Sarah." She writes my name on the cup and punches a couple of buttons on the cash register. I hand her the cash from my wallet.

"Thanks. That'll be right up," she says with a smile.

"Brenda, is it?"

"Yeah."

"Listen, I'm here for more than just coffee."

"Are you here about Kelly?" she asks.

"Actually, I am," I say—a bit taken aback that she'd know. It must be the matching blazer and skirt that gave away that I'm here for more than just a casual drink.

"We had a reporter here earlier asking about her. Which newspaper do you work for?"

I consider correcting her and then decide I'd probably get better information out of her if I'm just some reporter rather than the defense attorney of the man accused of murdering her co-worker, and maybe friend.

"I work for the *Gainesville Paper*. I'm Sarah Smith." I extend my hand for a handshake. She obliges. "Do you have a moment to talk?"

"I gotta start cleaning up in fifteen minutes... yeah, if you make it quick. I'll make your coffee and meet you at a table."

I nod and walk over to a table near the window. I take a seat and moments later, Brenda the barista is joining me with two cups of coffee. She sits across from me. "What do you want to know?"

Most people I talk to are criminals or witnesses and are usually never this forthcoming. It takes me a little off guard, but then again, I remind myself, *She thinks I'm a reporter*. I pull out a plain pad of paper and a pen.

"Did you know Kelly well?"

"Yeah, we've worked together for the past year and a half. I guess I know her in that regard, but not much about her homelife," she says taking a sip of her coffee. I jot down a couple of notes.

"Had you ever seen Kelly hanging around with any men here?"

"Yeah, occasionally her husband would come in and that Adam guy that's been in the news. He came here frequently too. I always thought they seemed a bit too friendly. Guess I was right about that."

"Right... what about anyone else?"

"Not really," she says.

"Did she ever tell you anything about Scott or Adam?"

"Anytime I'd ask about Adam, or as I knew him 'the cute writer,' she'd say he was just a regular."

"Did she have a lot of regulars?"

"Well, Adam—who I guess wasn't a regular after all," she says with a chuckle. I force a laugh to lighten the mood and help to remove myself.

"There was this other guy. I haven't seen him around in a few days. But if Kelly was working, he was here," she says nonchalantly taking another sip. "Think he had something to do with this?"

"Not sure. Just trying to report the facts. You said he was always here. What would he do while he was here?"

"Read or draw mostly."

"And you found that odd or was it just that he always seemed to be here when Kelly was working?"

"He used to ask when she'd be here, but then he got to the point where he wasn't asking no more, and that's because he seemed to have memorized her schedule. He was always staring at her. Kelly said he made her uncomfortable and she'd beg for me to take his table."

"Can you describe him, or do you know his name?"

"I can do you one better." She gets up from the table and walks to the cash register. She returns a moment later with a receipt.

Brenda slides it in front of me. "Jesse Hook. That's a copy of his receipt from a few days ago."

"Can I have this?"

"It's all yours... do you need my last name for the article?"

"Sure," I say pocketing the receipt.

"It's Brenda Johnson."

"Great. You've been very helpful," I say as I pack my stuff up.

"If you need any more quotes for your article, you know where to find me."

I give her a wave, quickly walk out of the coffee shop, and get back into my vehicle.

Jesse Hook, who are you? Are you the third set of DNA? Is that why you haven't come around since she was murdered? Are you the man we've been looking for?

Before I pull out of the café, I text Anne.

Hey, I need you to run a background check on a Jesse Hook. He should be located somewhere in the Prince William County area.

I hit send and moments later, I get a thumbs up emoji from Anne.

30

ADAM MORGAN

I still feel uneasy about the way things happened last night with Sarah and Sheriff Stevens. He scurried off quick, and then she did too. What were they in a hurry to do? Go see each other? I need to stop thinking like this. It consumed my thoughts until I fell asleep and then it consumed my dreams. I dreamt that Sarah and Sheriff Stevens were having an affair—that he fucked her in the back of his police car after they left here. But Sarah wouldn't do that. She's not that type of girl, at least I don't think she is. I think back to the first night I met her in that old dingy college basement. She was bored in the middle of a raging party. She didn't care to overindulge in drinks, try drugs, and she barely had any interest in me. She didn't care what others thought of her. She was just her. And now, she's Sarah Morgan—top defense attorney. What happened to the woman I fell in love with? What happened to the woman I married? She's a stranger to me now, and I'm sure she'd say the same about me.

Is our marriage over? Is she over me? I know I had an affair, but just because I slept with someone else doesn't mean I stopped loving my wife. *Oh God. What the fuck am I saying?* Who am I trying to convince that I'm still a good person? I know I'm not. And clearly, everyone else does too, including my wife.

I get up from the couch and cinch the plaid robe I'm wearing over a pair of pajama pants and a white T-shirt. I don't even remember changing into PJs. I wonder for a second if Mom changed me and I roll my eyes knowing she probably did. Immediately, the smell of bacon invades my nose. Mom is standing at the kitchen sink cleaning pans.

"Sweetheart, you're up. There's a plate of bacon, eggs, toast, and hash browns on the counter, all of your favorite breakfast foods." She smiles and points at the plate.

I stumble into the kitchen and plunge my fork into the food, shoveling it into my mouth. I didn't eat like this in jail.

"I'm going to do some shopping today, and I need to find a nearby hotel." She turns off the faucet and dries her hands. "As much as I would love to stay here with you, that loveseat is just not up to my standards, and I'm sure I'm going to have to see a chiropractor today because of it." She rubs her back and then sets a cup of coffee down in front of me.

"These trials can go on for a long time." I take a bite of toast. "You can go back to Connecticut, Mom."

"Nonsense. You're my son, and this trial should be speedy because you're innocent. We'll see to it that Sarah gets this done quickly." She nods encouragingly at me.

She picks up her purse and puts on her heels. "Just call me if you need anything. I'll be back later tonight," she says planting a kiss on my cheek. "Love you, cubbie-bear."

"Love you too, Mom."

~

It's a little after 11am, and I don't even know what to do with myself now. It's only been two hours since Mom left, and I already feel alone. A knock at the front door startles me. Through the peephole I see a petite woman with fire-red hair, hazel eyes, and a face full of freckles. She has a laptop bag hanging from her shoulder. I kind of recognize her, but not really. I decide to open the door anyway.

"Hi. Are you Adam Morgan?" She looks me up and down, surveying my disheveled appearance.

"Depends on who's asking." Knowing full well I don't care who is asking. I'd talk to just about anyone right now, anyone that would listen.

"I'm Rebecca Sanford. I'm a reporter for the *Prince William County Newspaper*."

I put up my hand, halting her from speaking any more. "My lawyer doesn't want me talking to any reporters. Sorry." I start to close the door.

She puts her foot in front of the door stopping me from closing it. "I know. Mr. Morgan, I'm just a big fan of your work, and I really want to get your side of the story."

"You've read my work?"

She nods. "I actually took the class on fiction writing you taught at the community college over a year back."

After we bought this lake house, I was approached to teach a class on writing at the local community college. I almost said no but had decided teaching might be a great career to fall back on since my writing was dead in the water. I only ended up teaching one semester though and then went back to full-time writing. I ended up overromanticizing the process as I despised most of my students and how little they cared. Plus, in most cases, their writing was fucking terrible and a chore to read.

"I thought you looked familiar," I say, although I'm not entirely convinced.

I look around, left, right and straight ahead to ensure no one sees me let her in. For all I know, Sarah has someone watching me. "Okay, come on in." I gesture in with a flick of my wrist, and she follows. "So, you're a reporter? My class must have done you good," I add with a chuckle.

She lets out a little laugh.

I tell her to have a seat at the kitchen table, and she does. She pulls out a notepad and pen. "Okay, how long were you and Kelly Summers seeing each other?" she asks, getting right to it.

I've already decided that if she wants a story out of me, she's going to have to help me. I can only do so much from a lake house in the middle of nowhere. "Ah, ah, ah," I say. "I'll give you an interview, but I need something in return." I'm not sure if I can trust this girl and this might prove to be a horrible idea, but I'm desperate and desperate people, well...

"Help you how? Like escape? I can't do that." She re-caps her pen as if she's done with this interview.

"No. I don't need your help escaping. I need your help getting some information on Kelly's past. I think I was framed. Someone else did this, and they set me up, and I think it has to do with her past."

Rebecca uncaps her pen and begins jotting down notes. "Why do you think it was someone from her past?"

I pour her a cup of coffee and set it in front of her. "Because she killed her first husband."

Rebecca's eyes widen, and she quickly writes it down. "Well, how come none of the newspapers have uncovered that then?"

"Because she changed her name and got married. It's quite the paper trail. She went by Jenna Way. She stabbed her husband to death or at least that's what she was charged with. The case fell apart during the trial when key evidence went missing, which I think her husband Scott Summers helped with. Everyone thought she did it, and she essentially got off on a technicality."

"Oh my God. That's awful." Rebecca takes a sip of her coffee, and I can practically see her brain working as her eyes stare off into the distance and her forehead crinkles.

"Well, who would want to hurt her?"

"My guess would be a family member or friend of her first husband. Someone who wasn't happy to see her get away with murder. The way she was killed was the same way she killed her husband—almost like poetic justice for the person who did it."

"What about her husband? I've heard rumblings in town that he may have been involved."

"I thought that too. And I think that's still a possibility. Although, she had said that he abused her while she and I were together, but he adamantly denies it. I really don't know what to believe there, but he does seem to have an anger problem, and he did suspect Kelly of cheating. So, he should be considered. Although, apparently his alibi for the night in question is his partner Deputy Marcus Hudson. Despite that, there's something in my gut that's telling me to look into her past."

"Got it." Rebecca sets her coffee down and proceeds to take more notes. "What about the third set of DNA that was found in her?"

"Is that public knowledge?"

"Not yet, but I have my ways." She gives me a coy smile.

"I really don't know who that third guy could be. Maybe a one-night stand? I couldn't even believe she was with another man other than myself and her husband. And I know how weird that sounds. Plus, someone threatened me. They sent a photo of Kelly and me together with a note that said, 'End it or I will.'"

"Who knew about you two?"

"Her husband Scott, I'm sure. Maybe his partner. I don't really know."

"What is it you need me to do?" she asks.

"Well—thanks to this," I pull up my pant leg showing off my

ankle monitor. "I can't leave this house, and it makes it difficult to investigate my own case."

"What about your lawyer?"

"You mean my wife?"

Rebecca lets out a nervous laugh.

"I'd say considering the circumstances I'm not sure she has my best interests in mind." I raise an eyebrow.

"Oh, that can't be true. I'm sure your wife is doing everything in her power to win this case for you," she says trying to feign optimism in her voice, which I find odd, considering she doesn't really know me, and she doesn't know my wife, but I suppose I understand the gesture.

"Maybe. But my life is on the line, and I'm not just going to sit here and have it taken away from me. Not without trying my damnedest to find out the truth."

"Understandable. Now, here's what I want. An exclusive interview and five thousand for my troubles." She holds out her hand to make a deal.

I look at her hand and then at her. I honestly didn't think she'd have the balls to ask for cash. She sure is a firecracker. I consider negotiating with her, but I don't have any other options, and I don't really have the time to be finagling over pocket change. "You got yourself a deal." I shake her hand.

She smiles, and I can tell she is pleased with herself. "What exactly do you need my help with?" Rebecca repositions her pen, ready to write down anything that comes out of my mouth.

"I need to find out the name of her first husband, and then I need names and numbers and maybe background reports, if you can muster that up, on friends and family he was really close with. I guess I'll start there. Can you handle that?"

"It shouldn't be a problem. You said her name was Jenna Way?"

"Yes, Jenna Way. From Wisconsin," I confirm.

"Got it. I should be able to pull all that within forty-eight hours. I'd ask you where you'd like to meet again, but I have the answer to that already. I'll be back, Mr. Morgan."

"Thank you, Rebecca. Oh, and before I forget..." I pull out a Folgers coffee can from a cupboard. I open it and pull out a stack of cash and hand it to her. "Here's half right now. I'll give you the other half when you bring me what I need."

"Hiding it in the coffee can... how clichéd." She takes the money and shoves it into her bag. "I'll be seeing you," Rebecca says as she lets herself out.

I really hope she didn't just take my cash without any intention of helping me or following through with the investigation. Not much else I can do so I guess I'll just have to take my chances. Time is ticking.

31

SARAH MORGAN

I head into work and I'm immediately intercepted by Anne on the way into my office.

"Sarah. Kent wants to see you. He says it's urgent," she says with a tinge of worry in her voice.

"Did he say why?"

"No."

"Fine. Here. Take my bag and hold my calls until I return, please." Anne nods and complies.

Kent is the other named partner at the firm. The Williamson in Williamson & Morgan. This was his show first, and he likes to remind me of that from time to time. While I may be the hot up-and-comer in the courtroom, he has been at this for decades and has contacts I couldn't dream of.

His secretary allows me to pass through with a "he's expecting you." His office is the only one in the firm that puts mine to shame. Straight out of a movie set, he had his walls finished with mahogany paneling and a large chandelier dangles from the ceiling. A boar's head hangs on the wall, a trophy from a recent hunting trip in Texas. This was with his big oil lobbyist friends to ensure that despite my defending Senator

McCallan he was still in their corner. Needless to say, I wasn't invited. The wall behind me has photos of him with every significant politician over the past two decades. Bushes, Clintons, Obama, you name it.

Two full walls of his office are floor-to-ceiling windows, tinted to his own specific requirements. He is not a fan of leaving his office, so he also has a twelve-person conference room table, bare bones as can be. No conference phone, no flat screen display for a computer: he runs his meetings old-school. If it can't be solved with a pen, paper, and a sharp tongue, then it isn't worth him getting involved.

"You wanted to see me, Kent."

"Yes, Sarah, please take a seat." He motions to a chair in front of the desk he sits behind.

"What's up?" I say, trying to keep it casual, which I know he hates.

"Yes, well your recent behavior and performance here at the firm have been... erratic, to put it mildly. You come and go as you please, you don't return calls, you miss meetings. Have you forgotten that as a named partner you don't have the luxury of focusing on one case, one client at a time?" He ends with what sounds like a rhetorical question, yet he will make me answer it anyway. One of his many charming habits.

"No, Kent, I have not forgotten. It's just that I am defending my own husband in a murder trial and as you can imagine—"

"That would be quite the conflict of interest? Cause you a tremendous amount of distress and distract you from your job? Yes, yes, I can imagine that. Which is why I wish you would have run it by me first." He is in full father mode.

"You know with our agreement that I don't have to run cases by you unless it is a corporate interest that conflicts with one of your clients. This is not a corporate case, and thus I am clear to take it as I see fit."

"Yes, you certainly did have the right to do that. But the question is, should you have done it? You don't think this might concern me as well? The other named half of the firm blowing off her duties, making us look unstable and flighty, anything but professional."

"That was not my intent at—"

"Well, it's what's happening, isn't it? Regardless of your intent." He pauses and stands to come around to the front of his desk and sit on the edge. "Look, Sarah, I'm not here to scold you. You are a big girl, and you are free to do as you please, for the most part. I just want to get a handle on this because it is making us look weak and spread thin, and don't think others haven't noticed."

"You're right. This is... harder than I anticipated. I just..."

"And who can blame you? I certainly don't. Hell, I can't imagine the stress. But that's my point. Look, I'll allow this charade to continue because I know nothing I say is going to stop you, but—hear me out—you need to end this, and end it quickly. For you. For me. For the firm. I'll get other people to cover some of your accounts in the interim, and I'll clear you from any new work for the time being. But get this taken care of."

"Thank you. I appreciate your understanding," I say, a bit angry but knowing that I won't win this argument. He isn't wrong.

"Oh, don't thank me yet. You see, since you aren't covering corporate accounts, you don't get to enjoy the monthly retainer fees they bring in, i.e., your portion of the profit-sharing is on hold until you end this case—"

"That's not in our agreement! You can't fucking—"

"Or what! You'll sue me? See how that goes for you. Look, this should be an incentive for you. End this quickly, the money comes back. Understood?"

I stare at him with fire in my eyes. I'm not going to answer him and quite frankly, I'm done with this conversation. I stand up and head toward the door.

"Oh, Sarah, one last thing."

"Yes, Kent?"

"Your secretary, Pam."

"It's Anne."

"Yes, yes, Anne. She isn't your sidekick to follow you around like a little dog on your every errand. She is being paid to be here and be a resource to the firm, not just you."

"Last time I checked, Kent, she was my secretary, and I pay half her salary…"

"Yes, and I the other half. So, if you would like to have her only half as much as you do now, be my guest. Or play ball and take care of this justice crusade on your own." He turns and sits back behind his desk again.

"Cocksucker," I whisper under my breath as I leave his office.

"Have a nice day, Sarah," his secretary chirps as I pass her desk.

"Fuck off, Nicole," I say without looking back.

In my haste, I bump into someone and am taken aback before I collect myself and look up. The gentleman I ran into is with another man. Both of them have oddly familiar faces that I struggle to place immediately. My memory recall is temporarily hamstrung by my anger.

"Woah, woah, woah, Mrs. Morgan, where ya off to in such a hurry?" The words come pouring out laced with a heavy Texan accent. Now I remember. These are the two executives from PetroNext, the very two who sat in to observe Senator McCallan's trial.

"Gentlemen," I reply, not answering their question.

"I suppose congratulations are in order," one of them says. It doesn't matter which one as they're spitting images of one another.

"I highly doubt you feel that way."

"Fair is fair, Mrs. Morgan. And you won fair and square... this time," the gentleman says to me, a smirk that can't be described as anything other than nefarious, growing across his face.

"Right... Why don't you both just run along into Kent's office so he can play nice. I have actual work to do. Later y'all." I blurt out. Not the smoothest of exchanges but I don't have time for them.

As soon as I'm back in my office, Anne pops in. "What was that all about?"

"Nothing," I say, without taking my eyes off my monitor.

"That bad, huh?"

"Can you just bring me some coffee?" I huff.

Anne nods and disappears quickly.

I didn't leave the office early. I didn't even leave for lunch. I stayed there all day like a goddamn hourly employee just to ensure my presence was known. Where does anyone at the office get off questioning me? I've worked harder than every other lawyer here, and I've earned my right to come and go as I please.

~

I close the hatch of my Range Rover, sling the reusable bags over my shoulders, and pick up an overstuffed box. It's dark out, and I'm careful to watch my feet as I walk in order to not trip on the way up the stairs of the porch. My heels click on each step, and once I'm standing at the door, I consider knocking—for only a moment. Instead, I reach for the handle, pull open the screen door, and let myself in.

"Hello?" Adam calls nervously from the living room. "Who's there?"

I don't answer and instead walk into the kitchen. He's sitting on the couch in the living room, dressed in sweats and a white T-shirt, sipping at a glass of scotch. He's made no effort to shave or comb his hair. Despite all that, he still looks handsome.

"Sarah? What are you doing here?"

I set the box and bags down on the island. "I brought you some provisions."

"Oh?" His face softens and he rises from the couch, slowly making his way into the kitchen, but still keeping his distance from me.

"Where's your mom?"

"She got a hotel room to stay in."

"I thought for sure she'd be the big spoon in your sleeping arrangement," I jab.

"Oh, stop." He chuckles. "She's not that bad."

I give a small smile and roll my eyes.

"You want a drink?"

"Yes."

He walks to the wet bar and pours me a glass of ten-year-old Laphroaig. He returns to the opposite side of the island and places it down in front of me.

"I figured you would need some stuff. I brought you New York strip steaks, more scotch, some bagels, smoked salmon, cream cheese, eggs, vegetables, macadamia nuts, and ice cream," I say as I pull out each item and begin putting them away.

"You didn't have to do that."

I look at him. There's a smile on his face. There's hope in his eyes. "I know."

He takes a sip of his scotch. "Thank you."

"I also brought you some writing supplies—paper, printer

ink, ballpoint pens, and some stationery." I unpack the other bag.

"You really didn't have to do that." He walks over and looks at the items. His eyes moisten.

"I know." I pick up the glass of scotch he set out for me and take a sip.

We stand there sipping from our glasses in silence. I don't know what to say to him, and I'm sure he doesn't know what to say to me. To think that we were once the love of each other's lives, linked as close as two humans can be, and now there is a chasm between us that is so deep and wide that it's difficult to even call across to the other side.

Finally, he speaks. "What's in the box?" He points at the cardboard box overstuffed with papers and folders.

I push it toward him. "I know you want to help, so I had Anne make copies of all the key evidence. It's all in there and it's yours to review."

He looks at the box and then at me. His eyes bounce all over me.

"I just want you to know that I'm doing everything in my power to win this case. You have to trust me," I add.

"I do trust you, Sarah."

I nod and give him a small smile. "I'm glad to hear that. I have to get going but let me know if you find anything or if you need anything else." I set my glass of scotch down and turn toward the front door.

"Sarah," he says, his voice is quiet, almost like a whisper.

I stop and turn to look at him. "Yes."

"Thank you... for everything." His voice shakes. "You really didn't have to do this. I... don't really deserve this."

My lip begins to quiver, but I bite down hard to stop it. I close my eyes for a second, and when I reopen them, they're wet. "No, you... well... I have to go."

Before I can take one more step away from him, he closes the distance, wrapping his arms around me, pulling me into him. I want to stop him. I want to tell him no. These are the same arms that used to hold Kelly. To be a source of strength and comfort to her. I know he doesn't deserve to hold me, but I don't fight it. I let him hold me. I bury my face into his chest and I cry. I practically fall apart in his arms. He cries too. He kisses the top of my head and squeezes me tight. He tells me he loves me over and over again. I look up at him—my cheeks are wet; my heart is pounding. Tears are running down his cheeks onto mine.

I pull him in for a kiss. He kisses me back. Our mouths open and close in sync. His hands run all over my body. He picks me up. My legs straddle his waist. He walks me to the island and sets me down, his lips never leaving mine. He moves to my neck and then to my collarbone, kissing every part of me he possibly can.

"I love you, Sarah," he whispers in my ear.

"I know." I pause. I stop kissing him and search his face for an answer, for what to say. Caressing his cheek with my hand, I finally speak as his eyes lock with mine, "I love you too."

He can't help but smile. "I love you so fucking much." His voice trembles and I stop him from saying anything more with a kiss, a hard and passionate one. His lips are soft and hot. His hands travel all over my body, pulling off my suit jacket, massaging my breasts, pushing up my skirt. My breath is ragged as his tongue and lips leave their mark up and down my neck.

He unzips his pants and pulls me closer to the edge of the counter. He bends down, pushing my legs apart and my panties aside—and then all at once, reality sets in for me, I push him away, my legs snap closed, I slide off the counter, pull down my skirt, and put on my suit jacket. He loses his balance and sits back on the floor before quickly regaining himself and standing. His eyes widen, and his mouth opens to begin his protest.

I put my hand on his chest. "I can't do this yet... I'm still mad at you for everything you did to me. I can't help but still picture..." I say trailing off. A tear rolls down my cheek. I wipe it away and sidestep him, quickly leaving the house.

"Sarah, wait!" His voice rings loud from the house, but he is trapped, an invisible perimeter preventing him from pursuing me.

I climb into my car and slam the door closed. What the fuck am I doing? I need to clear my head, and this is not the place to do it.

32

ADAM MORGAN

I'm sitting on the couch, sipping my second glass of scotch and eating a New York strip with my hands. Sarah left over an hour ago, and it took fifteen minutes to beat the memory of her out of my dick. It felt good to be close to her again. Like there was a chance at reconciliation, but she left suddenly. She's always leaving suddenly. Mom called to check in on me. She would have come over for dinner, but apparently she has a massage appointment. I have a feeling she's up to something though. She would never turn down dinner with me, her only son.

The phone rings. It's either Sarah or Mom. Those are the only two people that call me these days. I scooch over to the corded phone on the end table and with no caller ID, I'm forced to pick it up to find out who it is, like some mystery. "Hello."

"Adam?"

"Yeah, who is this?"

"It's me, Daniel. How the hell have you been?"

Ahh, good ol' Daniel. Daniel is my literary agent and has been with me since day one. In the beginning, I was a gamble. Then, I became a hot commodity and people tried to poach me from Daniel, but I stuck with him. Now, it's him who is sticking with me. I have been hearing from him at an ever-decreasing rate over this four-year lull, and I don't blame him. "Oh, hey, Daniel. Fine, fine. I've been fine, how about yourself?" I resituate myself on the couch to get comfortable.

"Forget about me. What's this I hear you're on trial for murder?"

"Yeah, unfortunately, it's true but I didn't do it, this is all..." I take a drink of scotch.

"That's great!"

"What? No, Daniel, I said it's true. I am on trial for murder."

"Oh, I heard you, buddy boy, and it's the best fuckin' news I've heard in ages."

"What? Why?" I press the phone harder against my ear to ensure I'm hearing him correctly.

"Think about it, Adam. This is a murder. You're a writer, put 'em together, and whattaya got? A tell-all, the likes of which has never been seen before."

"But, Daniel, I didn't do—"

"This could be your *In Cold Blood* except even better, cause I mean you don't have to interview the murderer... it's you!"

"Daniel, I didn't fucking kill—" I grit my teeth. What isn't he getting?

"I can picture it now, you doing press junkets from your cell, signing autographs at visitation sessions. Hmm, I'll have to figure out how the hell they'll let you go on a promotional tour but... wait... I got it! We can let them move you in a prison van with cops and everything, put you in an orange jumpsuit. Oh, the press would be fucking fantastic—"

"Daniel! I didn't fucking do it, okay. Listen to me, goddammit!"

"Geez, bud, relax. I know you didn't fucking do it. I mean you can be a ballbuster sometimes, but a killer? Hell, you couldn't hurt a fly. But regardless of how this turns out, the people don't need to know that. The way I see it is this; if you did kill her—"

"Which I didn't," I repeat. This fucking guy! Even at a time like this, his mind is always on making money. That's what makes him such a good agent, but also such a shit person. "I don't know, Daniel, I'm not really interested in being a would-be murderer when I didn't do anything."

"Look, you and I both know you've needed a spark for years now and then boom! This falls right in your lap. All I'm saying is, don't ignore it. You wanna send me some pages on it, I'll read 'em. If not, well... you can get back to finishing that 'next great American novel' I've been hearing about for the last half a decade. Up to you."

"Yeah, sure. Maybe."

"That's the spirit. Hang in there, kid. We'll grab lunch soon." Click goes the line.

I set the phone down and sink back into my seat, bringing the scotch to my lips. He's not wrong. This is a great story, and it's my story to tell. I know I didn't do this, but I can figure out who did. A whole true crime mystery for me to tell the world. A guaranteed *New York Times* bestseller. But what would I call it?

In Warm Blood... It Wasn't Me.

Fuck, I'm rusty. I take a pad of paper and a pen from the coffee table and start writing down everything that's happened, starting from the very beginning.

33

SARAH MORGAN

I'm going over the case files and waiting for Anne to bring me breakfast. She convinced me I should eat. I seem to have been living solely off coffee, water, and alcohol. I'm not sure who Adam and I are anymore. Husband and wife? Lawyer and client? Lovers? Enemies? I guess that doesn't really matter. All that matters is getting through this case, which has become increasingly difficult as the story was picked up nationally over the weekend. Reporters have been calling the office nonstop, and they even got a hold of my work cell. I bunkered down at our D.C. house and my office over the weekend, keeping a low profile, and focusing on the case files.

Anne informed me that the internet has gone wild with theories as to who may have killed Kelly. The majority seem to believe it is Adam, while several theories have arisen about Scott, the third set of DNA, a co-worker, another police officer on the force, and even the ghost of her ex-husband. I haven't paid much attention to them. The information regarding her killing her first husband and her being killed in the exact same way is what caught the public's eye. Many believe she got what she had coming, and others think she's being portrayed inaccurately. It's a polarizing case and there's not much agreement, which should benefit us when it comes to the jury.

A not guilty verdict is going to be a hard one to pull off, but perhaps we can get a mistrial through a hung jury. It may or may not be tried again after that, but we don't have a lot of time before the trial starts and at this point, that's our best bet.

The door is flung open and startles me. Anne scurries in carrying two smoothies, a bag of food from a local café, and a box of chocolates. She places everything on the desk in a hurry.

"What? What is it?" I ask.

"Bob's looking for you." Her eyes widen.

"And?"

"He's pissed."

Bob appears in my doorway wearing a nice tailored suit and a scowl. "What the hell is going on here?" He takes a couple of large steps into my office, so he's directly in front of my desk. Anne quickly shifts aside.

"To what do I owe the pleasure, Bob?" I smile.

"What's with the reporters out front? And what's this I hear you're representing your husband in a murder trial?" His face crumples.

"Yes, yes I am. My husband has been wrongly accused, and I'm doing some pro bono work on the case." I shift some papers around while paying nearly no mind to Bob.

"You can't do fucking pro bono on your own husband's case!"

"Yes, I can, and I am. I've already talked to Kent about it."

Anne lets out an awkward cough as if she had been holding it in to not make a sound. I glance at her and then look Bob directly in the eyes.

"Oh, have you? I'll also be talking to Kent about this and explaining to him how god-awful this publicity is for the firm." He points at me as he speaks.

"Do it, and I'll bury you, Bob," I warn.

He lets out a chuckle. "Ha. I'd love to see you try." He looks around my office. "Man, I'm going to look so good in here when they can your ass."

"You don't even look good in your own office." I return my attention to my case, shifting around papers. I know his threats are empty, but I don't need him ruffling up Kent's feathers again. I'm already on thin ice.

"Watch yourself, Sarah." He takes a few steps back and then turns to leave. I let him have the last word because it's all he's got. He can be mad over the publicity, but he can't be mad about me taking the case. I had to. It was the only way.

"Are you okay?" Anne takes a seat in front of me.

"Yeah. Don't worry about him. He's just overly protective of this place." I spot the box of chocolates with an attached card on the desk. "What's this?"

"It arrived as I was coming in."

I open the envelope and pull out the card. It reads, "This in no way compares to studying for the LSAT, but I know how you handle stress. Chocolate! XOXO, Matthew." I let out a small smile as I recall Matthew and I going on chocolate runs in the middle of our study sessions. I open the box, choose a piece, and pop it into my mouth.

"Want one?"

"Sure." Anne takes one for herself and takes a bite. "Who's it from?"

"Matthew." I take another one.

"I swear he has a thing for you." She raises an eyebrow.

"He's gay."

"Yeah, but he'd be straight for you," Anne says with a mouthful of chocolate.

"That's not how that works."

"He's at least bisexual." She curves the corner of her lip.

"Doubtful." I roll my eyes.

"Okay... oh yeah—I got the background check back on that Jesse Hook guy," she says as she quickly leaves my office and returns with a file folder. I take it from her and flip through it.

"Highlights?"

"Thirty-two, lives alone in Gainesville, dropped out of high school, no real job history. He seems to do freelance writing and painting on the side according to his Facebook page. No family in the area, not sure how he came to live around here. Never been married and no kids. Overall, he's kind of a creepy recluse."

"Registered phone number?"

"Yep. It's on the first page, and it matches one text and a dozen missed calls in Kelly's phone history. He texted her, 'I'm sorry' on the night of the murder and all the calls were sporadic a couple of days before."

"He could be our guy," I ponder.

"It's at least worth looking into."

"I'm going to head back into town. Will you call Sheriff Stevens and have him meet me at Seth's Coffee in about two hours?"

"Sure thing." She immediately gets up to make that call.

My phone buzzes. It's a text from Eleanor. Great.

I'm going out of town and will be back tomorrow. Nothing to concern yourself with.

I roll my eyes. If it was nothing for me to concern myself with then why did she text me in the first place? *Ugh. She's impossible.* I slide my phone in my pocket, close the box of chocolates, and put it in my tote bag. Before leaving, I take a few sips of the smoothie and a bite of my sandwich. I'm getting a bit tired of making this drive back and forth between D.C. and Prince William County, but I don't have the time to slow down.

I need to find out who this third guy is. He might be the

answer to this whole case, and he might know more than anyone else does about Kelly and her past. Until I can tie up this loose end, I will always be left wondering what it is that I don't know.

34

ADAM MORGAN

I heard from Rebecca, the journalist I'd asked to do some digging for me, sooner than I thought... actually, I wasn't sure I'd hear from her at all. She called me late last night, telling me she'd be over Monday afternoon. She works fast. She had said on the phone that she got everything I asked for. I don't know how she did it, and I don't care as long as it's right, and it clears me of this crime. I got up and showered, shaved, and dressed myself. It was quite the accomplishment as I've been nothing short of a slob these past couple of days. I even tidied up the place. I couldn't stand sleeping on the couch another night. My back is aching, but I guess the couch is better than the twin-sized bunk at the jail.

Since our mattress was thrown out during the crime scene clean-up, I ordered a new one online. I won't get much use out of it if I'm convicted, but in the meantime, I sprung for the most expensive one with the highest thread count sheets and the plushest pillows and mattress pad. If these are my last couple of weeks in my own bed, they're going to be luxurious. I haven't heard from Sarah since our encounter on Friday night. I had hoped she'd stop by again, but after the news picked up the story, I assumed she was lying low.

I'm sitting on the couch dressed in old jeans and a flannel top, flipping through my well-thumbed copy of *The Corrections*, wondering why my career hadn't taken the same path as Mr. Franzen's. But I only need to read one page of his writing to remember why.

The phone rings and I lean over to pick it up. I don't even get a chance to say hello. "Adam! It's Daniel. Great news! I already have multiple offers on the tell-all."

"You pitched the book? I didn't even agree to write it."

"Adam, you and I are one and the same. We both love money. Don't be dumb. This is the chance of a lifetime. I'm talking seven figures, movie deals, the whole shebang." He stops talking, waiting for me to agree. I can hear heavy breaths from his overexcitement.

My eyes light up, thinking of the money, fame, and power. A smile grows on my face the more I daydream of what my life could be, and then I can't stop my own response from leaving my mouth. "Fine. But I'm going to write the truth—none of this 'I'm the murderer' bullshit."

"That's perfect. People like true crime better these days anyway. I'm setting up an auction, so get to writing. I'll be in touch, buddy."

The phone clicks and I hang up the receiver, sitting there in a daze for a moment. *Holy shit. All my dreams are finally going to come true.* I take a seat at my desk, ready to pour the pages out. This story is going to make my career, it's going to make people know who Adam Morgan is. I crack my knuckles and open a blank word document. I type, *Adam Morgan: Murder He Wrote*.

There's a knock at the door. I turn in my seat and then it hits me. Damn, I forgot all about Rebecca and my investigation. I can't let anything get in the way of figuring out the truth. This book will mean nothing if I'm rotting in a prison cell or worse, dead. I close my laptop and rush to open the door. Rebecca walks in before I even have a chance to invite her. Her hair is in tight curls under her hat, and her cheeks are a rosy red.

"That was quick," I tell her as she removes her coat and hat and takes a seat on the couch.

"I work fast, and you don't have much time," she says, picking up *The Corrections*. She glances at it and sets it on the coffee table. "If only he could have been my writing professor." There's a smartass grin on her face.

"Then you wouldn't have been at a community college, now would you?" I snap back, my jealousy coming through. I can tell by her eyes she knows the comment did its job. Her perceptivity is impressive. "Anyway, you're right, I don't have much time. Can I get you something to drink?"

She shakes her head, and I join her on the couch. Rebecca pulls out a couple of file folders and lays them out in front of her. "You ready for this?"

I nod.

"Okay, so Kelly or Jenna's first husband's name was Greg, and they were married for a year and a half—got married young, like twenty. You know about the murder, the misplaced evidence, and the fact that Scott Summers helped her get away with it. The two left Wisconsin after the case was closed and wound up here in Prince William County, Virginia." She flips through the papers. I take pages here and there, reading them myself. Most of this I knew.

"Where's the new info? Like his family or something?"

"I'm getting there. Yes—both his parents are still alive. But I couldn't find much about them. The father works in commercial real estate, and the mother does a lot of volunteer work. They don't seem like they would have had anything to do with this.

They're in their sixties. It just seems like a bit of a stretch," she explains.

His sixty-year-old parents do seem a bit far-fetched. I mean, I couldn't imagine my own mom being involved in some vicious murder. But then again, Harold Shipman, AKA Dr. Death was murdering people well into his fifties, and that couple in Missouri picked up the hobby of killing drifters in their seventies. So, age doesn't really rule people out. If nothing else turns up, I'll have her dig deeper into where they were when Kelly was murdered.

"Here's the thing—Greg had a brother. His name's Nicholas Miller. Based on what I could dig up—which isn't a lot—I believe he lives in the area."

My eyes light up. *It has to be him. Who else would want to kill Kelly?* "Where does he live? Where does he work? Let's find him." This is it. This is my lifeline. This is my miracle. Everything is going to be okay.

"See, here's the thing. I called the home and spoke with the mother. The conversation I had with her is also why I didn't think the parents had anything to do with this. She was so friendly and nice. I enjoyed speaking with her. I might just call her regularly since my own mom is such a jerk."

"Okay, get to the point, Rebecca. We can talk all about your family problems after I'm cleared of this."

"Sorry. Anyway. I asked for Nicholas since when I pulled the background report on Greg, I saw he had an older brother. Well, the mother told me he had just visited and left the other day to head back to Maryland."

"Maryland. That's not Virginia," I say.

"Correct, but it's very close. There are so many cities, and towns he could be in that are less than two hours from here. He could have easily done this."

"How do we find him?"

"I'm still looking. I haven't been able to locate a Nicholas Miller, but I have found some others with that same last name. I was going to start there and see if anyone knows him. It's not that common of a name, so I might just get lucky," she says.

"Well, how 'not common' is it?"

"I have a list of seventy-two people with the same last name within a two-hour radius, and since you have nothing going on in the meantime, I thought you could help me tackle half this list." She hands me a page full of names, addresses, and phone numbers.

"There's like fifty names on my list. That's not half."

"I know. Because some of these don't have phone numbers, so I'm going to need to make some home visits. I wouldn't be complaining if I were you. Your life is literally on the line," she reminds me.

"Trust me. I know." I roll my eyes.

"Great. Well, you get to work on those, and I'll be back late tomorrow. Call me if you find anything."

"And you do the same."

"Oh, I will." She packs up her stuff.

Before she leaves, I call her name. She turns to look at me. "Be safe."

She smiles, nods, and then leaves me there with a page of phone numbers. One of these sets of numbers just might be my winning ticket—my very own lottery. I pick up the corded phone and start dialing.

35

SARAH MORGAN

A nne informed me on my drive that Sheriff Stevens was giving her grief about meeting me at Seth's Coffee. I'm not sure what his deal is, but I'm going to find out. I don't have time for his games. Time is running out, and he's going to help me whether he wants to or not. I'm not entirely sure what changed. He went from being flirty and telling me he would help me with anything to scurrying off suddenly at the lake house, and now ignoring me. I can't even recall what happened that made his whole demeanor change. Was it something Adam said? Did Adam threaten him?

Adam was acting a bit odd that night. But I just assumed it was because he's on trial for murder and if we lose, he'll get the death penalty. I'd be acting weird too.

I'm driving straight to the police station to catch up with Sheriff Stevens before he leaves for the day. I need his help finding Jesse Hook, and I need his police resources to discover everything there is to know about him and find out if his DNA matches with that third set. Plus, there's still that photo that someone sent Adam. Whoever it is knows something—and I'd still like to interview Scott Summers and his cocky partner, Marcus. They've both rubbed me up the wrong way.

I fly into the police station parking lot and charge right in through the front doors, wearing five-inch nude Louboutin heels and a white dress with a camel-colored trench coat. "I need to see Sheriff Stevens," I say to the woman working the front desk. She's dull and tired-looking. Haggard would probably be the best word for her.

"And you are?"

"Sarah Morgan."

"Let me see if he's available." She returns a few moments later. "Sorry, he's busy right now. You can come back later."

"Listen, lady. I just drove over an hour to get here. I am going to see him now!"

She rolls her eyes and just before she's about to speak again to tell me no or I'll have to wait, I scurry past the desk. She tells me to stop and follows behind. She's a bit plump and old, so she's no match for me even in my heels. I throw open the door to his office. Sheriff Stevens is sitting there eating a sandwich. He looks up at me and tosses his food on the desk. "Damn it, Marge!"

The receptionist appears behind me. "I'm sorry, sir. She just ran past me. She's a persistent little shrew," Marge says as she tries to grab my arm. I elbow her, and she clutches at her stomach in pain. I enter the office, smooth out my dress, and take a seat.

"I'm so happy you could squeeze me in." I smile.

Sheriff Stevens shoos Marge away, accepting defeat. "What do you need, Sarah?" he asks leaning back in his chair.

"Your help."

"I told you I couldn't put any more man-hours on this case. The charges have already been filed."

"What happened to you saying that you would help me

191

regardless and that you'd be there for me no matter what?" My eyes narrow.

"Things changed."

"What changed?"

"For starters, I've found no new evidence." He puts his hands in front of his chest, pressing his fingertips together.

"Because you haven't looked," I argue.

"Don't you dare question my investigation." He points a finger at me. "And I think Adam just may have done it."

My eyes grow wide. "Why would you think that all of a sudden?"

"That thought has always been there. I just thought there may have been other possibilities and there wasn't any that we could find. So, case closed."

"That's not how this works."

"Actually, you of all people should know that this is exactly how it works. That's the justice system for you." He shrugs.

I cross my arms showing how displeased I am with him. Of course, that's how the justice system works. I know that, and I don't need him telling me that. I need him to find out who the third set of DNA belongs to and whether or not this Jesse Hook knows more. He went from being this nice gentleman to this total asshole in the blink of an eye.

"Well, lucky for you—I've been doing your job."

"My job here is done, Mrs. Morgan. Now, you can leave my office." He points to the door.

"Then who's Jesse Hook? Did you look into him at all?"

He gives me a bewildered look. "Name doesn't ring a bell."

"Exactly. I thought so. Apparently this Jesse Hook was a bit obsessed with Kelly, practically stalking her. A co-worker of hers, Brenda, said that whenever she saw Kelly, Jesse was nearby. I wonder how close Jesse got to her and how much he saw of her that night or maybe he was there. Maybe he did it. Maybe he saw the man that did it. Or maybe he wasn't the other man in her life, but maybe he knows who that man is." I give him a smirk and raise an eyebrow.

Sheriff Stevens doesn't speak. I can see him mulling over everything I said. I toss the folder with everything we have on Jesse onto his desk. He flips through it. On the third page is a large photo of Jesse taken from an old newspaper where he placed in some art show. He has shaggy brown hair and a cold stare. He's not smiling, but he seems pleased with himself.

"I've seen this kid around," Sheriff Stevens says.

"And?"

"I'll look into it." He closes up the folder.

"I'd like to be there when he's questioned."

"Sarah, you're not a member of this police department."

"I don't care. I want to be there, and I'm going to be there. How long until you can get him in?"

He rubs his forehead in annoyance. He knows I'm not giving up, and he knows arguing with me won't do him any good. "Fine. I can get a car to bring him in within the hour."

"Perfect. I'll be in the waiting area. Text me when he arrives."

Sheriff Stevens nods. As I'm leaving his office, he stops me. "Want some company?"

"No, I think I've had just about enough of your company."

I leave his office and pull out my phone, sending Anne a quick text.

We got him. I'll be back late this afternoon.

36

ADAM MORGAN

I've made it through half the list with no luck. No one has even heard of a Nicholas Miller. I decide to take a break from cold-calling and pour myself a scotch at the wet bar. My decanter is empty, but there's two full bottles of scotch next to it, courtesy of Sarah. I pour myself a double, slam it, and then pour another. I slowly sip this one while I light the fire.

It's still bright out, but I don't care. I close the curtains and make the house as dark as I can manage with only the fireplace providing any light. It's how I feel right now—dark, hopeless, and just waiting for my time to pass. I sip slowly. Perhaps the slower I drink, the slower my time will pass by.

I sit there for a good twenty minutes, stewing in my own depression. Is this it for me? I make one mistake and my life is over. How is that fair? How is any of this fair? There's a lot of things I deserve, but jail or execution isn't one of them. I guess this is the life I chose. This is the path I decided to walk down. This is it.

After the scotch makes its way through my bloodstream, I try calling Rebecca, but I get her voicemail, and although leaving a voicemail isn't the cool thing to do these days, I do it anyway.

"Hey, Rebecca, it's me—Adam. I'm about halfway done and haven't gotten anything yet. Was hoping you'd be having better luck. Taking a break right now, but I'll start back up. If you want to come over for dinner, feel free to. I've got a couple of steaks in the freezer. Anyway, I'll talk to you later." I hang up the phone. That dinner invitation was the scotch talking.

I dial again. It rings and rings, and then Sarah's voicemail picks up. "Hey, Sarah. It's me—Adam. I've been thinking about you. I miss you. Please call me. I love you... Sarah..." I trail off and just hang up the phone.

I'm not sure why she's too busy to return a call to me. I called her earlier too, and she didn't pick up. I know things got weird on Friday night, but I thought we had a sweet moment. I thought we were making progress. I haven't touched the box of evidence she brought over. I still think someone from Kelly's past has to be responsible for her murder. If someone murdered the person I love, I would never let it go, ever. I would wait until I had an opportunity to get them back, even if it took years or my whole life. I truly believe Greg's brother has done that. It's the only explanation.

Then again, it could be Scott too. I need to speak with him again and really get a feel for him. He caught me off guard last time, but this time I'd be ready. I should see if I can get him to come to the house. Maybe have Sarah here too so she can get a read on him. That's always been her gift—reading people; however, she failed to do so all this time when I was seeing Kelly. She may have lost her touch.

And then there's that photo. Who could have seen us? Was it Scott? Or maybe someone close to him?

The front door opens and closes. Heels click along the floor and in walks Mom dressed in a long black peacoat and heels. She sets two bags of groceries on the kitchen table.

"Why is it so dark in here?" she asks immediately walking

around ripping open all the curtains, letting a flood of beaming light in.

I squint and rub my eyes, standing from the couch. "Jesus, Mom."

"You can't live in a cave." She walks back to the kitchen and begins unpacking the bags.

I slide the list of phone numbers into a pile and follow her into the kitchen. I don't want to explain Rebecca or my side investigation. She'll ask a million questions and insist on helping.

"What have you been up to today?" Mom asks.

"I was just doing some work. What did you get?"

"Just some treats for you—Lunchables, string cheese, Gushers, Go-Gurt. All your favorite childhood snacks." She smiles at me.

"I got some good news today."

She stops what she's doing. Her eyes light up. "They're dropping the charges? They found the real murderer?" Mom's nearly jumping up and down.

"No, Mom. My agent is working on a book deal for me."

Her excitement tapers, and she busies herself by opening a string cheese and handing it to me. She pats me on the shoulder and smiles. Instead of peeling it, I just take a bite out of the end. "It's a tell-all. It's huge, Mom. He's talking seven figures and a movie deal."

"Oh, honey. That's amazing. I'm proud of you. Your father would be proud too." Mom gives me a tight hug.

I'm not sure that's true, given my circumstances. "What have you been up to?"

"Running errands. I went and talked to a few lawyers as well."

"Why?" I raise an eyebrow.

"To make sure you have the best possible defense, and as it

turns out, every lawyer I spoke to agreed Sarah was more than qualified. Not sure I believe that. Probably just has to do with all the 'female empowerment' hype these days," she snarks.

"Mom. Stop."

"I'm surprised though. I thought lawyers were money-hungry ambulance chasers. Not one of them was even interested in taking your case. Something about it being a lost cause... but that's just because they don't know my son." She pinches my cheek affectionately.

"That's reassuring," I say sarcastically.

"I know you're innocent, cubbie-bear, and innocent people don't go to prison." She finishes putting away the groceries.

"That's not true at all. There's literally a nonprofit organization that helps exonerate wrongly convicted people."

"Regardless, you're not going to jail so you won't have to worry about that. I'll make sure Sarah gets this whole thing over with as soon as possible." She opens a pack of Gushers and hands it to me. "Now, I just came over to drop off some groceries before I leave town. I have a commitment I couldn't get out of, but I will be back tomorrow."

She kisses me on the cheek and leaves the house. I pop one of the candies in my mouth and bite down. The juice oozes out and arouses all my taste buds to a tart, sweet taste. Just how I remembered it as a kid. I toss the rest in my mouth, walk back into the living room, and pick up the list of phone numbers. I have to get through these numbers. Innocent people do go to prison, and I won't be one of them. I pick up the phone and begin dialing.

37

SARAH MORGAN

I t's about an hour later when Sheriff Stevens comes down to get me. His demeanor seems a bit more closed off, but when he speaks, he's kind. It's as if he is fighting a battle with himself about how exactly he should behave around me, how he should treat me, how he wants me to view him.

"We're ready for you, Sarah." He taps me on the shoulder just as I'm taking a bite out of a stale sandwich from the vending machine. I tell him okay and wrap up the remainder of it. He's returned to calling me "Sarah" as well. I can't read this guy, but I feel like he's hiding something or maybe just not sharing the full truth with me.

"We're going to put you in the viewing room while I question Jesse Hook."

As we walk, his hand bumps mine. He says sorry and smiles at me. I return the smile, and I don't know why I do.

"Right this way." He directs me into a small room with a large viewing window looking into the interrogation room, the same place Scott attacked Adam and the same room I learned of all of Adam's infidelities and lies. In a chair where Adam once sat is Jesse Hook. I recognize him from his photo even though it was taken years ago. His face is a bit scruffy now, and he's thin and lanky. His shaggy ash-brown hair doesn't appear to have been brushed in days. He's wearing an oversized zip-up hoodie and jeans. And he looks scared. That's what stands out most of all. The fear in his eyes.

Did he do it? Does he know who did it? What is he afraid of? Who is he afraid of? He seems like the nervous type and sometimes nerves read as fear, but this seems different. Maybe I'm reading too much into it—hoping it's more than it is, hoping he has the answers I'm looking for. I'm not one to wait around for answers. I seek them out. I hate this. I hate waiting. I hate not knowing. This little prick better know what I need him to know.

"I'll be right in there if you need me. Just tell an officer."

A moment or two later, Sheriff Stevens enters, taking a seat in front of Jesse. Jesse's eyes widen. He grows uneasy, shifting uncomfortably in his chair. I can see his chest rise and fall as he inhales and exhales deeply. He glances around. Sheriff Stevens hits the record button at the end of the table and takes a seat across from Jesse. He is calm and collected, but Jesse is starting to perspire. He is looking everywhere else in the room but at Sheriff Stevens. I even catch him looking at the one-way mirror, and it feels like he is looking directly at me—almost trying to say something to whoever is on the other side. I stop myself from bursting in and asking every question I haven't had an answer to since this case began.

"Brenda Johnson, an employee at Seth's Coffee, informed us that you had frequently been visiting the victim, Kelly Summers, days, weeks, if not months leading up to her death. Is that true?" Sheriff Stevens asks.

Jesse seems to become more comfortable at that question. He straightens up in his seat, brushes his hair out of his eyes, and folds his hands in front of himself on the table. "Yes, I knew of Kelly Summers as I do frequent Seth's Coffee, so that is true. I really enjoyed her service," Jesse says calmly.

Sheriff Stevens looks him up and down, almost evaluating and sizing him up. "You enjoyed her service?"

"Yes." Jesse nods.

"What do you mean by that?"

"She was friendly. She always refilled my cup, and I left Seth's Coffee satisfied every time."

Sheriff Stevens gives him a dirty look, and it's then that I wonder if Jesse is playing some sort of game with him. "What do you mean by 'satisfied?'"

"Well served," he answers quickly. I can hear Sheriff Steven visibly groan. Jesse appears to have taken hold of the confidence he didn't have earlier, and I'm not sure what changed.

"Since you were at Seth's Coffee a lot, surely you would have noticed Kelly Summers and anyone she had been frequenting there with or speaking with." Sheriff Stevens glares at Jesse.

"I'm sure I would have." Jesse folds his arms into his chest.

"Brenda mentioned that you may have been a bit obsessed with Kelly. That the attention was unwanted."

Jesse once again grows uncomfortable. His confidence drains from his body like a sand hourglass timer. "That's not true," he says with the last bit of assurance he has.

"What's not true?" Sheriff Stevens matches his demeanor folding his arms in front of his wide chest.

"I wasn't obsessed with Kelly. We were friends."

"Well, what kind of friend tells the other to leave them alone or begs their co-worker to intervene?"

"What are you trying to say?" Jesse's eyebrows pinch together.

"From the sounds of it, Kelly wasn't comfortable with your presence. She would ask her co-workers, specifically Brenda, to take your table whenever you came in, because quote, 'you made her uncomfortable,' unquote. Why do you think that is?"

Jesse's face turns a deep red. I can see him let out a large breath of air that blows his hair out of his eyes. "She's lying. Kelly and I were friends. She gave me her phone number and everything." He slams his fist on the table.

"Yes, we saw you had texted her on the night of her murder '*I'm sorry.*' What were you apologizing for?"

"I don't know. She hadn't been answering my phone calls. I figured she was mad at me for something." He regains his composure and just shrugs.

"It doesn't seem like you two were actually friends."

"But we were."

"Can you prove this? Your friendship?"

"Yeah, I can. I knew who her friends were or at least the people she was with a lot. One of them was a cop." Jesse juts up his chin and raises his eyebrows.

"You mean Officer Scott Summers, her husband?" Sheriff Stevens shifts in his seat and places his elbows on the table. The room is silent, while the two stare at one another. Jesse doesn't really move. He simply stares. My phone buzzes over and over and over and over. I stop paying attention to Jesse and Sheriff Stevens and pull out my phone. I have four texts from Anne. I open them up.

Adam had a redhead over today. Not sure who she is, but I'll find out.

Adam spent $10,000 at a mattress and bedding store.

Apparently, she's a reporter.

Adam has made twenty-two phone calls to twenty-two different phone numbers in the past twenty-four hours.

I finish reading through Anne's text messages and try to refocus my attention back on Sheriff Stevens and Jesse Hook. The mood seems to have shifted during my inattentiveness— shifted to what, I'm not exactly sure. But it has.

I know I told Anne to keep an eye on Adam. However, she's gotten so close it's making me uncomfortable. The number of calls. I said I wanted to know everything—but how much is too much? And this redhead he's hired to help him... ugh, Adam, once again, is hiding things from me. Would I expect anything less? No. Not even in the slightest. This is exactly why I have Anne making sure he's being watched at all times. I don't need any other surprises like Jesse here. I shift my focus to the interrogation room.

"And did you ever see Officer Scott Summers harm Kelly Summers?"

"Like verbally or physically?"

"Both. Kelly has mentioned to several people that he had harmed her both physically and verbally. Can you deny or confirm that?" he asks.

Jesse pauses, looking around and then back at Sheriff Stevens. "He was abusive, both physically and verbally. I witnessed both."

"Did you ever see Kelly with Adam Morgan?"

"Yes, I did," Jesse says.

My phone buzzes again. I look down at it and see another text message from Anne.

Bob is asking for you. He seems pissed... as per usual.

I text her back quickly:

I'll be there this afternoon.

The door opens, stealing my attention. I look up for a moment and return my concentration back to the interrogation room when I realize Deputy Hudson has entered. I really can't deal with him right now. "To what do I owe the pleasure, deputy?" I don't turn to look at him.

"Oh, we are starting with pleasantries?"

"Fine. What the fuck are you doing here?"

He smiles. "That's better. Oh, I'm just here for a little entertainment is all."

"Entertainment?"

"Yup. You see, for all of his shortcomings, Sheriff Stevens is actually quite excellent at this part of the job. I really do enjoy watching them squirm right before they break. It's almost an art."

"I might buy that. I mean, I enjoy the same thing too from time to time. But not this time. No, I think you are here for another reason." I turn to look at Deputy Hudson, trying to get a read on him.

"Yeah? Please enlighten me then, Miss Fancy Lawyer, with the thing that I apparently don't know myself."

"You are here to cover your ass. Make sure that if something you don't want being said is said in there that it isn't a surprise to you. So you have time to plan a way out. Because I don't know what you're up to, but your boss is in there handling this; and the whole conversation is being recorded and could be viewed by you later at any time. So, I'll ask again, what the fuck are you doing here?"

Marcus stares at me, tonguing the wad of tobacco in his gums. His eyes dart back and forth across my face. Now, he's trying to read me. Trying to find any indication of what his next move should be. "Maybe you're right. I can catch this anytime I please. And seeing as you have made it abundantly clear that you don't appreciate my company, I guess I'll be on my way." He walks to the door and opens it. "You have a lovely day, Mrs. Morgan," he quips with a smile plastered on his face.

I flip him the middle finger as a parting gift. I don't have any idea what he is up to, but it reeks of suspicion. I'll add him to my list of things to check out with this case.

When I return my attention to the interrogation room, Sheriff Stevens is getting up to leave. Jesse appears relieved. A moment later, Sheriff Stevens enters the viewing room.

"That went better than I expected," he says leaning against the wall.

"Are you just going to let him go? Is that it?"

I'm still torn between the text-conversation with Anne, the odd interaction with Deputy Hudson, and the interrogation I witnessed between Sheriff Stevens and Jesse.

"No. We'll still test him. We have cause, and he's here and as long as he's cooperative, we can. He seems to be, so you don't have to worry about that."

I nod, not completely satisfied with that answer but at this point, I'll take what I can get.

"Well, what do you think?" I close my notebook and look at Sheriff Stevens giving him my full attention.

"I think that Jesse doesn't really know anything. I think he just had a bit of an intense crush on Kelly and that's it. Did he like her? Yes. Was he close with her? No. But did he think he was close to her? Yes."

"He was obsessed?"

"Most likely," he answers.

"Did he say anything of value?"

"It doesn't sound like it," he says. "But we're also testing his DNA, and if there's a match between him and that third set of

DNA, that'll give us more insight and cause to hold him for more questioning."

That answer makes me feel like I understand things again even if I don't feel like I do. Something still doesn't feel right.

"Do you need a ride home?"

"No," I say. "How long until the DNA test comes back?"

"I'll expedite it to the lab—twenty-four hours."

"You'll let me know right away?"

"Of course." He nods.

I walk away trusting that he will. I'm not sure why he decided to help me suddenly when it seemed like he had given up on the case. What changed? Maybe he believes Jesse had something to do with Kelly's death or maybe he thinks Jesse just might know something. It has to be Jesse. He has to be that third DNA set. No other man was mentioned by any witnesses Sheriff Stevens or I interviewed. Unless, of course, Kelly kept that third man a complete secret from everyone. Why though? Why him? She didn't exactly hide Adam. Many in town knew about them. I hope the third set of DNA matches with Jesse. I'm tired of this wild goose chase, and I'm sick of not having all the answers. Now I have to put an end to whatever the fuck Adam is up to.

38

ADAM MORGAN

The scotch has stolen some of my memories. I hope I didn't obtain some pertinent information from the phone calls I made because if I did, I'm not sure I'd remember it. I've decided to start on the last phone number I could recall making.

A sandwich and chips did me some good as well as a power nap. I'm starting to feel like myself again—and by that, I mean, hopeless and depressed—but definitely sobering up. I'm facing the death penalty. There isn't much else I could feel. But I'm resisting the scotch for the time being.

I pick up the phone and begin dialing. The phone rings and rings and rings and just as the voicemail picks up, my front door swings open with a bang.

"Adam!" I don't even need to see her to know it's her. I could recognize that disappointed voice anywhere at any time.

I quickly hang the phone up and try to look nonchalant on the couch. Sarah enters the living room wide-eyed and angry.

Great. What did I do this time? It can't have been any worse than having an affair and being on trial for the murder of my mistress. "Hey, honey," I say with a bit of sarcasm.

I can tell by the look in her eyes, she sees me as no more

than a problem, a client that has to be dealt with. What happened to the Sarah I encountered on Friday night? The love that was once there seems to have vanished, and I can't blame her. Look at me, a scruffy, unkempt beard has taken residence on my face. I'm sure my bloodshot eyes have their bags packed. My hair is a mess, and I'm still in PJs and a robe. Plus, let's not forget about the situation I've gotten us in.

"Don't 'hey, honey' me," she says pointing at me. "What's with the redhead, the phone calls, and the ten thousand dollars you spent?" Her eyes narrow. Maybe she does care about me. She asked about the redhead first. Is she jealous? I haven't seen her jealous in quite some time. She just might love me after all.

"I can explain all of those things," I say putting my hands up.

"Then explain." She sits on the loveseat and crosses one leg over the other.

"Okay, the redhead: her name is Rebecca. She's a reporter—"

"A reporter? You're talking to a reporter? You do know you're on trial for murder and the death penalty is on the table?"

"I understand that, Sarah—more than anyone." I grit my teeth. This right here is my problem with Sarah, she treats me like I'm an idiot. What does she expect me to say to that? *Oh, damn. Thanks for reminding me. I completely forgot that I'm on house arrest pending my trial.*

"Do you actually understand that?" It's clearly a rhetorical question.

"She's helping me."

"She's a reporter. You're just a story, and you don't even know this woman. I have jury selection happening right now, and the last thing I need is anything in the media swaying them. You're lucky the media dug up Kelly's past because that's been good for you in terms of public opinion. But one more story that paints you in an unflattering light will destroy that. Do you understand?"

"Rebecca and I have an agreement. She's going to put my side of the story out, and I'm paying her to help me with my investigation." I sit forward and place my elbows on my knees.

"*My investigation*? What the hell is that supposed to mean? There is one investigation happening, and that's Jesse Hook. What is it that you think you're doing, Adam?" She bounces her foot up and down and readjusts her skirt. Her face becomes flushed, and she lets out an exasperated sigh. I know my meddling is bothering her because she thinks she knows best, and I used to believe that, but now I'm not sure.

"Who's Jesse Hook?"

"Exactly. You have no idea what's happening with your own case. That's the problem," she says with a bit of bite in her voice.

"I'm cooped up in this house. I can't leave. Therefore, if you don't tell me anything, I don't know anything, and when I don't know anything, I look for everything," I narrow my eyes at her.

"Is that a threat?"

"Why would you take that as a threat?" I'm bewildered by her question and her change of tone. She shifts uncomfortably in her seat and then straightens out her pristine outfit.

"No. Never mind." She gets up, picks up the box she brought over the other night and tosses it on the coffee table. "This is what you should be focusing on. I brought you everything."

"Who's Jesse Hook?"

She lets out a huff. "Jesse Hook used to frequent Seth's Coffee. A co-worker of Kelly's said he was obsessed with her and made Kelly uncomfortable, so we're looking into him."

"And?"

"We're testing his DNA. He just might be a match to that third set found in Kelly. Sheriff Stevens questioned him about an hour ago. I was there but got a little distracted. I'll review the tape of the interview."

"That's great to hear you were distracted while working on my case," I say sarcastically.

"Yeah, it's you that was distracting me. The redhead. The money. The phone calls. Will you please finish explaining that to me?" Her voice is laced with anger and annoyance.

"Like I said, Rebecca is helping me look into the family of Kelly's first husband. I think that part of her life is to blame for her death." I get up and pour myself a glass of scotch.

"That's a dead end," Sarah says pointedly.

"Why? Did you even look into that?"

"I believe the police did and that whole *someone from her past came back and got their revenge* just doesn't seem plausible."

"You 'believe the police did?' I would hope my attorney is not defending this case based on beliefs." I slam my drink and get myself another. I can't deal with her right now. She believes... since when did beliefs win cases. I need facts. I need evidence. What the hell is she doing?

"You know what I mean, Adam."

"Clearly, I don't," I challenge. Is she even fighting for me or does she know this is a lost cause? Did she throw in the towel the second she took this case? Is there no hope for me? I sit back down taking large gulps of scotch. The burning in my throat is the only thing that reminds me I'm still alive. The rest of me feels nothing.

"Weren't you the one convinced Scott had something to do with Kelly's death, and now you're convinced that someone from her past did? Which is it?"

"Scott said he never hurt Kelly and I think I believe him. Based on that, maybe he didn't have anything to do with it?"

"Jesse Hook confirmed he witnessed Scott physically and verbally abuse Kelly. Why would he lie?"

"Wait. He did? But Scott swore up and down he didn't." Why

the hell would Scott lie to me? Why would he care what I thought? Something isn't adding up.

"Who in their right mind would admit to abusing their late wife?"

She's right. I'm such an idiot. He just seemed like he was telling the truth. He seemed like he... he just wanted to help, and maybe he does. Just because he was abusive doesn't mean he killed her. I don't know what I'm saying. Of course, he could have. He has a temper. He's an asshole. He could get away with it. He's a cop for Christ's sake. Maybe I shouldn't write him off based on one conversation. This whole thing is a mess, and I don't know if I'm looking at the right person or even in the right direction. But I can't give up now. I have less than two weeks before my trial starts. There has to be someone out there who knows something.

"What's all this?" Sarah motions to the papers beside me on the couch. I should have put those away. She doesn't agree with me, and I think Kelly's past needs to be looked into. The papers are all the information Rebecca's given to me concerning Kelly's old life as well as the phone numbers I need to finish calling. Sarah walks to the couch and starts rummaging through them. She's quickly scanning everything in sight. If she doesn't believe this is worth looking into, then why is she looking?

"That's for my investigation," I say trying to collect it all into one pile. I don't need her going through this. If she's not going to help me, then she doesn't need to be here. I have work to do. She's looking at the list of phone numbers, perusing them one by one. What is she looking for? Or is she just trying to appease me? Trying to make it look like she's taking this seriously? What is her endgame? Her eyes linger a little longer than I'd expect. Then, she finally sets the paper down.

"Yeah, you're wasting your time." She pauses. "What did you spend the ten thousand dollars on?"

"What's it to you? That was my money—an advance on my book," I say defiantly.

"All right then. We'll be in touch." She gets up and starts walking toward the front door. Why is she always in a hurry? I have no idea who she is anymore. How did she know about Rebecca and the phone calls and the money? She's watching me, or she has someone watching me. But why? To help me? To hurt me? Or to keep me contained?

Before she leaves the living room, she stops and turns around. "By the way, if you end up in prison and you don't finish your book, I'll end up paying that advance back. So, please stop spending MY money, asshole."

"I thought it was our money, Sarah? We're married. Remember?" I snark back, folding my arms in front of my chest.

"Oh, was it our marriage when you were balls deep in some waitress?" She narrows her eyes at me.

I look away for a moment. She's got me there.

"Exactly." She stamps her foot.

"Regardless, you won't have to worry about your money anymore. I'm writing a tell-all, and there's already a bidding war for my book." I smirk.

Sarah's mouth drops open. "You have got to be fucking kidding me. I'm working my ass off on your case, and you're turning this whole thing into a goddamn circus, you and your delusional mother." She puts her hands up. "I'm done."

Sarah turns on her foot and leaves the house, slamming the door behind her.

39

SARAH MORGAN

I'm driving back to the city in a rage, my eyes focused on the spread of my headlights. I'm furious. I need to keep Adam contained. He's undermining the case, my investigation, and my career with his antics. I can tell he's drinking too much again. That bottle of scotch was nearly full when I was here on Friday, and now it's gone, and he's working on another. What the hell does he think he's doing? Talking to a reporter. Calling everyone that could have been related to Kelly's first husband. Writing a tell-all. I know he's discussing his case with his agent, and he's not supposed to be talking about it. He's jeopardizing the whole damn thing.

I slam my hand against the steering wheel in frustration. "Fuck! Fuck! Fuck!" I slam it again and once more for good measure.

I dial Anne via the voice command in my vehicle. She picks up on the first ring like she always does. "Hey, how'd it go with Adam?"

"Not great. He's working with a reporter on his own investigation, and he's writing a tell-all." I honk my horn at a person in a mini-van driving too slow in front of me. I swerve out of the way and flip them off as I drive by. It's a little old woman and a man. What is wrong with me? Adam has got me so worked up. I take a deep breath trying to remind myself that everything is going to be fine.

"Why?"

"Apparently, he doesn't trust what I'm doing for the case."

"But you're doing everything you possibly can. This is an uphill case."

"I even brought him over copies of all the evidence, so he could be involved," I groan.

"You did?" Anne's voice is meek.

"Yeah. But he's not even looking at it. I could use his help there, another set of eyes on it. He's been drinking a lot too and that must be clouding his judgment. I need you to get the phone turned off at the lake house. I don't want him destroying this case with his drunk dialing."

"I'll get it done. Anything else?"

"Yeah, set up a meeting with Bob tomorrow. I have to make sure everything is running smoothly at the firm as I don't want to end up in Kent's office again."

"You got it."

"I'm going home. I'll be back at the office in the morning."

"Sounds good. Take care of yourself, Sarah. I'll see you in the morning."

My phone buzzes. I quickly glance at it. It's from Matthew.

Dinner tonight? Say 7:30pm at The Capital Grille?

~

A formally dressed waiter escorts me through the restaurant to a table where Matthew is sitting. There's a bottle of opened champagne already set out, and Matthew is dressed in a beautifully tailored suit. He stands when I approach and hugs me, planting a kiss on each cheek.

"Sorry I'm late. Had to deal with Adam's antics." I take a seat.

"No worries. What's Adam up to now?" He pours a glass of champagne and offers it to me.

I roll my eyes, take the glass and drink the whole thing.

"He's drunk. He's calling dozens of random numbers. He's writing a tell-all, and he's working with a reporter on his own 'investigation.'" I throw up air quotes around investigation because that's how ridiculous it is to me.

"Not much has changed." Matthew laughs as he takes a sip of his champagne.

I refill my glass. "What's that supposed to mean?"

"Adam's always had a flair for the dramatics."

"I can't argue with that." I flip open the menu and glance around at it, even though I've eaten here dozens of times and I always order the same thing: porcini rubbed bone-in ribeye with fifteen-year aged balsamic.

"How's Eleanor?"

"Same as usual—bitchy, judgmental, rude, condescending... Did I mention bitchy?" I smirk.

"Of course she is," Matthew says flicking his hand at me.

"She brought up my parents!"

He tilts his chin down. "She didn't. What did she say?"

"Basically, that I should get over it."

He lets out a sigh and reaches across the table to squeeze my hand. "Ignore her. She's just a miserable bitch."

I give him a small smile, and he squeezes my hand reassuringly. We pick up our glasses of champagne, clink, and drink.

Matthew pauses and looks at me. "You know? I still don't understand why you're defending your husband in all of this."

"Because he's my husband," I sigh. "And regardless of what he's put me through, deep down I still love him."

"You do?" Matthew gives me an accusatory smile.

"Really, really deep down right now." I laugh.

Matthew laughs too. "It takes a strong woman to do what you're doing."

"But you think I'm crazy for doing it?"

He closes his menu. "Honestly?"

"Of course."

"Yes. You shouldn't have taken his case, and I don't think you're making the best judgments, most likely due to how personal it is to you. I know Adam's a little shit, but he does deserve a proper defense."

I snap my menu closed. "What are you talking about? What poor judgments am I making?"

"Don't get snappy with me. I invented snap." Matthew clicks his fingers.

I roll my eyes.

He clears his throat. "As I was saying. You're pushing this trial through quickly. Why?"

"I have my reasons, and they're none of your business."

"They are my business. I'm helping with the case, remember?"

I let out a huff. This was supposed to be an enjoyable dinner. Why is he questioning me or my intentions? I take a drink of champagne and set my glass down. "Adam and Eleanor want a speedy trial, and it's their right."

"You should advise them otherwise." Matthew narrows his eyes at me.

"My boss wants this case closed quickly. I'm not getting profit-share while I'm working on it," I whisper.

"That's not an excuse. Get him a different lawyer."

I slam my fist on the table, bouncing the silverware. "You

know I'm the only lawyer that has a chance in hell of winning this case."

Matthew leans back. "Take it easy."

"Sorry." I straighten up the silverware. "I just don't understand why you're challenging me. I thought you were my friend."

"I am, and that's exactly why I'm challenging you. I don't want your personal involvement to cloud your judgment. You're the all-star lawyer. Give me one good, lawful reason why you're rushing the trial." He folds his arms in front of his chest and cocks his head.

I glance at the table, around the restaurant, and then at Matthew. "Well, Kelly's twisted past leaked to the news, and if we can get the case in front of a jury while that information is fresh in people's minds, it'll help with reasonable doubt in Adam's case."

Matthew nods.

"We don't know who the third set of DNA belongs to and, in a way, not knowing can help us, because if we knew and that man had a solid alibi, then it'd mean nothing to the case."

Matthew nods again.

"Same with whoever sent the photo and the threat. A person can't have an alibi if we don't know who the person is."

He smiles at me. "That's all I needed to know. Sounds like your judgment is clearer than I thought. Now, let's eat," Matthew says just as the waiter approaches the table.

A couple of hours later, I'm walking into our—or should I say my—home in D.C. carrying my box of leftovers from dinner and a bottle of wine I picked up on the way home. Hopefully, Anne can get the phone at the lake house shut off by tomorrow. I can't have Adam ruining everything. I spend the evening sipping wine and reviewing all the facts of the case. I doze off around ten, which I didn't intend to, but... wine.

It's much later when I hear someone coming up the stairs. I have had a longing desire for... something, ever since this ordeal started. I've been unsatisfied for quite some time, and I need something, anything. I can feel the pressure in the air change slightly, and I know the door has been opened, I'm not the only person in the room anymore. I stare at the ceiling, but with no light, it begins to morph into clouds of blue and black, a swirl of something beyond. I start to lift off the bed, and the room becomes warm, and it feels more familiar than I have ever known. I can feel eyes upon me, circling me like prey in the darkness but I'm not afraid, quite the opposite. I'm dressed in lacy panties and a lacy bra, a piece of meat garnished for presentation.

The mattress presses down, and I feel breath on me. Soft hands slide up my stomach and then grasp at my breasts, massaging them. My breath quickens. I want this as bad as anything in my life. I can feel a cloying stickiness build up in my panties. A rubbing sensation grows as I begin to moan and then something is inside me. My every desire being fulfilled as if the thoughts in my head were being projected on the wall and deciphered. By the time I climax, I am more drained than I have been in days. Sleep quickly comes over me as I drift back down onto the bed, chasing a new sense of longing.

When I awake the next morning, there is a void just next to me in bed. I can't wait for the day when that hole is filled for good. A dam put in place to stop the endless flow of nothingness, all my desires carried in its current. I have decided that regardless of the outcome of the trial, I will divorce Adam when this is all over. I'm going to do what's best for me, and it's about goddamn time that I do. If he's found innocent, he'll have the opportunity to start his life over—I just won't be in it.

My phone buzzes and I pick it up. It's a text from Anne to say that Bob has moved our meeting up to 8:30am.

I text back that I'll be there. *Goddamnit, Bob*. I quickly get ready and haul ass into the office. I'm usually in much earlier than 8am, but with my late-night visitor, I got a delayed start this morning. Anne hands me a cup of coffee as soon as the elevator doors open. She looks bright and cheery despite our circumstances. Reporters have been trying to get into the building to interview me and have been calling the office repeatedly. Anne has done a great job of keeping them away.

"Good morning, Sarah. Bob's already in your office," she says with a look of pity. I glance at my watch.

"Why? It's not even 8:15am."

"I'm not sure. I tried to make him wait, but he insisted. Sorry."

"It's not your fault. Bob is well... Bob. Hold my calls while I deal with him."

Bob is staring out my window. At the sound of the door opening, he turns around.

"Nice of you to join me." He grins.

"You're fifteen minutes early." I place my bag on my desk and shuffle around him to get to my seat. "What do you want?" I sit down and start sorting through my papers.

"I want to talk." He walks to the other side of my desk and sits down.

"We don't talk, Bob," I say pursing my lips.

"We do now. I want to know what's going on with your husband's case."

"It's none of your business, and it's being taken care of." I take a sip of my coffee.

"What can I do to help?"

"I don't need your help and why would you want to help anyway?"

"Because the whole thing is a bad look for the firm. I want it closed and buttoned up nice and neat."

218

"I'm handling it."

"Then why am I getting phone calls from reporters?"

I regroup some papers on the desk. "Well, you're in charge of PR for the firm, so that's probably why, Bob. But if you really want to help, I need you—"

I'm cut off mid-sentence from his ringing phone. He puts his finger up and pulls it out. He looks at the number and gives an odd, yet inquisitive look. He answers the call.

"Bob Miller," he says into the phone. Then he is silent for a few moments. "Wrong number." He hangs up the phone.

"Reporter?" I ask.

"Something like that." He pauses. "Now, what were you saying?"

"Since you're familiar with the reporters in the area. I need you to take care of a Rebecca Sanford."

"Take care of her how?"

"She's been interfering with the case, and I need that to stop. Can you handle that?"

"Can I handle that? That's cute, Sarah. Consider it done." He laughs. He stands up from his chair. "I'll be around if you need me." He walks out of my office.

Anne shuffles in right as Bob leaves. "What was that about?"

"Oh, just Bob being his usual cock(y) self." I roll my eyes.

"By the way, the phone company just called and confirmed the phone at the lake house is being shut off."

"That's great. One less thing I have to worry about," I say while scanning over a handful of papers.

"Did you find out who Adam was calling?" Anne asks.

"It's nothing to worry about—everything is taken care of." And I hope I'm right. Adam better not have interfered with the case. I'm having a hard enough time as it is. Anne nods and leaves my office when the phone on her desk rings. A few moments later, she's talking to me through the intercom on my desk phone. "Sheriff Stevens is on line one."

I take the call.

"Nice to hear your voice, Sarah," he says.

Great, we're back on a first-name basis. "What can I do for you, Sheriff Stevens?"

"I'm just calling to let you know the DNA results came back on Jesse. He's not a match."

Shit. How could it not be him? I was convinced it was him. If not him, then who? Maybe this third set of DNA has nothing to do with the case; maybe it does. But I will never be okay not knowing. I have to figure out what the fuck I'm still missing.

"Are you sure?"

"One hundred percent."

"Now what?"

"Not a whole lot I can do since the case is closed, but I'll keep my ear to the ground for you and let you know if I find or hear anything."

"Thanks," I say feeling defeated.

"I'm sorry, Sarah. I know things have been... difficult, but if you need anything, please let me know."

"Yeah. Thanks, sheriff," I say, and I hang up the phone. I slam my fist against the desk. I can't deal with his back-and-forth, wishy-washy thing we have going on. I'm not sure what his angle is. Is he trying to help me or is he trying to help himself? I can't worry about him though. I'm running out of time, and I'm not any closer to getting the answers I desperately need.

40

ADAM MORGAN

I spent most of last night drunk dialing, so much so that I
have to call some of those numbers again. What the fuck is
wrong with me? I can't even help myself. Rebecca is supposed to
stop over this morning or at least that's what I remember her
telling me last night. I could be wrong though. Regardless, I have
five phone calls left to make, and I best do that before she
arrives.

I woke up and showered for the first time in days, trimmed
up my beard (I decided to keep it), and got dressed in somewhat
presentable clothing, jeans, and a T-shirt. There's a fresh pot of
coffee, and I've just sat down on the couch with the telephone in
front of me.

I dial the first number, and I get the voicemail for a woman
who says her name is Gretchen. I cross that number off the list.

I phone the second number and a woman answers. She
doesn't know what I'm talking about. I cross her name off the
list.

I dial the third number, and a man picks up. He also has no
idea who I'm referring to. He's a bit rude and hangs up on me.

The fourth number is an old man who has a hard time

speaking. He sounds like he has had a laryngectomy. I hang up on him as he tries to tell me his life story. He's old and lonely, and it sounds like he's in the same boat as me—we don't have enough time.

The fifth and last number answers on nearly the first ring. He answers so fast that I miss his name—I'm thinking Rob. But I can't be sure. Since I don't pick up what he says, I immediately go into explaining.

"Hi. I'm looking for Nicholas Miller. He's the brother of Greg Miller and brother-in-law to Kelly Summers. My name is Adam Morgan. I desperately need to speak with Nicholas. It's a matter of life or death," I say. This is my last call. I hope to God this person knows him. If not, Rebecca didn't get me all the names, or I fucked up when I was drinking and dialing. God. I'm such an idiot. I'm out of breath. I've broken out in a sweat.

"Wrong number," he says, and then he abruptly hangs up.

I slam the phone down. "FUCK!" I slam it down a few more times. How is this happening? I hope Rebecca found something. She had to have found something. I slam the phone down again and punch at the coffee table. I get up and pour myself a cup of coffee and return to the couch. I wish this were scotch. I take a drink before the coffee has cooled, and it burns my tongue and throat. It's not the same feeling as scotch. It's painful. But it makes me feel alive. I pick up the papers and scan through them, hoping that one phone number will stand out. Obviously, none of them do. I toss the papers back on the coffee table and take another drink of scalding coffee.

I have to get a hold of Rebecca. I need her here. I can't do this without her. I need to know that she's found something. She's my last hope. I pick up the phone and put the receiver to my ear, but there's no dial tone. The line is dead. I tap the switch hook several times, trying to get a dial tone, but nothing. *Shit, I broke the damn thing.* I lean back into the couch, covering my face with my hands, pulling at my skin. This can't be happening. This can't be my life.

There's a knock at the door. I jump up and jog to it, swinging it open immediately. It's Rebecca, and I couldn't be happier to see her. I give her a hug, and it's awkward, but I don't care. She kind of pushes me away, and we break the embrace.

"What's gotten into you?" She shrugs me off and pushes past me. She tosses her bag on the couch and helps herself to my cup of coffee.

"Please tell me you found something."

"Maybe." She takes a seat.

"What do you mean maybe?" I pace the living room waiting for her response. This is it.

She's my last hope. I'm running out of time, and Sarah and I are clearly not on the same page. She's chasing some Jesse guy and thinks my theory is completely off-key. I broke the phone. I can't leave this God-forsaken lake house, and my trial starts in nine fucking days. Rebecca takes a few sips of my coffee and places the cup on the table. She pulls a stack of file folders from her bag, separates three from the stack and tosses them on the coffee table.

"These three have the closest connection to Kelly's past life and all live within a 150-mile radius of Prince William County. Each folder contains a bio, a photo, and background report. Two of them have criminal histories. One doesn't. This is all I had time to get, but it's a good start."

I pick up the folders and open the first one. I hope one of these sparks something, but I'm not sure how or if it will. I need more than a good start. I need a finish line.

I open the first folder. It's a middle-aged woman by the name of Cheryl. She lives one and a half hours south of here. Two kids. Several speeding tickets and one disorderly conduct charge. She's hard looking with thin lips and a pointy nose.

"That's Cheryl. She's Greg's cousin," Rebecca explains.

"What are your thoughts on her?"

"She's related and lives close enough to commit the crime, but I don't think she and Greg were all that close and it seems she has enough problems of her own."

I'm content with Rebecca's explanation, so I close the folder and toss it on the coffee table. I open the next one. It's a picture of a middle-aged man with dark eyes and dark brown, well-styled hair. My first thought is, *this guy looks like a real prick*. His name is Nicholas Robert Miller. He has no criminal history, and he looks familiar, but I can't place him. I've seen him before.

"What's this guy's story?"

"He's Greg's brother. Lives in D.C. No criminal history. They were obviously close. He's definitely a possibility, but I didn't have time to look into his alibi for that evening. Depending on that, he could be a prime suspect," she says.

"He looks familiar."

"Yeah?"

"Yeah, I just can't place him—but I've seen this man before."

"If he had anything to do with this, he would have been watching you and Kelly. Maybe you've seen him in the area, like at Seth's Coffee."

"That's a possibility, but I feel like I've spoken to him."

"Maybe you did." Rebecca raises an eyebrow.

I close my eyes trying to pick that moment out from my memory. I've spoken to this man before, but where? Where and when would I have had a conversation with him? I try to recall all the times I sat at Seth's Coffee, flirting with Kelly, watching her, and waiting for her to get off work. I had occasionally spoken to others in the café. Would I have seen him there? Would he have approached me? I can't recall. I look at the photo again. My eyes staring into his. I've had a conversation with this man before, and I recall it being heated. I remember not liking this guy, but I don't know why. I look at it a few more moments, and when I can't pull the memory, I set the folder on the table. I leave it open, hoping that any glance will spark something.

Taking a deep breath, I open the next folder. I don't recognize the woman in the photo. Maddie Burns. She was Greg's ex-fiancée. Petite with long brown hair and very homely-looking.

"Fuck!" I throw the folder onto the ground.

"What? What is it?" Rebecca asks.

"It's none of these goddamn people. You were supposed to help." I point at Rebecca and stare her down. She nearly jumps from her seat. Her eyes widen as I lose my temper. At the wet bar, I take a long swig of scotch.

"Maybe your wife is right then. Maybe it's not someone from Kelly's past," Rebecca offers.

I take another long swig. "It has to be. It fucking has to."

"Not necessarily. What's this?" Rebecca motions to the box on the coffee table.

"It's all the evidence from the case. Sarah brought it over." I take a seat beside Rebecca, feeling defeated.

"Have you looked through it?" She leans forward pulling out the box's contents.

I just shake my head. It's all over for me. I drop my head into my hands.

"Isn't this the photo with the threat you were talking about?" Rebecca holds it up. "The one you received two weeks before the murder?"

I hadn't seen it since the day I found it in my mailbox.

She flips it over and over, examining it. "This has to be something," she says. "It's too convenient to be nothing."

I look down at the table and another handwritten note catches my eye. I look back at the photo Rebecca is holding.

"Wait," I say. She stops moving it. I take the photo from her, flipping it to the side with the writing, and then I grab the Post-it note stuck to the top of one of the evidence folders. I hold them up side by side.

The note says, "Here are the copies of the case files you asked for."

"What is it?" Rebecca asks.

"Don't you see it?" I look at her and then back at the writing on the photo and note.

"See what?"

My eyes trace the curves of the letters over and over again. "They're the same handwriting."

This is Sheriff Stevens.

41

SARAH MORGAN

T his third set of unknown DNA is still not sitting well with me, and I don't want to go into this case not knowing who it belongs to. I don't need any more surprises. I stayed up all last night reviewing every connection I could find to Kelly as well as the interview Sheriff Stevens had with Jesse Hook. I know I zoned out a bit and missed something. The tenseness of that interrogation and the way the mood shifted from tense to relaxed and back struck me as odd. It was almost like there was a power struggle between Jesse and Sheriff Stevens. Why that is, I don't know. Maybe they both know something I don't. When I talked to the sheriff yesterday, he didn't seem all that shocked that it wasn't Jesse's DNA. But then again, that is the nature of his work. He wasn't convinced from the get-go. Still, there's something Jesse said that made me think twice and if I'm right about this, it would explain why no one saw Kelly with this third man and why this third man used a burner phone.

I rub my forehead and take a drink of the lukewarm coffee from my desk.

"Anne!"

She enters immediately wearing a pencil skirt dress and her hair in a low bun. "Yes, Sarah—do you need some more coffee?"

"Actually, that'd be great." I look at my half-empty cup. "But can you get Sheriff Stevens on the phone?" Anne nods and disappears. I wait a few moments and then pick up the phone.

"This is Sheriff Stevens."

"Hey, it's Sarah."

"To what do I owe the pleasure?" There's an ounce of flirtation in his voice.

"I have a lead on the third set of DNA."

Sheriff Stevens coughs and for a moment, I think the line has gone dead. "I told you, Sarah—I want to help, but the case is closed. There's nothing more I can do."

"Then I'll just have to look into it myself," I say preparing to hang up the phone.

"Fine. Who's your lead?"

"I reviewed that interview you had with Jesse, and I noticed that Jesse said he always saw Kelly with a cop."

"Yeah, so—her husband Scott is a cop," he interrupts.

"True and that's who I assumed he was talking about, but what if he wasn't? What if Kelly was having an affair with Scott's partner, Deputy Marcus Hudson?"

"That's quite the accusation, Sarah. Do you have any proof of that?" He sounds irritated, and I guess he has every right to be. In the past week, one of his deputies has been accused of being a wife beater, and now I'm accusing another deputy of having an affair with his partner's wife, and possibly murdering her. It doesn't really have the wholesome look you'd want for a small-town sheriff's department.

"No, but Kelly would have known Deputy Hudson very well. They could have easily grown close, and it explains why he used a burner phone and why they were never seen together in public. That's something you would want to hide," I explain.

"I'm not bringing Deputy Hudson in for questioning nor testing his DNA without any evidence. That's ridiculous, Sarah." He raises his voice.

"Then let's bring Jesse in again. Let's ask him to specify."

"Sarah, this is over. There is no *let's*. This is my investigation, and it's closed. Please do not call me again." Sheriff Stevens hangs up the phone.

I slam my phone down. "Fuck."

Anne enters the office with a worried look on her face.

I drop my head into my hands and let out a groan.

"Are you okay?"

I pick my head up and look at her. "No. I'm not." I flop my hands on the desk.

She scurries to me and takes a seat. She takes my hand for comfort. "What's wrong?"

"Everything. My marriage is over. My husband is on trial for murder. I'm not getting any help from the Prince William County Sheriff's Department, and I've hit a dead end in the case. I'm going to lose."

Anne tilts her head in an endearing way and places both her hands on mine, gently rubbing them. "It's all going to work out in the end. I promise," she says, and I think she means it or at least believes it. How would Anne know if everything is going to work out? She's my assistant. I'm the lawyer. I'm the one with the experience. I'm the one dealing with Sheriff Stevens. I'm the one with the cheating and potentially murdering husband. I'm the one going through all of this. I want to scream. I want to flip over my desk, but I won't. I have to be calm and composed.

I take a deep breath before speaking. "This third set of DNA —I have to find out who it belongs to."

"Why isn't Sheriff Stevens looking into that further?" She releases my hands, and we lean back in our chairs.

"He says the case is closed."

"Won't the fact that we don't know who that DNA belongs to bode well with the jury? Like a mystery—like it could be this other person? It'll leave room for reasonable doubt."

"It could, but it's risky. If we know who that person is, we can build our case around it, pointing the suspicion at that person. I think I may have a lead."

"Who?"

"Scott's partner, Deputy Hudson. Heck, maybe they killed her together. They are each other's alibis after all. But I think she was sleeping with his partner."

Anne's eyes widen. "Why do you think that?"

"Something Jesse said and the fact that no one ever saw her with a third man. If it were Deputy Hudson, they would have kept it a complete secret. Plus, the burner phone."

"I mean if you can't prove Deputy Hudson was the third set of DNA and Sheriff Stevens won't cooperate, couldn't you point the suspicion to Scott, her husband? The texts he sent that night were pretty damning." Anne rubs her chin.

"That's part of my case, but the prosecution will call him to the stand and try to paint him as a grieving hero. The jury will most likely feel sympathetic toward him and have respect for him as a member of the police force. We don't have anyone saying otherwise, aside from Jesse—who was Kelly's apparent stalker. His word is as good as worthless."

"Is there a chance Scott did it?" Anne raises her eyebrows.

"As far as I'm concerned, there's a chance anyone could have done it. Heck, Anne, you could have," I say lightly.

Anne lets out a nervous laugh. "Why don't you... umm... talk to D.A. Peters? Wouldn't he want to know this?"

"That's not a bad idea, Anne. I'll slip that hunch I have about Deputy Hudson into discovery, and I'll make sure to put his name on the witness list. D.A. Peters will look into it thinking I have something on him, but he'll end up doing my work for me."

"That is brilliant."

"I should probably meet with him first and see if I can plant some seeds before he requests any of our discovery. Can you see if he's available to meet this afternoon?"

"Absolutely." Anne gets up from her chair, eager and ready to help in any way possible. She's the one person I can always depend on, the one person I can always trust.

42

ADAM MORGAN

I'm pacing the living room back and forth, grabbing at my hair, scanning for objects that I could destroy to vent my anger. How could I not have known? How could I not have seen this sooner?

"Do you know who wrote it?" Rebecca asks for the tenth time.

"I have a pretty good fucking idea." I want to punch something just to get some relief.

"Okay, well then who is it? We just found a big clue here. This is good news!" Rebecca is trying to calm me down, but it's no use. I'm seeing red. A lying bitch is messing with my life. She's trying to ruin me. She threatened me. Jesus Christ. She probably killed Kelly. For all I know, she's manipulating the fucking evidence as we speak. Rebecca's face pleads with me, eyes wide open, straining to know the answer.

"It's Sarah's assistant, Anne," I finally say.

"Shit..." Rebecca looks at both notes. She returns her gaze to me. "And you're sure?"

"Look at the writing. Of course I'm fucking sure." I shove both notes in her face, a few inches from her nose.

She swats them away. "Easy. I'm on your side remember."

I take a deep breath and a step back from her.

Rebecca looks me up and down. "She sent the threat. But if she killed Kelly, what would her motive be?"

"How the fuck should I know? I'm not a murderer. Remember?" I throw my hands up.

"Well... think," Rebecca presses. "This isn't the time to fly off the handle, this is the time to think."

I rub my head, willing the answer to come to me. "She's obsessed with Sarah, and she's never really liked me. Maybe she wanted her all to herself."

"If she's obsessed with Sarah, perhaps she'd do anything for Sarah. Like kill her cheating husband's mistress?" Rebecca raises an eyebrow.

"Don't you dare. Sarah would never fucking do that." I point at her and narrow my eyes. I could literally hurt Rebecca now. I'm glaring at her as I pace back and forth. I can see the uneasiness in her face. How easy would it be to lunge across the room and take her to the ground? Wrap my hands around her throat, crush her windpipe with my thumbs as I watch her eyes fill up with blood and the life slowly leave her. I could be in control of something again, finally. I could validate the fear that is on her face.

Her voice is trembling when she begins to talk. "Listen, Adam. I didn't mean it that way. I just have to ask the hard questions sometimes, especially if I'm going to be of any help to you."

I don't return the smile, but I do stop scowling at her. *She's not the enemy*, I remind myself. *She's just trying to help. She's just trying to understand the situation.* But I don't have time for her to understand. I don't have time to sit here. I need to leave. I need to confront Anne. I need her to confess what she did. I need this all to end.

"So, what now?" I try to divert myself from doing anything rash. Focus on Rebecca. Listen to her. Stay here with her. This will all get sorted out. She's helped me so much already. I stop pacing, and I stand there in the middle of my living room frozen in time. Rebecca is no longer tense, but she is concerned. She glances at me, then at her bag on the table and the set of keys next to it. I follow her gaze. Is she trying to leave? Does she think I'd do something to her?

"I can take all this stuff to the police station, and I'm sure they would have to reopen the investigation." Her eyes are full of hope.

I'm not sure whether that hope is for her or for me. "But the case is closed," I say.

"Yes, but you haven't been convicted. The police have a responsibility to look into all suspects of the case."

"But what if they don't? What if they refuse? What if it's too little too late?"

"Your lawyer can still use it in the case. It definitely could work for creating reasonable doubt amongst the jury," she explains.

My lawyer. You mean my wife? Does she know Anne's the one that sent the note? Is she involved? I start pacing again—harder and faster. *She can't know, can she? Fuck. I can't do this.* As I walk, my eyes keep catching the set of keys like a small glimmer of hope, and when it happens, it's like no thought goes into it. I just do it. I don't look back. I grab the keys and run out of the house, jumping into Rebecca's Chevy Cruze.

Rebecca chases after me. "Adam, what the hell are you doing? You're on house arrest. You can't leave. Wait!"

I close the door defiantly and put the car in drive. I slam my foot on the gas pedal, the tires spin out, kicking up dirt and leaves—and then I'm pulling away from the house. My ankle bracelet begins to buzz and flash.

43

SARAH MORGAN

I'm sitting in one of the many conference rooms within Williamson & Morgan. Anne scheduled a meeting with D.A. Josh Peters and Matthew has joined me. A stack of boxes covers part of the table—my discovery or, really, lack thereof. It's there to throw the prosecution off and hopefully, get them to uncover things I was unable to thanks to the Prince William County Sheriff's Department no longer cooperating. Everything in those boxes has been carefully curated by Matthew, Anne, and me today to get D.A. Peters to do our dirty work. He should be here any minute. This meeting is intended to throw him off. I know he thinks this case is a slam dunk—and it is, but I need him to believe there's some possibility of the prosecution losing. I need him to think I have something up my sleeve and that he needs to find out what that is.

Matthew takes a seat at the head of the conference table. "Am I playing bad cop?" He gives a small smirk.

"Always."

"And are you sure you want to be toying with the prosecution right now?" He raises an eyebrow.

"Are you questioning my strategy again, Matthew?"

"Just checking your judgment."

There's a knock on the door. Anne opens it, carrying in a tray full of snacks, soda, and water. "Right this way," she says to D.A. Peters who is following behind her.

"Who's this?" He gestures to Matthew. "Discovery is only for council."

"This is Matthew. He is assisting with this case."

Matthew stands and holds out his hand. "I'm doing more than assisting."

"Does he even have a law degree?" D.A. Peters asks me as if Matthew isn't in the room.

"Yes, he and I went to Yale together."

"Which is why I'm a lobbyist now, not some D.A. that went to George Washington night school." Matthew smirks and takes his seat.

D.A. Peters doesn't respond to Matthew's quip. He sits down and directs his attention to me.

"Anyway, thanks for coming down here on such short notice," I say.

He nods. "Of course. What is it you wanted to discuss? Might I remind you, the plea bargain is off the table."

Anne gently closes the door behind her as she leaves.

"We wouldn't take the plea bargain even if it were on the table." Matthew gives him a stern look.

"Okay, then what is it you're looking for?" D.A. Peters clasps his hands together.

I point to the stack of boxes, and then I slide a few more folders toward him. "This is our discovery so far. There will be more."

He glances at the boxes and then pulls the folders toward him, flipping through them quickly. He closes them back up and looks at me.

"You might want to take a closer look. Not sure they taught

you this at night school, but evidence is the most important part of a law case," Matthew retorts.

D.A. Peters rolls his eyes, paying no mind to Matthew's bad cop routine. "You could have sent these over to my office. I didn't need to come down here."

"I know that. I just wanted to give you the courtesy." I smirk.

"The courtesy of what? This case is open and shut."

"Is it, counselor? Because from what I've found, it's not. That's where my courtesy to you comes in. You've been good to me, and I didn't want to embarrass you in that courtroom, so I'm giving you nearly all of our discovery early."

He glances at the boxes again and at the folders in front of him. A look of suspicion begins to creep into his eyes as he tilts his head in either bewilderment or disbelief, I'm not sure which. I fully expected this reaction though: I would have the same. I quickly press on. "Oh, I almost forgot." I slide another folder to him. This folder contains the transcript of a conversation between Jesse Hook and Sheriff Stevens. I highlighted areas that I need D.A. Peters to see. I need him to want to talk to this witness. I need him to get more information out of this witness.

He opens the folder up and scans it. "Who's Jesse Hook?"

"Exactly," Matthew says. "Not so open and shut, is it?"

"Jesse Hook is—" I say. There's a scream from outside the conference room.

44

ADAM MORGAN

An hour ago, I got in the car, and I didn't stop driving. I had tunnel vision. I was full of rage. The outside world careened by me but only in various hues of crimson and scarlet, as if the blood boiling in my veins had grafted itself onto every single object I was seeing. And I knew leaving the house was going to have consequences, but I didn't care—I still don't care. I need to see this through. I need to get to the bottom of all of this. I'm running out of time and this is my last chance, my last opportunity to learn what really happened that night at the lake house, to discover who is responsible for Kelly's death, and to free myself from this nightmare.

I'm a few steps away from throwing the doors open and coming face to face with Anne, the woman I've known for years, the woman who threatened me, the woman who most likely killed Kelly, and the woman who is trying to frame me for it. How could she? How could she get so close without me knowing? Why was she at our lake house? I know Sarah has let her stay there in the past for vacation, but why was she there then?

She's never been a person I looked at twice. She was there,

seemingly innocent, but now I see the cracks in her—I see who she really is: a vengeful monster. Her quietness is now plotting and manipulative. Her politeness is cunning. Her entire wholesome demeanor is just a façade for who she truly is: a bitch of the highest order.

The photo and the Post-it note are clutched in my hand. I throw the doors open and I scan the office. A couple of people look up, some look scared, others are unphased by my disheveled appearance. I walk further into the office. I am looking for one person and one person only. I know where she'll be. It's where she always is. Sitting, plotting, waiting. I round the corner and notice her desk is empty. *Fuck.*

Then, there she is walking toward me, chatting with a man beside her and carrying a stack of folders. She doesn't notice me at first.

The man she's walking with is familiar. I've seen him before. Well, obviously I must have seen him before—but I feel like this "before" was recent. She looks up and notices me, standing only ten feet away. Her eyes widen like those of a deer in headlights—like a deer that is about to be introduced to 3,000lbs of steel careening toward it at 60mph. The man beside her notices she's stopped dead in her tracks and follows her gaze to find me. His eyes widen and then narrow. He recognizes me, and for a gleaming second, I recognize him, but then I lose it as my attention refocuses on the she-devil in front of me, the woman attempting to steal my life, the woman who killed Kelly.

"Adam, are you—are you okay?" Anne stutters.

"You!" I point at her as I close the gap between us, ready to tackle her, ready to hit her, ready to... I don't even know what I'm ready to do. She screams. It pierces the stale office air.

"You fucking killed Kelly. You framed me. I know everything, you evil bitch!" Just as I reach her, I'm knocked to the ground.

One punch to the side of my face takes me out completely. Anne is crying and standing behind the man who sucker punched me.

"What the hell is going on here?" Sarah runs in with Matthew and another man trailing. I recognize the man from my trial—D.A. Josh Peters.

"Bob, what did you do?" she asks as she sees me writhing on the floor.

"He came at Anne." Bob points at me. That's Bob. Oh yes, I know Bob. He's the one who's been giving Sarah shit for the past couple of years and gunning for her job any chance he can get. He's a fucking dick. I never liked him even before Sarah had problems with him. He's smug, and he's always treated me as if he were better than me. Any office party Sarah dragged me to, he was there to remind us all how great he is.

"What the fuck, Adam? What are you doing?" Sarah's lips barely move as she speaks through clenched teeth. She's embarrassed by me, I can tell. Anne cries like the conniving bitch she is. Bob and Matthew try to comfort her. Sarah makes sure she is okay. D.A. Josh Peters is still trying to understand the situation, but I can see there's a look of triumph because this is all looking good for his case—unless, of course, I can prove Anne is behind all of this.

"Her," I say pointing at Anne. Everyone looks at her. Anne gives a *who me?* look. "She took the photo. She wrote the threat. She killed Kelly!" I toss the photo and note by Sarah's feet. Sarah reaches down and brings them both to her line of sight. Eyes are wide, mouths open. My accusation has taken everyone by surprise. It's a moment before anyone speaks. Anne shifts uncomfortably, scratching at her arm. Sarah redirects her attention to Anne.

"Is this true?" She holds the photo and note up.

Anne stutters. She looks down at the ground, shuffling her

feet. "Yes. I went there to take some photographs, like the ones I showed you. But I saw them, Kelly and Adam... together."

"Jesus Christ," Sarah huffs.

"But I didn't kill Kelly. I wouldn't. I couldn't. And I wanted to tell you. But I couldn't, so I just... I sent the threat. I wanted him to fess up." Anne shakes her head, trying to convince us all, but mostly Sarah, that she's telling the truth. I don't buy it for one second.

"She's dangerous, Sarah. The threat. She threatened mine and Kelly's life. Can't you see? She has to be behind all of this," I plead.

"No..." Anne looks at Sarah. "It wasn't a death threat, it was an 'I'm going to tell Sarah if you don't' threat."

"But you didn't fucking tell me, Anne." Sarah spits venom. She's upset. She feels betrayed. I can see it in her face. She's mad as hell. It's clear to me she didn't know Anne knew about the affair. Anne hangs her head and cries harder.

"How could you not tell me, Anne? You're my assistant. You're my friend. You're practically family." Sarah's voice quakes.

"I-I-I-" Anne stutters.

"Everybody freeze!" Sheriff Stevens draws his gun. Deputy Hudson and Officer Scott Summers are standing on either side of him with guns drawn too.

"Fuck." I put my hands up. Everyone else puts their hands up as well. Sarah appears annoyed as does Bob. *God, where the hell did I just see him?* I rack my brain trying to recall. Sarah hasn't dragged me to an office party in quite some time. Maybe he was at the courthouse. Maybe he gave an interview on the case, and I saw him on the news or in the paper. *Shit. I've seen that smug face, and it was recent—so recent it scares me, because I know it's important, but I can't recall.*

"Adam Morgan, you're under arrest for violating the terms of your bail and fleeing house arrest," Sheriff Stevens says as

Deputy Hudson and Officer Summers pick me up from the floor, handcuffing me.

Sarah shakes her head in embarrassment and disgust.

"Wait! Anne—Anne sent the threat. She killed Kelly. Arrest her." I get one hand free pointing at that little weasel.

Sheriff Stevens exchanges a glance with Sarah and Scott Summers. Scott instantly turns red and is already manhandling Anne, no questions asked. Anne screams as Scott tries to handcuff her.

"Wait a minute!" Bob yells. "What the hell do you think you're doing?"

"You heard him. She had something to do with my wife's murder. She's coming with us," Scott says.

"You can't just arrest her," Sarah pipes in. Matthew and D.A. Peters back her up.

"Sarah? She lied to you." My eyes grow wide in disbelief.

"I'm going to get to the bottom of this. But she has rights." Sarah shakes her head.

Anne thanks her.

"Don't you fucking speak to me," Sarah warns.

Anne shrinks and lowers her head.

"What do you want to do, boss?" Deputy Hudson holds me in place by the cuffs.

"This is a fucking nightmare. We're bringing her in for questioning. If she doesn't want to come, we'll get a warrant," Sheriff Stevens says.

Anne raises her head. "I'll go. I have nothing to hide."

"Yeah, fucking right. Lying bitch," I say under my breath but loud enough for everyone to hear.

"That's enough," Bob exclaims.

And it's at that moment that I realize where I saw Bob recently. It's the look on his face that brings back the image. My mouth drops open. My eyes grow wild. This motherfucker. "It's you!" I point at Bob's smug face.

"Me... what?" he asks.

"You. You're Nicholas Robert Miller. You're Kelly's ex-husband's brother."

Sarah whips her head at him. Sheriff Stevens is rubbing his head. Scott's anger has yet to subside and is only intensifying every moment he's here. D.A. Josh Peters looks confused, and I don't blame him. Matthew steps aside from Bob.

"I'm not being pulled into this," Bob says matter-of-factly.

"You killed her, didn't you?" The question is rhetorical.

"I'll hear no more of this nonsense." Bob's face tightens.

"Is that true, Bob? Are you Kelly's ex-husband's brother?" Sarah asks.

Bob hangs his head. "Yes, but I had nothing to do with any of this."

Sarah lets out a gasp.

"Jesus fucking Christ. This case was supposed to be closed," Sheriff Stevens says in exasperation. Scott begins breathing heavily and then in an instant, he's on top of Bob, pummeling away. Sheriff Stevens and Deputy Hudson scream at him to stop and pull him off. After a cacophony of shouting and tangling and untangling of polyester the chaos subsides and heavy panting begins to fill the space.

"I'll have your fucking badge for this, you ape-pig piece of shit!" Bob yells at Deputy Summers, blood spraying from his mouth. Bob doesn't appear to be anywhere near physically capable of taking on the good deputy *mano a mano*, but if looks could kill, Scott would be side by side with his dearly departed wife.

"Please Mr. Miller, accept our sincerest apologies. That behavior was completely uncalled for, and Deputy Summers here will be put on unpaid leave immediately." Sheriff Stevens tries to immediately smooth things over.

"Fuck you all! You just made a huge mistake the lot of you," Bob screams. It seems there's no calming him down and Sheriff Stevens wisely just nods and lets it go.

D.A. Josh Peters turns to Sarah. "I'm going to hold off on discovery because it appears you have more to present. Just call my office, and I'll have someone come pick up everything when it's ready." He ducks out quickly, not wanting to be caught up in the mess, I imagine.

Sarah nods as he starts walking away. Matthew rubs Sarah's shoulder, trying to comfort her. That should be me rubbing her shoulder, not fucking Matthew.

"All right, everyone let's go. We're going to the fucking station now!" Sheriff Stevens loses his composure.

I guess it's back to my old stomping ground after all.

45

ADAM MORGAN

I knew before my rampage started that it wasn't going to end well for me. I'm a fucking idiot, and I'm sure Sarah is going to take every opportunity to remind me of that. Now, though, my main concern is the extreme pain exerted as a pair of handcuffs are squeezed and twisted so tightly that the skin is beginning to roll back off my wrists like shavings from a pencil sharpener.

"You don't have to pull that hard," I plead to Sheriff Stevens.

"Respectfully, Mr. Morgan, I don't really think you are in a position to decide what is or isn't best. So, if you could just kindly shut the fuck up and come with me back to central processing, I would surely be grateful." There's enough condescension in the sheriff's tone to humble even the toughest of customers.

I want to come back with a clever quip, but my judgment tells me that it will serve me no good. I just do as I am told. At least I'm in better shape than Bob is right about now. The thought alone causes a small smirk to grow across my face.

"This should all be fairly familiar to you, Mr. Morgan. However, unlike last time, we will not be quickly trying to get you out of here so you can be on your merry way after a night or

245

two. Something tells me you'll be in for a little while. But hey, what do I know? I just bring the bad guys in. I don't make the laws," Sheriff Stevens informs me.

For some reason when he calls me Mr. Morgan, it is more of a slight than if he just referred to me as Adam. Almost as if the familiarity of that first-name basis isn't something he wants with "scum" like me. "Mr. Morgan" is projected with the cold distance of a faraway observer as if I was on another planet receiving radio signals.

"Sadly, it is all familiar," I say. I try to keep my sarcasm in check as all I want for this night is for it to be over.

"Hopefully, one way or another, it will be your last time with us." This could be taken as kind or as evil, and I'm not sure what to make of it. Is he cheering for my conviction? Is he still convinced after everything he has seen that I did this? *Fuck. If he thinks that, then what will a jury think?* I feel the beginnings of a panic attack, but I do a breathing exercise and focus on the realization that I can't solve anything, not here, not now anyway, and I come back down to earth.

"I'm gonna leave you with these guys for a minute," Sheriff Stevens nods at a couple of blue-uniformed gentlemen with unpleasant expressions. "I just have to ask though... why? You knew you had the ankle bracelet on. You knew we would find you. You knew it would only make things worse. So why?"

"Because I didn't do it, and no one is listening to me."

"I see." Sheriff Stevens stands still for a moment looking down at the floor as if he will somehow find an answer hidden within the pattern of the gray paint flaking off the roughly poured concrete floor. He then looks up at me and opens his mouth to speak, but all that comes out is a breath. He closes his mouth, shakes his head, and walks back toward the entrance of the station.

"Mr. Adam Morgan, is it?" one of the deputies asks.

"Yeah, that's me."

"Are we gonna do this the easy way or am I gonna have to drag you by those goddamn handcuffs to cooperate, because I'm good either way, but you scream 'flight risk' to me," the deputy says with a full-toothed smile, all while smacking his gum as loud as possible for emphasis.

"I won't be any trouble this evening, sir." I'm too tired to fight anymore.

"Smart decision."

I wonder what Sarah must think of all of this. I mean I know the obvious parts. The anger, disappointment, shock at my stupidity, but what about what I was saying? She must know deep down that I wouldn't have made that all-for-nothing excursion for no reason, knowing full well it would land me in a world of hurt. I just hope somebody, anybody, will finally start listening to me. But based on that scene at the office, the only person who thinks I'm not insane, Scott Summers, decided to go Rodney King on a respected defense attorney and now looks more like Mike Tyson than a distressed widower.

Just how fucked am I at this point?

I'm not sure I even want to know the answer.

46

SARAH MORGAN

The visitor's lot is nearly empty when Matthew and I arrive at the station. We walk toward the entrance. Matthew gives me an encouraging look and a nod as he holds the door for me.

"You've got this," he says.

"Thanks." My lips form into a small, tight smile.

I walk into the waiting area, shoulders back, chin held high. I'm going to need to muster up all my strength and confidence to get through this evening.

"May I help you?" Marge asks through bulletproof plexiglass.

"I'm just waiting."

"Need you to sign in," she says, pushing a clipboard under the plexiglass.

Matt and I walk over and scribble down our info. We take a seat in the reception area, waiting for Bob and Anne to arrive. I'll deal with Adam after I've heard both their interviews.

"Think they'll come?" Matthew asks.

"If they're innocent, they will," I offer, although I'm not

convinced them showing up would have anything to do with their innocence. But as they say, innocent people don't run.

Less than twenty minutes later, Anne and Bob arrive. They sit on the opposite side of the waiting area. Bob stares off into the distance rubbing his temples, and Anne is still intermittently crying while hanging her head in shame. My face is twisted in a way that clearly conveys disgust, and the only question that repeats over and over in my head as I glower at Bob and Anne is, *who are these people?*

Time slowly melts as the four of us float in purgatory. Our only punishment is being in each other's company. The awkwardness of the situation and Anne's shame mixed with Bob's anger are palpable and make the time drag even slower. I never thought I would be feeling this, but I'm really looking forward to seeing Sheriff Stevens.

Just when I think things couldn't get any worse, the front door of the police station opens and in walks Eleanor, dressed in all black, looking like the Grim Reaper. I stand, ready to fill her in on everything that's transpired while she's been gone, but before I can even get out a phony welcome, she's standing directly in front of me with lips pursed so tightly it looks like her filler might ooze out.

"How could you let this happen? I was gone for one day!" She practically spits in my face.

"Eleanor. Your son is thirty-six years old. He's a grown adult and responsible for his own actions. I can't watch him 24/7."

"No, you obviously can't. And that's probably why he was unfaithful to you." She raises her chin.

I take a small breath. *Don't hit her. Don't hit her. Don't hit her.* "That's really not fair. I'm doing everything I can for his case." I stand a bit taller, trying to make myself bigger than her.

"There shouldn't even be a case. He's innocent. But now he's

249

going to face charges for assault and bail jumping because you couldn't keep an eye on him."

"Eleanor. Just stop. You're being ridiculous." I shake my head.

"Am I? You couldn't even keep an eye on your own mother... and look what happened to her." The corners of her mouth curve into a grin as if she's pleased with her little comment.

Anne lets out an audible gasp. Bob shifts uncomfortably in his seat. Matthew half stands but then sits back down. I'd love to knock her out and bash her skull into the ground over and over again until I see brain—if she even has one. But I don't need to defend myself for murder as well. I have to put an end to Eleanor's involvement in this case and in my life, and I know just what to say. I take a deep breath.

"Your son is a liar, a cheater, and possibly a murderer. Your coddling and over-the-top mothering has gotten Adam into this mess. The best thing you could do as a mother is to take note from mine and kill yourself."

Eleanor's eyes widen to a new level and her mouth gapes. She raises her hand and slaps me hard across the face. "You wouldn't know a mother's love, you little bitch."

It stings, and I put my hand to it. When I take my fingers away there is a smear of blood from where her ring made contact with my cheek.

Eleanor takes a step back. Her teeth are clenched, and the fire in her eyes is still burning strong.

Matthew stands and wraps his arm around me, inspecting my face. He turns to Eleanor and says calmly, "You should go. You won't be able to see Adam tonight anyway."

The security door adjacent to the reception area beeps, and a large figure crosses the threshold. "What the hell is going on here?" Sheriff Stevens glances at myself and then Eleanor. She straightens herself up, tilts her head into the air and does an about-face, scurrying out of the police station back into whatever five-star hole she is occupying.

"It's nothing. Let's just get this over with," I say as I pull my hand from my face.

"You sure? That's quite the mark you got there."

I nod.

"Have they all been checked-in, Marge?" Sheriff Stevens asks the receptionist.

"Yup," Marge replies without even looking up from her paperwork.

"All right, you guys can come with me." Sheriff Stevens extends an arm as if to say, *please cross the threshold and let me show you what I have in store.*

We follow him down a narrow, painted concrete corridor. Matthew and I walk side by side, while Bob and Anne trail behind us. The walls are white on top and red below. The color contrast is jarring on the eye, and that is precisely the effect intended on people being helplessly escorted to various interrogation rooms.

The sheriff brings us all into one room and begins speaking to us without offering any of us a seat or taking one himself. "First, I want to thank all of you on behalf of the Prince William County Sheriff's Department for volunteering your time to assist with an ongoing investigation. I must remind all three of you that none of you are under arrest and under no circumstance are you required to speak to us. That being said, if you do volunteer to share information with us, it will be recorded and may be used in the course of the investigation. If that is clear and acceptable to you all, do you still wish to proceed?"

Nods all around the room supply him with his answer.

"Good. Well as I said, it is most appreciated. Before starting, Mr. Miller, you sustained injuries today because of the horrible actions of Deputy Summers. I'm sure you can imagine the level of duress that he is under and the emotions he is dealing with. However, his behavior was unacceptable, and there is no excuse for it. I just want you to know that he has been placed on suspension without pay and is under internal review. Pending the outcome of the findings, we may have to terminate his employment. I am telling you this because I want you to know that we are taking the matter very seriously." Sheriff Stevens looks right at Bob and asks, "Mr. Miller, do you wish to press charges, as is your right, against Deputy Summers?"

"No, I do not," Bob answers confidently. "I know he must be dealing with a lot right now and what Mr. Morgan was accusing me of must have been rather upsetting to him. While I am not happy with his behavior, I do not wish to press charges."

"I can't say I'm not glad to hear you say that, Mr. Miller. Scott can be a bit of a loose cannon, and his behavior was horrible, but deep down he is a good sheriff."

Bob just nods, clearly wanting to get this all over with.

"All right, then. We will be separating the two of you." He points at Bob and Anne. "I will have two officers escort you into separate rooms." A pair of officers enter. "If you would please follow them." Sheriff Stevens drops back into an open-armed stance as if playing Christ at the center of the table in *The Last Supper*.

Anne gives a quick glance at me. I purse my lips giving her neither direction, nor communication. Bob walks out with his chin slightly up in the air.

When everyone exits, Matthew and I are left face to face with Sheriff Stevens.

"So..." he opens the exchange, "quite the shitshow in the upper echelon today." A sardonic grin is plastered on his face. I know he likes to have the upper hand and see me squirm. He is going to milk this show for all it is worth now that he has me back on his ground. I'm not going to cave to him though.

"Yeah," I respond.

"If only some officers of the law would have responded faster when an alarm went off telling them a man accused of murder who is on house arrest went barreling off his designated premises at 100mph, then maybe this all could have been avoided. But hey, it's hard to hear alarm bells over the loud chewing of doughnuts," Matthew quips.

I glance at Matthew and let a small smile sneak into the corners of my mouth.

"Who are you?" Sheriff Stevens asks.

"Matthew Latchaw," he thrusts his hand for a handshake, establishing dominance.

Sheriff Stevens folds his arms in front of his chest. "Our officers followed protocol to the best of their ability and were mere minutes behind Mr. Morgan upon him leaving his domicile. You both should be thankful for how fast they did in fact respond. The scene at your office could have been far worse." There's a serious tone to his delivery.

"Maybe so. But if Scott Summers hadn't been there Bob might still be able to walk normally this evening," I chime in.

"Deputy Summers actions were... regrettable as I noted. His behavior will be dealt with."

"What's the plan?" I ask wanting to move this process along. My cheek is burning and I need a stiff drink.

"We'll question both Anne and Bob. Frankly, I'm just crossing the Ts and dotting the Is as this case is closed on our end."

"You have to admit this is a weird connection. Bob has motive, and Anne threatened Adam. So, I'd appreciate it if you did more than just cross the Ts and dot the Is," I say sternly. "And I'd like handwriting analysis of the note in comparison to Anne's."

"You're right. It's definitely suspicious. If either of them were involved, we'll find out." He tries to match the seriousness in my tone of voice. "No need on the handwriting analysis. She's already admitted to writing the note."

"Have you heard of false confessions? I'll need the handwriting analysis." This sheriff's police work is sloppy at best, and I'm unsure if it's due to ignorance or if it's intentional.

He presses his lips tightly together and nods.

"May we observe the questioning of the two persons of interest?" I ask. "Their testimony will ultimately be pertinent to my case."

"Sure. I don't see why not."

I can't tell if he thinks he is doing me a favor or is just in an agreeable mood. "Would you mind staggering the interviews then? So we can observe them both?"

Sheriff Stevens raises his eyebrows at my question, "I suppose we could," his voice trails up very high at the end, "but you do know that will greatly increase the time you are here for the evening, right?"

"Obviously." Matthew rolls his eyes.

"I understand," I say with clear confidence in my voice.

"Okay then... sure. I'll let the deputies know. Do you have a preference of who first?"

"Let's start with Anne."

47

ADAM MORGAN

What the fuck is taking so long? And where the hell is my mom?

I called her as soon as they finished booking me. I pace back and forth in the interrogation room, a place I have become quite familiar with over the past two weeks. They better find something on Anne and Bob. This is my last hope, and I need Sarah and Sheriff Stevens to believe me. They have to believe that I didn't do it, just enough to thoroughly look into Bob and Anne.

The door is thrown open with such force it slams against the concrete wall and bounces back into Scott Summers. He winces in pain and then shuffles in, flinging the door closed behind him. He looks like a wild animal, flushed, breathing heavily, eyes bloodshot, lips pursed. "We need to talk," he says sternly.

I put my hands up showing that I'm not looking for a fight.

"Relax. I'm not going to hit you."

I put my hands down and fold my arms, waiting for him to speak. I don't know what he's here for.

"I don't have much time. I shouldn't be here. Tell me

everything you know about Bob and Anne." He gives me a fleeting look. There is hope and anger in his eyes.

"I don't think you did this, and I know I didn't," I start.

"I don't give a damn about your theories. Just tell me the facts!" He takes a couple of steps closer to me and grits his teeth.

"Okay. Okay." I tell him everything. Everything I know about Bob, about Anne, about Kelly, everything. This is my last desperation play, so there's no use not putting all my cards on the table.

"How did you find this information out?"

"I can't tell you my source," I say.

"I don't give a fuck about protecting your source. You'll be locked up until the trial for the shit you pulled today. I'm all you've got. If you want to get out of this whole mess. Tell me." His patience has worn thin. He's broken out in a sweat, and he's glancing at the door and the one-way mirror frantically. I'm sure he's not supposed to be here. There's no way they'd keep him around after the shit he pulled today. He attacked an attorney, one of the best in the D.C. area. You don't just walk away from that, even if your wife was murdered.

"Fine. Her name is Rebecca Sanford. She's a reporter for the *Prince William County Newspaper*." I hope to God Scott is telling the truth about not being involved with his wife's murder; otherwise, I just gave him a smoking gun for my guilty conviction. Without Rebecca, I don't have a chance in hell of getting out of this. Unless Sarah is working on another angle for my case.

He nods at me and tells me he'll be in touch. I don't know if I believe that, but I'm hopeful. Even when you have nothing left in your life, hope is the one thing that can never be taken away. Scott leaves abruptly without another word. I take a seat at the table and wait. I've gotten pretty good at waiting.

48

SARAH MORGAN

I headed to the bathroom to clean up my face before returning to the observation room looking in on the interrogation room Anne is sitting in. She sits alone, scared, nervous—guilty, maybe. She taps her fingers on the table, then fiddles with the hem of her shirt, then twirls her hair. She doesn't know what to do with herself. Matthew is leaning against the wall behind me, watching Anne and me. I told him he could go. This isn't his mess, nor his problem. But he insisted on being here, on helping me with this case.

"That was pretty messed up what happened out there with Eleanor," he says.

"Yeah, it was."

"I can't believe you told her the best thing she could do as a mother was kill herself. That was cold."

I turn back and look at him. "I needed to say something to push her over the edge, enough that she would hit me. This whole charade of us going back and forth needed to end. It's exhausting and it's not helping the case."

"So, you took one for the team?" He crosses one leg in front of the other.

I turn back to the one-way glass. "You could say that."

I've dealt with Eleanor's cutting remarks, insults, condescending comments, and overall bullshit for more than a decade. It felt good to watch her lose her shit and finally come down to earth for once. The slap was worth it.

Sheriff Stevens enters the interrogation room and takes a seat across from Anne. He offers her water. She declines. He explains her rights. She nods. He tells her that the conversation will be recorded and may be used as evidence. She stares at him blankly and then he begins his interrogation.

"Where were you the night of October 15th?"

"I went out for drinks with my boss, Sarah Morgan."

"Is this a common occurrence?"

"Yeah, Sarah and I are friends... or at least we were," she says sheepishly.

She's got that right. Friends tell you if your husband is cheating.

"How do you know Kelly Summers?" Sheriff Stevens leans back in his chair.

"I don't."

"But you knew of her before her murder?" Sheriff Stevens taps his fingers on the table.

Anne swallows hard and nods. "Yes, not her name or anything. I just saw her with Adam."

"And what were you doing in Prince William County?" He cocks his head.

"I had been there in the summer for vacation, and I loved the scenery for my photography, and I thought it would be even more beautiful in the fall. I wasn't expecting to see what I saw. I was just taking some photos. It was completely innocent."

"Innocent?"

"Well, it was," Anne says.

"But you decided to take that information and threaten Adam with it?"

"It wasn't my best judgment." She frowns. "I just didn't want to be the one to tell Sarah. I didn't want to hurt her." Anne fidgets with her fingernails.

"*End it, or I will* sounds like a death threat. Would you agree?"

She hangs her head. "I can see that now. But that wasn't my intention. I had planned on telling Sarah if Adam didn't end it or didn't tell her himself."

"Did you ever see Kelly with anyone else?" Sheriff Stevens asks.

Anne glances around the room.

"What an odd question," Matthew says from behind me.

"It is. Isn't it?" I glance back at him and then return my attention to Anne and Sheriff Stevens. What is he getting at? What's his angle?

"No." Anne crinkles up her forehead.

"And where were you on the evening of Sunday, October 15th?"

"Like I said, I was having drinks with Sarah Morgan until around midnight." Anne stares intently at Sheriff Stevens.

"She knew about Adam's affair in the weeks leading up to the murder, and she didn't say anything. Maybe if she would have told me, this wouldn't have happened. Kelly would still be alive. I would have confronted Adam. We'd either be working toward reconciliation, or I'd be prepping divorce papers, but either way, he wouldn't be on trial for murder." I turn to look at Matthew for a moment.

He nods his head. "What's done is done."

I let out a sigh and redirect my attention back at Anne, glaring at her through the glass. *I can't believe she didn't fucking tell me.* A piece of my brain is telling me to erupt at Anne and before I can quiet it, I'm bursting through the door of the interrogation room.

"Sarah please..." but Anne's words are cut short as I dive headlong across the table and tackle her to the ground. I start pummeling her face, pretending she is the manifestation of everyone who has fucked me over in my life. My knuckles and rings gouge into her skin. Sheriff Stevens tries to pull me off, but I elbow him in the nose and send him reeling. As Anne slowly climbs back to her feet, she tries to cry for help, but her mouth is so full of blood all that comes out is a weak gurgle and pink mist. I run over, grab her by the hair, begin to spin her around in circles, and then I release her straight through the one-way mirror. Pieces of glass rain everywhere, and I pick up a particularly jagged piece as I continue my rampage toward Anne...

I blink repeatedly bringing my mind back to reality. I see Anne and Sheriff Stevens sitting in the interrogation room. I need a break from this shit. My head is in the clouds right about now. Everyone I thought I could trust, I've learned I can't. I don't even know which emotion to pick, and I decide that getting some fresh air is my best course of action. I quickly get up.

Matthew asks if I'm all right. I nod and walk down the hall to find Marge still with her nose in her paperwork.

"Excuse me. Marge, is it? I'm heading outside for some air if that's okay?"

"This isn't kindergarten, ma'am. You don't need my permission to walk in and out of a building," Marge replies, still without looking up from her work.

"I just thought you would... Never mind." I walk out the door. "Bitch," I say under my breath.

Outside, the air feels like I've jumped into a cold pool as I cross the threshold of the sheriff's department out into a temporary escape. I take in a deep breath and blow it out with force as I close my eyes for a second and try to clear my head. I'm trying to think of pure whiteness, a blank word document with not a single line of legalese on it. The monuments in D.C. just after being cleaned. My brain tries to mimic the color and clear itself, but rather than a purge I come face to face with a dark pool of *ifs* and *whys*.

A wave of bullshit that comes crashing out of the depths and grabs me with a half dozen tentacles, trying to pull me down into the viscous blankness. I dig my heels in, but it is no use, I am helplessly dragged forward, no escape, no light within, but just as I am about to cross the event horizon, I open my eyes.

My heart rate has accelerated. This respite from the circus is anything but. I look up and see the myriad of dots painted across the nothing night sky stretched behind. I am envious of their isolation. "At least no one bothers you," I say as a tear begins to well up in the corner of my eye. But no, the dam I have built up to stave off my emotions, for this case, for my career, for my marriage, it needs to hold... at least for a little while longer.

I dry my eye and turn to walk back inside.

Standing in the doorway is Matthew. "I wondered where you had gone to."

"I just needed a minute—"

He walks to me and wraps his arm around my shoulder.

"You think you fucking know people." I shake my head.

"Look, for what it's worth, I think Anne's intentions were in the right place." He rubs my shoulder.

"Don't!" I warn. I really don't want to hear about Anne's intentions. I've been betrayed by nearly everyone in my life.

Matthew lets out a small sigh and never one to quit, he continues, "Like I was saying. Anne isn't... how would you say? The strongest of people. She is a follower, not a leader. You have no idea how much that girl idolizes you, Sarah. So, the idea of her being the one to turn your world upside down. She just... couldn't do it. She was too scared of being the dead messenger that you would just leave in your wake and never remember again. People do lots of stupid things under extreme duress, but I'm telling you right now, I know when someone is lying or not, and that woman in there, she truly loves you and would never mean to hurt you."

I let out a large breath I didn't realize I was holding in. I know Matthew's right. Anne is like the little sister I never had, and our relationship is more than a subordinate and a superior. More than a meal ticket and a mouth to be fed. More than a rung on a ladder to be climbed and an ambitious young woman. But that doesn't change one thing, I am still enraged, and maybe just a little bit hurt.

"I know she does," I say grudgingly.

"There you two are." Sheriff Stevens says as he pushes open the door. "I wrapped things up with Anne. We'll still do the handwriting analysis as you requested, but based on that initial interview, I think she's clean."

Matthew drops his arm from my shoulder, and we take a few steps toward Sheriff Stevens.

"Regardless of how upset I am with her, I have to agree with you," I admit. I want to be mad at her, and I still am, but Matthew and Sheriff Stevens are both right. There's no way she had anything to do with this, and her threat to Adam and dishonesty with me came from good intention.

"Should we move on to Bob?"

Matthew and I nod, following Sheriff Stevens back into the police station.

49

ADAM MORGAN

S cott wants to help me? Part of me isn't surprised. If he really doesn't believe that I killed her—which he shouldn't, because I fucking didn't—then as someone who lost the person he loves most, he should stop at nothing to bring the true culprit to justice.

But... on the other hand, Scott has been known to let his temper get the best of him, and he is an asshole. Would it be so surprising for a piece of shit like that to pretend like he believed me just to win back some credibility with the department, all while pushing my head underwater with his boot even further? The shitty reality is that beggars can't be choosers and right now, Scott is all I have left.

But should I be doing this to myself, really? My mind is almost reaching a state of ultimate enlightenment as I am able to hold two conflicting thoughts at the same time.

On the one hand, I know that hope is the only thing that I can cling to and the only thing that can't be taken from me, so I should hold on to it for dear life, right? But on the other hand, I'm not naïve. I know my chances are slim to non-fucking-existent. Why torture myself into thinking something is there that isn't.

It's as if one half of me has been told a secret about our inevitable demise, and instead of warning my other half to steer clear, I devise a plan to lead us both down to it.

Another possibility does cross my mind. What if Scott is the killer? All of this erratic behavior, the loose cannon, bereaved widower act is both a cover for the truth and a convenient outlet for the fear and "caged animal" emotions running through him. If that is the case, then I am giving him even more ammunition to use against me. And not only that, but I have led him straight to the one person on the outside who was willing to help me uncover the truth. With me stuck in here and no one watching Rebecca, Scott can hunt her down and dispose of her just as easily as he did Kelly. Really though, at this point, short of a miracle, I am fucked either way. So, who cares what happens on the outside? All I can do now is just sit and wait...

Or maybe not.

50

SARAH MORGAN

W e walk back inside with Sheriff Stevens. My anger hasn't entirely dissipated, but at least I am trying to process everything. While I can be angry that Anne withheld information from me, she isn't the one who made Adam fuck Kelly and certainly isn't the reason someone killed her. Her motives, while slightly misguided, were not nefarious. That is enough of a kernel of redemption to start bringing my blood pressure down to a more human level. I'm not naïve though, and I still have to brace myself for another potential bomb, as it is now Bob's turn to speak.

Marge changes her tune when Sheriff Stevens walks through as opposed to some annoyance in the form of yet another attorney.

"Hello again, sir. Returning to the dungeons? Would you like me to buzz you through?" she says with a smile. She is clearly amused by her own choice of wording and pleased to have the opportunity to aid the good sheriff in any way.

"No, Marge. It's fine. I can scan myself through. And how many times have I asked you, please, not to call it that, especially in front of visitors?" he says with an imitation stern tone that suggests a mere show of reprimand as opposed to actual anger.

"I'm sorry, sir. I'll try and remember better in the future." There's a wry smirk across her face.

Sheriff Stevens winks at her so slightly I wonder if I'm only imagining it.

He scans us through with his badge and leads us back to the interrogation rooms. Past the same eye-accosting walls, we move in lock-step across the cheap flooring. This time at the next intersection though, we take a left, instead of a right.

Bob is sitting behind the one-way glass, clearly agitated by the wait. He's looking around as if searching for someone or something to vent his frustration at. His legs bounce as he fidgets wildly and perspiration has built up near his hairline. He isn't used to being on the other side of the table.

Sheriff Stevens stops before leaving us. "Are you ready for me to do this? If not, we can wait a little longer and make him sweat some more." His smile is meant to be disarming, I'm sure.

"No. I'm fine. I just want this over with," I respond. I am both drained and anxious to just leave. My confident lawyer persona has all but vanished for the night, and I need to go home and recharge it. I'm in a vulnerable spot without my armor, and Sheriff Stevens is not the person I need around. I'm just glad Matthew is here. We sit down in front of the glass.

"All right then." The sheriff nods and heads into the interview room.

Bob's head immediately snaps toward the door, his eyes narrow, and the fidgeting legs come to an immediate halt. Bob might be a blow-hard and a bit of a cock ninety-nine percent of the time, but he is a good lawyer and a ruthless cross-examiner. He looks like he doesn't want to leave this station without the gratification of a fight.

"Good evening, Mr. Miller. I'm sorry to keep you waiting so

long. Can I get you anything to drink? Water? Coffee?" Sheriff Stevens knows the tough guy act that immediately caved Anne won't work on Bob. He starts with the nice guy routine to perhaps keep things civil.

"Save your apologies and your pleasantries. I don't need refreshments. This isn't my first rodeo, so let's just skip the bullshit."

So much for the civility play.

"Very well then." Sheriff Stevens chuckles to himself as he takes a seat, amused by Bob's bravado. "Let's start with what you know about Kelly Summers."

"What about her specifically, Sheriff Stevens?" Bob knows what the police can and cannot use in court. He knows what looks like fishing or speculation versus actual evidence. Sheriff Steven's questions will need to be tight as a drum or this will go on all night.

"I apologize. For a second, I forgot I was dealing with an attorney. No fluff questions then. Did you know the victim Kelly Summers in any way prior to the start of this case?"

"Yes, I did."

No extrapolating will be found in any of Bob's answers. Part of me is disappointed knowing that Sheriff Stevens likely won't get any new information about my case out of Bob. But on the other hand, I am relieved to know that I don't have another surprise coming my way.

The door of our room opens and in walks Deputy Marcus Hudson, smug as ever. His shoulders are held high and there's a shit-eating grin on his face.

"What are you doing here?" I ask.

"Observing this interrogation as I have every right to do." He stands behind, towering over Matthew and me.

"Every right to, but no reason to..." Matthew scoffs at him. "You fucking reek of suspicion."

Deputy Hudson laughs. "Be that as it may, I'm the law around here."

"Just keep your mouth shut and let me do my job—and you better be ready to be the law when I call you to the stand," I say without even looking back at him.

Deputy Hudson groans and I hear his feet shuffle, and the air around me becomes less stuffy. I glance over my shoulder. He is leaning against the wall with his arms crossed in front of his chest. His shit-eating grin is now a scowl.

I redirect my attention to the interrogation room.

"Would you care to explain how you knew Kelly Summers or, better yet, Jenna Way?" Sheriff Stevens asks.

"She was married to my brother," Bob replies.

"Your brother from Wisconsin?"

"Correct."

"Whom she murdered?"

"I didn't say that. She was never found guilty of such a crime so any statement coming to that conclusion would be pure speculation," Bob says with a tinge of contempt in his voice. It would appear Sheriff Stevens has found the right button to press.

"I'm sorry. Let me rephrase. Your brother whom she was married to, who then wound up murdered and then she fled the state, nowhere to be found." Sheriff Stevens depresses his finger slightly further onto the big red button marked "Dead Brother" that lies just under Bob's skin.

"Yes, she was married to him. Yes, he was murdered. Whether or not she quote fled the state as opposed to just leaving under standard circumstances is, again, speculation." His frustration builds further.

"Gotcha, gotcha, gotcha. Did anyone ever end up being charged as it pertains to your brother being..." Sheriff Stevens runs a finger across his throat to signal Bob's brother's death.

"No. No one was charged in my brother's..." Bob pantomimes the action back to Sheriff Stevens, spit coming through his clenched teeth as he answers.

"Man... Fuck. That's gotta suck, huh? I mean your brother's life just gets extinguished. Poof. And whoever did it to him is just walking around. I mean that's really gotta chap your ass. Especially, someone as familiar with the justice system as you. But hey, then again on your side of the aisle, it's your job to defend those very types. I mean, hell, for all you know, you've helped that same person out of a pickle right under your nose. I mean, it could be anybody, right? That's statistically possible, isn't it, counselor?" Sheriff Stevens ends his line of questioning with an up-pitch in his voice and his head cocked, waiting for an answer.

Bob is now a shade of red, typically reserved only for fire trucks or perhaps the inside of a volcano. He sits silently for a long time while his legs slowly start to bounce again. The room becomes thick and dense—like the night air right before it is about to snow. Finally, Bob lets out a long breath and a single tear begins to well up in his left eye, mere centimeters from the vein in his forehead that seems poised to blow.

"Sheriff... I am here for questioning under your supervision voluntarily. I am not under arrest and have not been charged with any crime. As such it is my constitutional right to both refrain from answering any questions as well as leave under my own power and not to be restrained or kept against my will. I am, of course, happy to comply and cooperate with law enforcement in any manner where I could be of assistance in the pursuit of lawful justice, and as such, am more than willing to answer any further questions, in writing, submitted to my office. As a civil servant, I thank you for your time, and I will be leaving now." Bob then stands and leaves without looking at Sheriff Stevens.

"Excuse me, sir—but we aren't done..." Sheriff Stevens blurts out, but the door is already closing, and the words fail to reach their target as if frozen in midair and then shattered to pieces on the ground. I quickly stand up and open the door to the hallway.

Bob walks past me. He sees me but continues without a word, knowing full well that I witnessed everything. He gives me a look of contempt so deep that I can actually feel pain from the cut he surely hoped it would make in me.

Sheriff Stevens comes out looking down at the floor. He stops for a moment and then turns to me, looking for some sort of affirmation for his line of questioning.

"What the fuck was that?" I say to him.

"He wasn't helpful."

"Yes, he was! By even being here, he was. Just cause he wasn't some pushover or afraid of you doesn't give you the right to do what you did." I try to keep my voice quiet enough so Bob can't hear, but loud enough so Sheriff Stevens can know my anger.

"I thought I could get something out of him. I was just trying to find an angle to provide some help," Sheriff Stevens says with a hint of pleading in his voice.

"Well, you didn't. Instead, you borderline tortured a man about his fucking dead brother. You found a wound, stuck a knife in, and amused yourself as you slowly started twisting. He isn't on trial here for murder, he was trying to be agreeable as best he could. But do you think he will help now?"

"Sarah, I was just trying—"

"Save it. I hope you feel big. In fact, how about you take some of that bloated tough-guy cocksureness and go do your fucking job and find out what really happened." I turn on my heels and walk down the hallway. Matthew is only a few steps behind me. Sheriff Stevens says something, but I've tuned him out so thoroughly I couldn't even begin to guess what he said.

Out in the lobby Anne is sitting in a chair crying and Bob is pacing. They both look at me when the door opens, and I consider for a moment offering them a ride home, but I don't trust either of them. Sheriff Stevens didn't get to the bottom of anything with Bob, and thanks to his line of questioning, I have no idea whether or not he's involved. And Anne's still on my shit list.

"You have to sign out on the register if you are all officially leaving!" Marge yells through the silver tinted mouth slats lodged in her glass bulletproof separating wall.

"Fuck off, Marge," I say over my shoulder.

I glance at Bob and Anne for a moment and then avert my eyes. I can't look at either of them right now. Out in the cold night air, Matthew and I head toward my car in silence. A trend that continues the entire car ride home.

51

SARAH MORGAN

After two double Tito's, both of which I consumed in under thirty minutes while reviewing case documents, the sting in my cheek begins to lose its potency. That bitch of a mother-in-law really clocked me one and the gaudy jewels that adorn her knuckles didn't help either.

She cut me more than surface level with that dig about my mother, especially because she wasn't wrong. I didn't know love from my mother, at least not since my father passed. He was the glue that kept us all together, the one who encouraged me in life and brought joy to my mother. He was the man of the house in the most traditional sense possible, straight out of a Norman Rockwell painting. My father was the sole breadwinner and was the only thing keeping our little nucleus rotating smoothly. But that came to a screeching halt. We lost everything with one unfair act. A father, a husband, a provider, a protector, the only person who pushed me to be more and kept me engaged with life, and the only person keeping my mother from nose-diving off her plateau of happiness and into a sea of depression.

When he was gone, we had nothing: no money, no income, no spark of life. My mother couldn't hold a job because she was so depressed that she slept all day and rarely ate or spoke. In my eyes, she merely saw the reflection of the woman she used to be. Where I once was a collective joy for her and my father, I was now only a symbol of pain and loss. I resented her for this. Not just that though. True, she abandoned me emotionally when I needed her the most, but she also showed weakness in ways that I no longer could feel sympathy for but rather anger and embarrassment. Whenever my mother did speak, it always devolved into a fight.

"Just get out of my house! I can't stand to look at you."

"Your house? Your house!? This isn't your house, it's Dad's. You've never worked a day in your life. You were so pathetically reliant on one man that you now have nothing and know how to do nothing. You are weak and pathetic, and you can't even keep it together for the two of us. You're supposed to be the adult here, not me!"

"How fucking dare you! You have no fucking idea what it's like..."

Scenes like this played out over and over but with less and less frequency as my mother became more and more nocturnal and made fewer and fewer appearances outside her cave of sorrow. I assumed something nefarious was afoot when the refrigerator started becoming less and less full, and past due notices began arriving in the mail.

Like most addicts, at first, she was very good at hiding her behavior. But eventually, the life insurance money ran out, and the welfare money must not have covered her mounting addiction needs. Then items went missing from the house. And random visitors accompanied her home in the evening, men whose faces I never saw but I knew them intimately from their tone of voice and primal noises of both frustration and ecstasy.

By the time I was fifteen, we had lost the house and bounced around between women's shelters and motel rooms. I waitressed

early mornings before school and on nights and weekends to
afford the necessities like food, clothing, and shelter, while my
mother prostituted herself to afford her growing addictions. I
stayed under the radar at school by keeping out of trouble and
maintaining a high GPA. I preferred taking care of myself than
living in some foster home.

On my sixteenth birthday, I found my mother's body in a
cockroach-infested motel room we had been staying at. She had
overdosed on heroin, her gift to me. I would no longer have to
care for her, work forty hours a week to support us both, have to
fight off the men that thought I would be a sweet indulgence
after she had passed out.

I stared at her pale, thin body for over an hour, a hollow,
lifeless shell. Four empty needles were stuck into her arm. I
packed up our things and walked to a pay phone to call 911. That
was the last I ever saw of my mother, and I vowed to never be
like her.

But even my mother still did more for me than Eleanor has
for Adam. My mother made me wise, made me independent,
made me learn how to fight for myself.

Eleanor made Adam weak, her love smothering out his
ability to exist on his own. My mother and Eleanor aren't so
different, the way most addicts aren't, the only difference is that
Eleanor is still feeding her addiction, while my mother's took
her long ago.

52

ADAM MORGAN

Moments after Scott Summers stormed out of the interview room, I notice the door slightly ajar. I stand and pace, listening intently for anyone in the hall. I tap the large mirror, seeing if anyone is in there watching me.

After a few minutes, I work up the courage to do something I'm most certainly going to regret. Pulling open the door slowly, I peek out into the hall and I'm met with silence. I creep out of the interview room and make for the front of the building, crossing paths with no one.

Before entering the lobby, I spot Marge at the front desk muttering to herself as she pushes papers around. She picks up her coffee cup and disappears into a side room.

It's now or never. I move quickly but silently, glancing back only once as I jump the barrier, cross the lobby and exit through the front doors. Sarah's car is still in the parking lot. I turn right and head down the street. I'm not sure where I'm going or what I'm doing, but I can't stay here. I have to find Rebecca. She's the only one that can help me now.

53

SARAH MORGAN

I didn't bother to set an alarm after last night's clusterfuck, and I instead just let myself sleep until I naturally woke up. It was the first good night's rest I've gotten since I took on the case. After a nice long shower, a cup of French press coffee, and a big savory breakfast, I feel I can handle everything again.

Bob and Anne are at the top of my to-do list. But there's also the matter of Adam and his ridiculous outburst. Then there's the third set of DNA, and I still have to smooth everything out with D.A. Peters before the trial. Christ, I don't even have my fucking defense strategy laid out yet. But if anyone can do this, it's me. I mean, it has to be me.

I drive to the office. I'm not even sure if both Bob and Anne will show up today, but knowing them, the odds are pretty good. Anne will want to spend the entire day groveling at my feet until I forgive her. Bob will not want to appear broken or defeated in any way to his subordinates at the firm.

I'm sure I'll be reprimanded by Kent at some point. Lucky for me, Kent was out of the office yesterday, but the news will get to him quickly.

Not thirty seconds after I enter my office, I hear a faint knock on my door frame. Anne is peeking into my office, the lower half of her torso still out of view in case she needs to make a quick dash to escape my wrath.

"May I come in, Sarah?" she asks sheepishly with a heavy vibrato in her voice. This is the hyena approaching the downed wildebeest while the lion is still eating. Maybe the lion will share. Or maybe it will decide to have two meals this morning.

"Yes, Anne, you may," I say, taking a deadpan and emotionless tone to convey my reserved and cautionary judgment of her as a person.

"Look, I just wanted to say I'm sorry again. I'm sorry for not telling you about Adam and Kelly. I'm sorry for breaking your trust. I'm just sorry, and I understand if you want me to leave. I can have my desk emptied by end of day."

I say nothing. I let her sweat.

She bows her head and begins to back out of my office, fully defeated.

"Anne, stop," I call to her. She lifts her head, and I see hope in her eyes. I should let her go. I should let her quit all by herself. It'll save the firm money. It'll save me the headache. But I know she meant well. I know at the end of the day, she is loyal to me. And whether I like it or not, I still need her. I don't have time to find another assistant in the middle of this trial.

"Is Bob in the office this morning?"

"Yes, he is, would you like me to call for him?"

"No. Not yet, Anne. But in the meantime, please set up a meeting with D.A. Peters for later this afternoon." Anne smiles at me and nods and turns to walk out the door. "And, Anne," I add.

"Yes, Sarah?" she asks with all the anticipatory excitement of a puppy waiting for a command.

"From this point on, until I'm ready, you are just my

assistant." I let the words hang heavy as I swivel my chair away from her.

"Yes, Mrs. Morgan," she murmurs as she leaves my office.

My phone buzzes, and I pick it up. A text from Eleanor:

We still have to work together for my son, but I'm not keen on seeing you anytime soon. Your words were vile, and I apologize for allowing them to get the best of me.

I toss the phone on the desk without a response.

54

ADAM MORGAN

My feet are absolutely killing me. I can't even begin to guess how many miles I have walked. Last night, after I left the station, I just started walking, knowing I would have to get as far away as I could. Putting a significant distance between myself and the station would be important, but so would getting out of my orange jumpsuit and finding some shelter, all while avoiding main roadways.

A few hours into my escape it began to rain. Of course, it started to rain. I had underestimated how far out in the middle of nowhere the station truly was, and after what felt like at least five miles of walking, I still had yet to run into a house, or store, or any car I felt comfortable enough to flag down.

I then remembered that Rebecca had said she lived locally. I mean she did write for the county paper after all. I thought that if I could just find a map, I might be able to figure out where the fuck I am.

As the pitch black of a starless and rainy night settled into its darkest point, I realized that as there were no street lamps, I had no real idea where I was going.

279

I moved deeper into the woods from the edge of the road to try to find some form of shelter. This proved to be quite the task with visibility no further than three feet in front of me. After a good fifteen minutes of walking in what I'm sure was a big circle, I came to a partially downed tree which had caught between the massive trunks of two other trees. It looked relatively stable and gave some shelter from the rain, so I decided to set up camp underneath it. I had no illusions about finding some big leaves or branches to improve my structure: I'm not fucking Bear Grylls after all.

Sitting under the downed tree, I couldn't help but think it was just waiting until I fell asleep to finally surrender to gravity and add me to the ground as another decaying piece of fertilizer. I supposed that wouldn't be the worst end for me. The D.A. and the state would undoubtedly applaud it. I could picture the press conference. "Yes, it is true. Mr. Morgan escaped custody the other evening; however, he did not get far, and, in the end, nature decided to exact the justice that the state had already been seeking."

A great cold began to creep through me. I tried to scoop mud and dirt into barrier walls along my sides to keep the water out, but this proved futile and I eventually gave up. Shaking and all alone, I was left with nothing to do but contemplate how I got into this position.

Some elements are obvious. Yes, I was cheating on my wife in our own marital bed, so I guess there's all the good shit that comes with that. But no, this is something more. Lots of people cheat on their spouse, well... some people cheat on their spouse. But I would imagine the more common end to those trysts is divorce, not fucking murder.

Whoever did this must have known us both and very well at that. They knew about the lake house. They knew I spent large chunks of time there without any additional visitors. They knew Kelly came to see me and often spent the night. They knew how to get in, how not to make a noise, where we would be. They knew practically everything. This person must have been patient, calculating, and very sure of themselves. This was no quick plan. This took time.

Scott would have had that time. Scott would have the training and knowledge to cover this all up. It's his job for Christ's sake. I mean, I can picture him now. Almost a limitless amount of time to patrol the area, scout her work, my house, and here I am helping him.

But is it that simple? The scorned husband? How does the Bob connection fit in then? And Anne knew about us? And they work together. That can't just be coincidence, right? I'm trying to connect the dots on how it could be possible for all three of them to be in this together.

Maybe Anne was the one who told Deputy Summers in the first place. Yes, that makes sense. She might have wanted Deputy Summers to be the one that confronted Kelly since Anne couldn't seem to tell Sarah or face me herself. But she probably didn't anticipate Scott's response. But what about Bob? He would have wanted Kelly dead more than anyone. I mean she killed his fucking brother...

The numbness that had been holding me let loose for a second, and I began to realize the number of insects accumulating on my hands and legs. My first reaction was to flail and remove them all, but then I remembered where I was. This was their home, not mine. They were seeking warmth and shelter the same as me, so how could I blame them. I wanted to be one of them. Every morning I would have a purpose. Trekking into the woods, searching for building material and food to bring back to the colony. I would have friends, a team, a clear sense of direction. For all of the wrong I did, my sloth, my lies, my infidelity, I didn't deserve this. Ant Adam would be born anew. At night I could rest knowing I put in an honest day's work. Fill my belly. Once in a while plant my seed in the queen. Really not much different than my own life. Just not aimless. And finally, fair.

~

I wake completely soaked and colder than I have ever been. My muscles do not want to respond. They are frozen in stasis, hoping warmth will come to them. My brain assures them that that will not be the case and finally they release. I head in what I think is the direction of the road. My guess turned out to be correct as I hadn't walked as deep into the woods as I thought I had.

As I continue to tread, I notice that my hands are caked in dried mud. The patina begins to crack and shed itself into a slow falling helix of flakes. *My own dirty Hansel and Gretel trail*, I think. Then I look back and realize that dirt falling into dirt leaves no trail.

From time to time I flinch as a large drop of water, having pooled in the leaves high above, catches the back of my neck. This subtle reminder doesn't let me forget how weak and cold and alone I am. I look up into the canopy to search for some sort of illumination and warmth, but this is blocked by the very leaves that are crying upon me. They deny me any such respite but continue to point their arms away, encouraging me to do no more than leave them alone.

After the most lonely and miserable walk I have ever taken, I begin to hear a steadier roar of traffic. Instead of one car every twenty minutes, I hear one every few minutes. I must be close to something, and my body is screaming for me to run out into the road and cry for help, but I also must still be cautious. I am on the run and still in my jail garb.

I continue walking and soon realize I am near the intersection of two highways and all the standard establishments that accompany such a splendor of human convergence. A gas station, a truck rest stop, and a handful of fast food spots. I assess my appearance and decide that the truck rest stop is my best bet. If I get lucky, maybe one of the truckers will have left their cab unlocked. I could pop in, borrow some clothes, sneak into the rest area and take a quick shower. Then I could move freely about the area.

During a brief pause in the traffic I cross to the parking area of the truck stop. I am trying to sneak as best as I can, but it is broad daylight, and I must look like a miniature sasquatch.

I check the first truck after scanning for any onlookers and try the door. Locked. *Fuck.* I move to the next vehicle and the next with no success. Finally, on my fourth go, I find the door locked but the window wide open. I reach in and lift the lock from its resting place and let myself in. I quickly climb past the two front seats toward the back bench. At first, I am surprised that I am only catching the smallest whiffs of cigarettes, stale sweat, urine, and pork rinds, before realizing that the magical scent masker is none other than myself.

I find a small duffle bag under the bench and reach inside. I pull out some underwear, a pair of jeans, and a green checkered flannel shirt. "That'll do," I whisper to myself.

I hop down from the cab and close the door quietly and relock it. I then turn toward the rest stop bathrooms but am frozen in my tracks as I see two men walking in my direction. They are smoking cigarettes and chatting and haven't noticed me yet. But it is only a matter of time. I scan the area quickly.

There's a gravel ring at the edge of the parking lot that gives way to a field of tall cat-tails and wheat grass; the darker woods set further in the skyline behind it. When I look back, I am met with squinting eyes and the slow but steady walk of someone who is approaching with caution, shoulders slouched down, head cocked forward.

"Hey!" one of them yells.

"What are you doing?" the other shouts.

I panic. I have no answers for them that will suffice. Especially not with my appearance. I do the one thing I can and run towards the field.

"Hey, motherfucker, we're talkin' to you!" the first trucker yells as they begin to pursue me.

They continue yelling as they chase me, but my mind is a blur of panic, and I only catch bits and pieces: "...cocksucker!" "Stop..." "...faggot..." "I'll kill you!"

I hit the tall grass, but don't stop. With my hands holding on to the stolen clothing I can't protect my face and the stalks scratch and cut my cheeks as I run. The constant battering makes my eyes water and swell closed. I don't stop running until I am deep into the woods again and I can no longer hear the voices behind me. I find another tree to hide behind just in case and slump down to catch my breath.

After what feels like a reasonable amount of time for people to quit searching, I think about getting dressed and moving on. There's a small tickle on the back of my hand, and when I look down, there's an ant crawling across my skin. "I know, bud. I know," I say to him.

As I change out of my prison garb and into the confiscated trucker get-up, another drop of water strikes my bare back and sends shivers up my spine. I look up and watch as the branches dance in a slight breeze that rolls through. Waving at me, taunting me. The arms pointing out once again to leave the way I came.

"Yeah, I don't wanna be here either," I say looking skyward.

New clothing fully in place. I go back to the rest area to see if the truckers have gone. I still need to find a map or get to a phone, but for that, I might have to wait till night.

55

SARAH MORGAN

I arrived early at the small café D.A. Josh Peters agreed to meet me at. Usually, I'd arrive a few minutes late to show that my time is more important than his. Not this time though. It is I that needs the favor. Things were going smoothly until Adam fucked everything up by coming to my office and attacking Bob and Anne. I had Josh wrapped around my finger. He was about to do my job for me—find out who that third set of DNA belonged to. Now I'm left with more work, and I've lost the upper hand.

I tap my fingers on the square wooden café table. The hum of those around me, the whirring of a coffee machine and the clanking of dishes is a nice break from the noise and worry that has filled my head since before the case started. I swirl the straw around my peach mango smoothie. I couldn't eat solid foods now if I tried. My stomach is in knots. My anxiety at an all-time high. My patience is worn thin.

I spot D.A. Peters as he enters. He doesn't look around for me and instead walks to the counter to order. He's late. He knows it. But he doesn't care. He knows he's at an advantage. We're days away from the start of the trial, and I've never been more unprepared for a case in my life. I blame Adam and his antics for throwing me off. I blame Anne and her lies. I blame Bob and his odd connection to the victim. Maybe I shouldn't have taken this case on. I'm the best when it comes to criminal defense, but maybe I'm not the best for this case. I thought I could help Adam.

As D.A. Peters finishes flashing his perfectly symmetrical grin at the cashier, he spots me sitting off to the side. His smile partially disappears, but there's still enough of it there for me—enough I think to sway him into helping me, at least, I hope. He gestures to the menu asking me if I want anything. I shake my head and hold up my smoothie. He nods, takes his receipt and joins me at my table, taking a seat across from me.

"Mrs. Morgan, to what do I owe the pleasure?" He unbuttons his suit coat.

I pause before speaking as I can't sound too eager. Casual is the name of the game. I take a sip from my smoothie. "Just wanted to see if you were ready for court..."

He gives me a quizzical look. He's not buying it. I am so fucked. "I've been ready. But that's not really why we're here is it, Sarah?" He raises an eyebrow.

I lean back in my chair. A waitress interrupts us, setting down a basket of chips with a sandwich and a black coffee in front of Josh. Her cheeks flush as she smiles at him. I can tell he has that effect on ladies and why wouldn't he? He's a good-looking man. Maybe that's the angle to play here. He tells her thank you. The waitress lingers for a moment, then steps away not before looking back at him twice.

"Are you sure you don't want anything?" He gestures to his food.

"Oh, there's plenty of things I want." I deliver this in my most flirtatious voice. Either he doesn't pick up on my signal, or he ignores it. He shrugs and dives right into his sandwich.

In between bites he warns me, "When I'm finished with this, I'm finished with this conversation. So, you might want to spit it out. I'm not playing any more of your games."

I let out a huff. "Fine, what do you know about the third set of DNA?"

"Nothing." He takes a sip of coffee.

"And that doesn't bother you?"

"I don't need that third set of DNA for a conviction," he says matter-of-factly.

"But—"

"But you need it," he interrupts.

"Maybe I don't."

"You know as well as I do. A jury will look at the third set of unknown DNA as circumstantial. I mean it's one of three. The victim slept around, that much is true. If you knew who it was, you could build the case around it. Prove reasonable doubt. Prove that other person had more motive than Adam. I know how this works, Sarah. You're between a rock and a hard place. You might want to start coming to terms with the fact that you're not winning this case," he says coldly.

"There's always Scott."

"There is." He doesn't let anything else on.

"Think he did it?" I ask.

"Who?"

"Scott."

"Honestly, I don't know who did it. Scott, Adam, that unknown DNA. All I know is Adam is a slam dunk."

"And you wouldn't care that you're potentially putting away an innocent man?"

"That's for the jury to decide." He wipes his face with a napkin, stands up, and buttons his suit coat.

"What about the connection between Bob and the victim? What do you make of that?" I ask.

288

"Circumstantial."

"Then the whole fucking case is circumstantial," I say through gritted teeth.

"The dead body found in your husband's... or should I say the bed you shared with your husband negates that. See you in court, Sarah." He holds his head up high and walks out of the café.

What a smug prick. That didn't go as I had planned. I was hoping to get more out of Josh. I wanted to know what his angle was and what his case was going to be built on. I don't think he knows who that third set of DNA belongs to and even if he did, he wouldn't include it in discovery. It would only help me. I pull out a pad of paper and scribble down a list of names. All the men I can think of that had any contact with Kelly, all the men that could have slept with her, all the men that could have killed her. I take a picture of it with my phone and then crumple it up and put it in my pocket. This would typically be something I would ask Anne to do, but I can't trust her—at least not yet.

I leave the café and quickly dial Matthew. He answers on the first ring, "Hello, darling."

"Hi, Matthew. I need a favor."

"Anything."

"It's not exactly legal," I say quietly as I walk amongst strangers down the sidewalk.

"Oooo, now you're starting to sound like one of my clients." His voice is determined, yet light and airy, something only Matthew can achieve. "But still anything."

"I'm going to text you a list of names. I need you to get a DNA sample from each of those men. Hair, saliva, skin... I don't care how you get it. I just need you to get it." I say as I'm nearing my office building.

"Getting DNA from men. My specialty." He chuckles.

"Then have them all sent to the lab and run against the

unknown DNA found inside Kelly. I've already added you as co-counsel, so you shouldn't have any issues." I hold the phone tightly to my ear and whisper, "Make it look legal, routine. Make sure you're discreet and make it quick."

"Sarah, you know these won't be admissible in court." His tone becomes serious.

"I'll make them admissible."

"Seriously, what are you doing?"

Again, he's questioning me. Fucking Jesus. I should have asked Anne to take care of this, but I can't trust her, and I'm not sure I can trust Matthew either.

"I just need to know," I press.

"But this isn't the way," he pleads.

"Goddammit, Matthew! Are you going to help me or not?"

"You know I am. I just hope you know what you're doing."

"I do. Talk soon." I end the call just as I reach Willamson & Morgan Law Offices.

56

ADAM MORGAN

G etting back into the rest area at night proved to be much easier. I camped out for a while, making sure the excitement from earlier had died down. The truckers were gone and no cops ever showed up. I can only guess that the truckers had their own reasons for not wanting the authorities involved for what amounted to probably less than forty dollars of stolen clothing.

I eventually was able to shower at the rest stop, snag some leftovers from the back trash dumpster—gross I know, but the trucker's jeans didn't come with a magic wallet full of cash in the back pocket. Then I crossed the street to the gas station.

The clerk looks up from his smartphone for a brief second just to acknowledge my presence with a head nod and then returns to his mindless entertainment.

I head to the restrooms hoping for a pay phone but knowing that this would be a rare find these days. Sure enough, there isn't one. I then turn back and head toward the wall rack that contains local pamphlets, postcards, calendars with loons on them, but most importantly, road maps. I pull one out of its slot and find where I am. I then try to recall where Rebecca had said she lives. I use the lake house as a marker point and trace my way to her. Finally, a bit of luck: she is less than three miles from where I am, not far off the highway.

I slip the map into my waistband and pull my shirt over it. I don't want to steal from this guy, but I don't really have a choice. Besides phoneless escaped convicts and maybe the elderly, who the fuck needs paper maps anyway?

I decide that a call to Rebecca with a heads-up of my arrival might be wise. Best case scenario, she comes and picks me up and saves me hours of walking. I go to the clerk and he says without looking up, "Can I help you?"

"Yeah. I lost my phone and really need to make a call right about now. Can I borrow yours for a second?"

"Five bucks," the clerk responds, still staring at his screen.

"What?"

"Five bucks. You wanna use my phone; it'll cost you five bucks."

"But I don't have any money on me."

"Then no phone," he replies quickly. He then looks up. "If you have no phone, and no money, then what are you doing in here anyway?"

"Well I'm a bit lost, and I was hoping you might have a pay phone."

A smile begins to grow across his face, and he starts to laugh, "A pay phone!? Dude, where did you walk in from? 1997?"

I just stand there, not sure what my next move is, but when he stops laughing, he presses the home button on his phone, clicks on the "call" app, and hands it to me.

"Fuck. I haven't laughed like that in a while. Make it quick and don't wander off," he says, a slight shine of tears cascading down his cheeks.

"Thanks."

I turn my back on him and try to remember Rebecca's number from memory. After a few moments, it comes to me. I punch it in and let the phone ring. After four rings the call goes to voicemail. The positive though is that the recording is in fact Rebecca's voice, so I remembered correctly. I skip the voicemail and try her one more time. Again, no answer.

I type in another number, glancing back at the clerk as the phone rings. He's busy reading a magazine.

"Hello."

I press the phone firmly to my ear. "Daniel. It's Adam."

"Adam, my boy. The auction's still going strong. Ends next week and we gotta lotta nice offers. Wait! I heard you were in prison again. Something about bail jumping. This book is going to be spicy," he says.

"I've escaped."

"Oh, shit. You can't be calling me."

"I need your help."

"Adam, I can't help you. I'd be an accessory. Just take some good notes for your book." He ends the call abruptly.

Shit. I dial another number, and she picks up on the first ring.

"Mom, I've escaped."

"Oh heavens. Where are you?" There's panic in her voice.

"It doesn't matter. I'm going to meet you at your hotel later tonight. I need cash."

"Of course, sweetheart. You don't belong in that prison anyway."

"Just don't tell Sarah."

"I have no interest in speaking to Sarah, and I have half the nerve to slap her again."

"Again? Mom, you didn't?"

"Hey what's taking so long there, bud?" the clerk asks over my shoulder.

"I have to go." I end the call, delete the call log and click the screen off, handing him back his phone.

"Sorry, thanks for your help."

"Girl won't answer, Mr. Pay Phone?" There's a smile on his face.

"Something like that."

Out in the night air, I decide that a walk it shall have to be, and I begin my journey, keeping the highway near my line of sight for reference. After a few hours, I arrive at what I'm pretty sure is Rebecca's neighborhood. Without a phone though I can't call and ask for an address. I decide to try to spot her car in the driveway, crossing my fingers that she doesn't keep it in a garage.

It would appear Lady Luck has finally bared her head to me. I spot Rebecca's Chevy Cruze in the driveway of a ranch-style home. The police must have returned it to her rather quickly after I technically stole it. I hope this is real and hysteria and delusion haven't set in yet. I stumble to her home and knock on the door with such fervor, willing her to come to the door quickly before a neighbor spots me. I should be all over the news by now, but knowing Sheriff Stevens, he'll attempt to keep it hush-hush until he finds me. I've seen numerous signs in front yards on this hellish journey that say, 'Vote for Sheriff Stevens.' It appears he's up for reelection and the last thing he would want right now is the county thinking he let a killer escape from under his nose to run loose in their backyards. I escaped over twenty-four hours ago. I'm sure he's fuming. I'm sure they're looking. I'm sure my time is limited.

Rebecca pulls open the door with frustration. I hadn't realized I'd been pounding on it for nearly a minute. She has a towel wrapped around her body and her hair is drenched. Her eyes widen when she sees me. "What the hell are you doing here?" She glances around the neighborhood and pulls me inside.

"I need your help."

She closes the door and locks it, peering out the side panel window once more. She's skittish, even more than I am. She's scared. I can see it in her eyes, in her demeanor, in the goosebumps on her freckled skin.

"You can't be here." She pushes me aside and walks into the kitchen. She leans against the counter, pulling her towel tighter around her.

"I know. But you're my last hope," I plead.

"Did you tell anyone about me?"

"No... well, yes."

She rubs her arm. She fidgets. Her face flushes. "What the fuck, Adam!"

"Sorry, I panicked."

"Who?"

"Kelly's husband, Scott." I hang my head.

"When?"

"A day ago."

She pulls at her hair. "Someone's been watching me. Been following me." She paces.

"How do you know?"

"They were in my fucking house. I keep getting these phone calls. They started yesterday."

"I'll help you." I grab her and try to pull in for a hug.

She shrugs me off and pushes me back. Tears fall from her eyes. "You can't even fucking help yourself," she yells.

"I'll fix this."

"I should have never gotten involved. I have to leave. I have to disappear."

"It's fine." I grab her wrists. She tries to wiggle away. I don't let her. I pull her in, and I hug her tightly. She stops resisting.

"We'll go to the police together. We'll tell them everything you've found. I won't let anything happen to you." I pull out of the hug and look her in the eyes trying to reassure her. Leaning in, I kiss her. It's a kiss of comfort, at least I think it is, at least I hope she knows it is. I kiss her again and again until she stops crying.

When she's calmed down, I think that I have helped until a flash of anger spreads across her face.

She pushes me hard. I stumble back and catch myself before I fall to the ground. "Get out! You have to leave!"

"Please, Rebecca. Let me help you."

"You can't help me. Get the fuck out of my house."

I put my hands up and back out slowly. It's not anger on her face. It's fear. She's scared, and I don't know if it's me she's afraid of or someone else. She's right. I can't help her. I can't even help myself.

Before I can even make it to the front door, I see the strobing of red and blue lights across the front window. "Did you call the police!?"

"I'm sorry. I didn't know it was you." Tears stream down her face.

"Who did you think—" but I'm cut off as a loud pounding starts at the door.

"Police department! All parties come out of the house with your hands up!"

I open the front door slowly, one hand in the air while the other turns the knob. Before I can open it all the way and raise my other hand, I am seized by the shirt collar and thrown to the ground outside. A knee is pressed into the small of my back, and a thick pair of hands grab my wrists and places me in handcuffs. As I'm pulled to my feet and dragged to the squad car, my eyes catch the faint glimpse of a shadow moving in the bushes behind Rebecca's house. I look away before it registers in my mind and I snap back to see it again, but it's gone. With the lights flashing in my eyes and no water for two days, I can only guess the things I might be seeing.

I surrender without a fight and take my place in the back seat, ready for my ride back to the station. I look forward out the front window of the car, losing my thoughts in the spiraling lights and begin to pass out. At least this part I do deserve.

57

SARAH MORGAN

U nless Matthew pulls through for me, I'm fucked.

I received a text from him last night saying, "*Got it.*" I didn't ask for any more information. What I'm having him do isn't legal, so I'd rather not leave a trail of information leading to me. I'll have to wait. I'll have to be patient, and I'll have to hope that one of those goddamn names is a match. I'm on the couch in my office looking out the window at the city, something I never take the time to do. But right now, I have time.

There's a knock, and before I can tell whoever it is to enter, the door opens and in walks Bob. He's carrying a few folders that he has to shift in his arms as he closes the door behind him.

I let out a groan.

"Tell me this is all almost over," he says taking a seat beside me, completely uninvited, but I'm too tired to fight with him.

"It should be. Court starts Monday. I have Matthew working on something that will help."

He nods and places the folders on the coffee table. "I thought I should let you know Sheriff Stevens cleared me."

"Well, I suppose that's good news." I glance at him and then return my gaze to the skyline.

"I was in Wisconsin. He verified my flights, and I have twenty plus witnesses that can verify my whereabouts."

"You don't need to convince me, Bob."

"I just thought you'd like to know... for the case."

We sit in silence for a few moments.

"What about Anne?" I finally ask. I know Bob is more informed than he should be about this case. He doesn't want anything to reflect poorly on the firm, and he's still upset about Adam's outburst and how it made him look.

"She seems to be cleared," he says.

"Seems?"

"Yes."

I don't question him any further. There's no way Anne could have done this. She doesn't have it in her. She's meek and kind. She couldn't even tell me that Adam was cheating on me. How the hell could she pull off a murder?

"The police also checked my bank accounts to rule out that I paid someone to off Kelly."

I nod.

"I'm clear there as well."

"Okay. Is there a reason you're telling me all of this, Bob?"

"I just want to make sure we're on the same page. We are on the same team, after all, Sarah. You know that, right?" he questions. His face softens. His face is never soft in the office. It's always stern. Always condemning. Always masked with anger or discontent.

"Yeah, I know, Bob."

"And I spoke to Kent about the incident. He understands that you aren't to blame for what happened in the office with Adam."

"Thanks. You didn't have to do that."

He tries to give me a look of comfort. He stands and leans over placing his hand on mine. He gives it a small pat. I nearly pull away. It feels strange but oddly comforting.

"This will all be over soon," he says, and he starts to walk out of the office.

"Bob," I call out to him. Stopping him mid-exit.

"Yes?"

"I'm sorry."

"For what?"

"Sheriff Stevens. His line of questioning the other night. I had no idea he was going to take it there, and it was completely inappropriate." My phone rings jolting me and interrupting our conversation.

"It's... fine," he replies. "You should get that." And he turns and leaves my office.

I pick up the phone from the coffee table. "Sarah Morgan."

"This is Sheriff Stevens. I wanted to inform you that your client escaped from our premises sometime yesterday. We think we've located him. We need you to come down to the station." The line clicks dead as he hangs up abruptly.

"Motherfucker!" I throw the phone down and grab a coffee mug from my desk, whipping it against the wall. It shatters into a million pieces.

58

ADAM MORGAN

Back at the station, a familiar scene of yelling and finger pointing unfolds before me. The saliva of countless sheriffs and deputies giving orders rains onto me. To say they were gentle in their handling would be quite false indeed, but I suppose this is the treatment a murder suspect who has escaped and been recaptured deserves, so I don't complain.

Before I had a sort of status: only my hands were cuffed in front of me, and only during transfers. That's gone. Now both my hands and feet are cuffed and attached to each other. I am never left unsupervised and barely allowed to speak without being met by a chorus of yelling.

Of the things that have been screamed at me since my return, the few that stick out are, "...transfer to max holding..." "...fucked up one too many times!" and "...your attorney will be here shortly before your transfer." The last one is particularly disappointing as I once again get to play the fuck-up in front of Sarah.

After what seems like a very, very long time enduring verbal abuse, albeit deserved, I am informed that my attorney has arrived, and I am transferred to an interrogation room and handcuffed to the table.

Not long after, Sarah and Sheriff Stevens enter.

The first words out of Sarah's mouth are, "Is that really necessary?" as she points to my hands cuffed to the table.

"Don't even fucking start with me," Sheriff Stevens says. His anger is visible all over him.

"Fine," Sarah huffs.

"Look, the only reason you are here is to avoid any issues in court as far as the handling and rights of your client. He is going to be transferred to a maximum-security holding facility until the trial and additional charges will be brought against him for escaping."

"I understand. My client's behavior was inexcusable in this instance. While we maintain his innocence on the charges related to the murder of Kelly Summers, there is no denying his behavior over the last forty-eight hours."

They are both speaking as if I am not even in the room. But given the situation, that is probably for the best.

"Fine, duly noted," says the sheriff. "I will leave you with your client now. You have ten minutes, and then we are transferring him to Sussex State Prison. You can schedule all future visits with them." Sheriff Stevens leaves, but not before giving me a look that says, *You're going down, asshole*.

Sarah turns back to me once the door is closed. "What the fuck could you have possibly been thinking?"

"Sarah, I can explain—"

She holds up a finger to stop me. She begins to rub her temples with her eyes closed, her head bowed. I can only imagine what is going through her mind.

"Do you have *any* idea how much you just fucked everything up? Thanks to you, even if by some miracle I get you off on the murder charges, you are still going to serve jail time for escaping police custody and evading the authorities. We are talking *years* in prison. Do you even get that?"

"Sarah, you don't understand—"

"No, Adam! You don't fucking understand! Let's just look at the facts for once. Fact: you escaped from jail. Fact: you are on trial for murder. Fact: you went to the house of that reporter, who you don't even know."

"I do know her. She's helping me," I argue.

Sarah sets her bag down and draws a folder from it. She slides it across the table. "No, you don't know her."

I look down at the folder, but with my hands cuffed to the table, my attempt to open it is laughable. Seeing me struggle, Sarah leans over and does it for me. There's a picture of Rebecca clipped to the left side and on the right side, there's some sort of a report.

"What's this?"

"That's Rebecca Sanford. Only she's not a reporter, she's a private investigator—and she was hired by Scott Summers."

"What? That's ridiculous! Why would he do that?" I try to throw my hands up, forgetting I'm handcuffed.

Sarah slams her fist on the table. "Listen to me, Adam. She was never actually helping you. Scott didn't trust the narrative any more than you did. What don't you get about that?"

"I don't know. I just thought she was on my side." I hang my head.

"The only person on your side is me." She folds her arms in front of her chest and taps her heel on the floor.

"I know."

"Your antics have given the prosecution so much ammo. You've made yourself look like an imbecile, like a wild animal that would do anything—even kill—to get his way." Sarah shakes her head.

"What can I do to make this right?" My eyes fill with tears. *How could I have been so stupid?*

"You can go to prison. You can keep to your fucking self, and you can stay there until your trial is over." She picks up her bag and throws it over her shoulder.

I don't say anything. I just nod. She walks to the door and before she exits, she turns back to me. "Adam."

I look at Sarah hoping her words will be kind. Hoping she'll forgive me and understand where I was coming from and what I was doing even as dumb as it was.

"I guess someone else might advise you to start praying in this situation because you're going to need a miracle to get out of this. But you know I don't believe in God, so you're on your own for the time being." She leaves, letting the door close behind her.

59

SARAH MORGAN

I can't do this shit anymore. The chips just keep stacking up against me. I close the car door and enter the dimly lit office building. It's late, but Anne said Matthew had a courier deliver a package earlier: the DNA results are waiting for me on my desk.

I can hear the buzzing of a vacuum cleaner. The only ones here this late are the cleaners. It's past 9pm. The trial begins on Monday. I ride the elevator up to the fourteenth floor. Motion sensor lights flicker on as I walk.

Before I make it to my office, my phone rings. I scramble to find it in my purse and without looking, I answer it quickly just to silence it.

"What's this that a mother can't visit her own son in prison?" Eleanor seethes.

I regret not looking at the caller ID before taking this call. "His visiting privileges were revoked due to his escape."

"That's nonsense. When do I get to see him?"

"You can see him on trial days, but you won't be able to speak with him."

"You've mishandled this whole thing, Sarah. I don't know how you got to where you are! You screw up all the time. I have half the nerve to report you to the bar, and they'll—" I hang up. I go to her contact information page and tap *block this caller*. I let out a sigh of relief, dropping the phone back into my purse.

On my desk is a large sealed yellow manila envelope. What's inside it may make or break me. I hesitate before dropping my bag on the floor, kicking off my heels and walking to my desk. I pick up the envelope and twirl it in my hand for a moment. It all comes down to this.

Pulling the metal clasp open and peeling back the flap, I slide out a small stack of paper. I quickly scan and flip the page, scan and flip the page, scan and flip the page and then my breath catches. A small gasp escapes. My mouth curves to a grin.

"I knew it. It's a fucking match."

60

ADAM MORGAN

A guard escorts me into the courtroom. I'm wearing a nice suit and I'm clean shaven, but the pair of handcuffs sullies my appearance. All of this is to try and make a good impression on the jury—to look innocent. I am innocent, but I need them to think that too.

Sarah stands at the table. She's smiling. I haven't seen her smile in a long time. I hope she has something up her sleeve, something that'll save me. If she does, she hasn't made me privy to it. I can't really blame her. I've broken her trust countless times.

Scott went missing over the weekend and hasn't been located by authorities. Perhaps that's the angle she's using. I shouldn't have trusted Scott or Rebecca. I haven't heard from her since the night I was arrested.

Matthew is also here, sitting in the front row, right behind Sarah. My mother is sitting in the second row looking proudly and fondly at me. I smile at her. I also notice right before I turn and take my seat that Deputy Marcus Hudson is in the back, looking very dapper in his dress blues. Why is he here? Sarah must be intending to call him to the stand or at least has made him think she will. Maybe this is the ace in the hole she is hiding.

Anne and Bob are in the back row. A rush of anger surges over me, but I settle it, remembering that they were both cleared. I still think at least one of them had something to do with this. D.A. Josh Peters is standing at the table across the aisle from Sarah, looking smug as usual. His demeanor concerns me, but I trust Sarah will knock him down a peg.

I smile at Sarah. She nods. The guard removes my handcuffs. Sarah and I take a seat but only for a few moments.

"All rise. Department One of the Superior Court is now in session. Judge Dionne presiding. Please be seated," says the bailiff.

"Good morning, ladies and gentlemen. Calling the case of the People of the State of Virginia versus Adam Morgan. Are both sides prepared and ready?" Judge Dionne says.

"Ready for the People, Your Honor," D.A. Josh Peter says.

"Ready for the defense, Your Honor," Sarah says.

"Will the clerk please swear in the jury?"

This is it. My entire life comes down to this. My life is in Sarah's hands, the judge's hands, the jury's hands, anyone's but mine. It's up to them now. Sarah, my sweet Sarah, taking on the world while I'm still struggling to live in it—better yet, stay alive in it.

It's time now for Sarah to begin opening remarks. She practiced these many nights in our home with me over the years. I know how good she is at this and how important it is for setting the tone. I'm hoping now that she will muster her best performance to date because I'm going to need it.

"Good morning, ladies and gentlemen of the jury. My name is Sarah Morgan, and it is my privilege to represent Adam Morgan in this case before you today. Yes, you heard that right, Morgan."

Sarah turns her body towards me in an open stance and

points at me with her whole palm open. "Adam is not only my client." She looks back at the jury. "He is my husband."

Half the jury is agasp at the situation they have just learned they are in. I'm not sure yet if this is a good thing or a fatal mistake on our part.

"You have heard the prosecutor explain what he hopes will be proven throughout this proceeding, but what the prosecutor did not tell you is all the facts that we know right now. I can easily stand here before you today asking for a verdict of not guilty, no bluffing or showmanship required. Why? Because I know for a fact that Adam Morgan did not kill Kelly Summers." Sarah pounds her fist on the railing in front of the jury box, punctuating her statement and snapping the jury to attention.

"Did Adam Morgan have an affair with Kelly Summers? Yes, yes he did. Did he love her? Yes. He has said so himself. And both of those things, as his wife, hurt me beyond belief. They anger me beyond belief." She turns and looks at me with a mixture of anger and heartbreak in her eyes. She looks as though she could scream and cry simultaneously.

"Between us, I want to see him reap the consequences of his transgressions. But the transgressions he did commit, not the ones he didn't. Did he have an affair? Yes. Did he love another woman outside his marriage? Yes. But did he kill that woman? No, no he did not." Sarah's voice comes down almost to a whisper. I have seen her do this before, the decrescendo before the climax. Lulling the jury as she wants.

"My client, my husband, had an affair. But loving someone other than your wife does not make someone a murderer. The prosecution," Sarah points to D.A. Josh Peters, "will paint Adam as a cheater... and as his wife, I know for a fact he is. We won't even try to refute that point, but there are other facts beyond that. Facts the prosecution will gloss over. Facts the prosecution will try and make you not notice at all."

Sarah walks down to the end of the jury box and stands before juror number one. She brings her hand up in the air, the back of her fist facing the jury, and begins to raise her fingers one at a time as she recites what she knows to be true.

"One. I know for a fact that Scott, Kelly's husband, threatened to take her life on the night of her murder.

"Two. I know for a fact that Kelly's real name was Jenna Way —and Jenna Way... well, Jenna is quite the interesting woman indeed. Jenna was accused of murdering her first husband, Greg Miller, before mysteriously fleeing the state of Wisconsin, and then magically ending up in Virginia with a new name, new hair color, whole new everything."

The jury begins to murmur. I look over at D.A. Peters. He is rolling his eyes, but his posture is giving way. This is not the stage he wanted set, not for his slam-dunk case.

"Three. I know for a fact there are numerous people who will be presented throughout the case, from Kelly's—or should I say Jenna's—past life that had motive to kill her in order to get justice for Greg.

"Four. I know for a fact Kelly was sleeping with at least three different men, all in a very short period of time. How might I know that, you ask? Because the medical examiner found sperm carrying three different DNA profiles inside her vagina."

Two of the older female jury members lean back with looks of disgust on their face. It pains me to hear Kelly made into such an unlikeable subject. Disloyal, a liar, flighty, violent, a whore, and maybe even a murderer. But I know this has to be done. I know this is what Sarah has to do to make the jury sympathize with me and not the dead woman. A woman I loved.

"And five. I know for a fact Kelly had a stalker by the name of Jesse Hook who frequented her place of work just to get a glimpse of her."

Sarah brings her hand back down and walks toward me. She

gives me a look that I haven't seen before. A look that says, *You owe me for this because you don't deserve it.* She isn't wrong. To tell the truth, I don't know why she is helping me. But I do know without her, I might as well walk right to the electric chair.

"The prosecution believes Adam Morgan killed Kelly Summers. And beliefs are just that, beliefs. What we are looking for, what we need in a court of law, are facts. And I have just presented you with five things that I know to be facts, and I will happily add one more. Six. Adam Morgan did not kill Kelly Summers. Thank you."

61

SARAH MORGAN

I was just packing to leave and go back to D.C. The trial ended yesterday as jury deliberations began. In cases like this, they can take weeks, especially with the death penalty on the line. I hear frantic pounding on my hotel room door. I open it without even checking the peephole and find Anne standing before me, panting and flushed red. I'm about to ask what she is doing here, why she is in the condition she is in, but she speaks first with sharp abruptness.

"The verdict is in," she says out of breath.

"What? Already?"

She nods. "That's not good, right?"

"No, not usually." I grab my jacket and purse and bolt out the door, blowing past Anne. She follows me all the way down to my car and hops in the passenger seat as soon as I unlock the doors. Anne is back in my good graces. It took me a while to forgive her, for her to earn my trust back. But she did. She's stuck with me through this whole trial, all the way up until the very end, which seems like it might be today.

"Are you okay?" Anne asks.

I look at her from the corner of my eye. My hands are

grasping the steering wheel so tightly, my fingers are white. "I will be."

"Regardless of how this turns out, you did everything you could."

"Thank you for saying that, Anne." I give her a small smile. She returns it and nods.

~

I don't get ten feet into the courthouse before I run right into D.A. Josh Peters. It's almost as if he was anticipating my arrival.

"You ready for this?" he asks. I can tell by his demeanor that he's not all that confident. I'm scared shitless. A quick deliberation can go either way in this case. I merely nod at him and head toward the courtroom. I pass Bob and we exchange sympathetic glances. He knows as well as I do what this could mean.

I walk to the front of the courtroom and take a seat. Matthew is already waiting in the first row behind my chair and he gently squeezes my shoulders when I sit down. He leans forward and whispers into my ear, "It'll all be okay. No matter what happens." I look back at Matthew, but my eyes meet Eleanor's. She's sitting right behind him. We haven't spoken since the night I blocked her phone number, but we have been seeing each other in this courtroom. She never misses a trial day, and she's always looking proudly at Adam as if she were attending his little league games. Eleanor gives me a brief glance and then refocuses her attention on the door her son will soon walk out of.

Adam is escorted into the courtroom and seated next to me. His expression is bleak. I know he wants me to tell him everything is going to be okay, but I can't. I don't know that everything is going to be okay. But I also won't try and scare him unnecessarily. I simply rest my hand on his for a moment, offering the last little bit of comfort I'll ever offer him, regardless of how this turns out.

Judge Dionne takes his seat. The jury enters the courtroom.

"Will the jury foreperson please stand? Has the jury reached a unanimous verdict?" the judge asks.

The foreperson stands and says, "Yes, Your Honor."

Adam places his hand on mine and squeezes it.

The clerk retrieves the verdict from the foreperson and hands it to the judge. He reads it over silently to himself.

I can feel Adam's heartbeat in his hand. It's fast, loud, panicky.

Judge Dionne returns the verdict to the clerk. "Will the defendant please rise?"

Adam stands, letting go of my hand.

The foreperson clears her throat. "We the jury, find the defendant..."

62

SARAH MORGAN

11 YEARS LATER

I know what you're thinking. Did I do everything in my power to save Adam? To try and save the man who ruined our love and our marriage. I ask myself the same question sometimes. And the only answer I have ever come up with is that I did what I had to do. To survive.

Today is the day of Adam's execution. I stopped writing or visiting him over ten years ago, right around the time he went insane. Every visit became more explosive than the last, and I couldn't do it anymore. He had lost all hope after his conviction, and a human without hope is a wild animal. I needed to move on, and I did. If Adam hasn't, well, that choice will be made for him today.

I've come to say goodbye. I've come to give myself some closure, or at least I think I have. Adam may not have murdered Kelly Summers, but he is paying for his crimes.

I glance up at the large concrete and brick building in front of me, a maximum-security prison, but for Adam, it might as well be a coffin. The sun is shining bright today. There's a clear blue sky, and I can hear the birds chirping. I walk up the steps to the building carefully in my white pencil skirt and white blazer.

An angel of death descended upon this lowly place. My hair is a shimmery golden blond, long and down. I wear it down these days and let it be free. It's how I try to live my life too, uninhibited and less rigid. I guess some things do change after all.

I enter the building and go through security. It takes nearly twenty minutes because this is a maximum-security facility, but I don't mind, not in the least bit. I'm able to speak to Adam before he is executed, since I was the lawyer on his case, and I am still his wife. Yes, we're still married. Adam refused to sign any divorce papers and I didn't fight him on it. I figured giving him a shimmer of optimism was worth being married to him for longer than I cared for.

I plan to remarry tomorrow as I will be a widow by the end of the day. We're having a wedding on the beach with close friends and family. It's going to be beautiful. From now on, everything in my life is going to be beautiful.

After removing my jewelry, my purse, and cell phone, I'm escorted through the main lobby, down a small hallway and into a holding room. They will soon bring Adam in to speak with me. It's a small concrete room with a table, two chairs, a clock on the wall, and a CCTV camera in the upper corner. There's nothing else, not even a one-way mirror. I was told I would have ten minutes. Ten minutes is all I need. I tap my long red nails on the table, careful not to chip them as I just had them freshly done for the wedding.

The door swings open and Adam is standing there, filling most of the door frame. His beard is long and scruffy, but it doesn't look bad. His hair is cut so short it flashes between visible and not, depending on the light. He appears to be a bit thicker, not in a fat way, more of a stocky way. But his eyes tell the real story. Prison has not been kind to him. While being known as the murderer of a cop's wife didn't hurt his "cred" inside, they still could see what he was, a soft artist. A broken man out of his element. Chum in the water as the sharks slowly circle and close in. I can't imagine what he's been through in here.

His face lights up when he sees me. He is completely devoid of his boyish charm. He is a man who has been beaten down for a decade. I give a partial smile back. I can't say I'm happy to see him, but I'm also not sad to see him either.

"You came?" He takes a few more steps into the room. His arms and feet are shackled around his waist so his steps are quite small and more like a shuffle.

"Of course."

The prison guard directs him to the chair. He removes most of the chains and cuffs, aside from one from his right wrist, which he hooks to the table. Adam takes a seat and smiles at me.

"Ten minutes and no funny business," the prison guard says.

I nod at him and Adam thanks him. As soon as the door closes, Adam slides his free hand across the table, hoping that I'll reciprocate. I pause for a moment, looking at his cracked, beaten hand and at his even more beaten face, and then I acquiesce. My hand encloses his, and he begins to cry. I can do nothing but stare back in wonder, like a spectator at the zoo, observing some foreign species.

"How have you been?" he finally says as he fights back all the emotions of a life stolen.

"I've been... good."

"You stopped writing and visiting?"

I can't tell if it's a question or a statement, so I just nod. "I know... it became... too hard."

"I understand." He hangs his head.

I squeeze his hand lightly. He smiles at what he probably thinks is a gesture of affection, but it is merely the closing of a countdown that started long ago. Ten of those little squeezes of my hand, each expels one more minute that I have to endure with him. I've always been good with timing. It's how you deliver a perfect opening or closing statement at court. It's how you hit the perfect pauses during a cross-examination. It's why I'm so good at my job. It's all about timing. He squeezes my hand back. I don't care to be involved with him in even the most germane of romantic interactions, but I've endured worse from him... much worse.

"Did you ever find anything more on the case?" he asks with a pleading tone, touched with hope.

"Adam," I sigh out to him, "why even bring that up? It won't do you any good."

"You were never curious enough to look back into it? To try and save me?" His voice begins to rise in tandem with his eyebrows.

"Of course, and I have, but there was never any new evidence—there was no way to get the case reopened. You know that. I went over that with you six months after the trial ended." I squeeze his hand for the second time.

He lowers his head feeling defeated all over again. Did he really think I'd spring in here with new evidence and he'd magically get released at the eleventh hour? That kind of thing only happens in the movies. It doesn't happen in real life. After a few awkward moments of him staring at the table, he lifts his head back up and looks at me. I squeeze his hand for the third time. He squeezes back. I wish he'd stop that.

"What about that third set of DNA?" There's a small air of excitement in his voice.

"What about it?"

"Do you know who it belonged to?"

"Adam, we went over it. There wasn't enough evidence to bring it into court." I sigh.

His face scrunches up, anger setting into his eyes—the wild

beast is returning. He takes a deep breath, smoothing out his face again. He's finally coming to terms with it all. I squeeze his hand a fourth time. This time he doesn't squeeze back. Instead, he gives me an odd look.

"Listen, I didn't come here to rehash the case. I came here to say goodbye and to tell you that I love you." I loved him at one point, so it's not hard for me to mimic saying those words to him, even if they're not true anymore.

He drops his head and whispers under his breath, "I love you too, Sarah." Silent tears begin to stream down his face.

I squeeze his hand a fifth time.

63

ADAM MORGAN

S arah came to see me today. I've wanted to see her for so long, I've lost count of how many years it's been. And now here she finally is, right in front of me, and it feels... bittersweet. She doesn't seem to be herself, at least not the Sarah I remember. She is cold and disinterested. And for some reason, she keeps squeezing my hand in a way that doesn't convey love or affection but rather, something else. At first, I thought it was for comfort, whether for her or me, I wasn't sure. But the timing of the squeezes is off. No, actually the timing of them is perfect, right down to the second. One every single minute. Why is she doing that? I know this isn't an easy day, I should fucking know more than anyone, but... it doesn't seem to be affecting her, at all.

She looks beautiful today. It's almost painful to take in, given the circumstances. Her hair hangs freely down to her shoulders, and her lips and nails are painted a bright red. She's dressed in all white, like an angel, but it hardly seems appropriate the more that I think about it. I choke up thinking about her and me together and all the time that we lost. The fact is that once she walks out this door, I will never see her again. I've tried not thinking about it all these years. Sure, I knew this day would have to come eventually, but it's not something you want to dwell on. Lethal injection for a crime I did not commit. That last part is what stings the most.

No further evidence was ever found in my case, so my fate has remained unchanged. It was the perfect crime and the perfect set-up by whoever did this. I gave up hope a long time ago, yet for some reason, I thought on this day, maybe by some miracle, Sarah would walk in with a bombshell discovery to blow the lid off whatever conspiracy was sealing me in; my knight in shining armor here to save me. Her outfit certainly matched the part.

I know now that won't be happening for me. My life is already over, I'm just on borrowed time, walking dead through these halls. Perhaps in the afterlife, if there even is one, I'll learn the truth of what happened to Kelly Summers and finally have some peace about all of this. But probably not.

She squeezes my hand again. It's the sixth time. I've been counting.

"So, did you move on?" I finally work up the courage to ask.

"I don't think anyone ever truly moves on from something like this, Adam."

She's been answering with these vague "non-answers" the whole time she's been here. Not letting me back in for even a second. Her defense systems are fully activated.

"Do you think things could have been different for us?" I ask.

"What do you mean?"

"Like if the trial turned out differently. If they found the real killer. Would we have had a chance?" I try to contain the desperation in even asking the question.

"I'd like to think so." Her eyes lock with mine as she tilts her head and begins batting her eyes, it almost seems... forced. Like she's saying what I want to hear, but why? I really don't know, but that's the one thing about Sarah, she's always thinking, calculating. There's never not an ulterior motive, another angle to the play. She's always in control... of everything.

"I'd like to think so too. I think we'd have been happy. I think we'd have finally started a family of our own." There's hope in my eyes, but there's none in hers.

She smiles and squeezes my hand for the seventh time. "Do you regret what you did?"

"What do you mean?" My head perks back up from the table as my eyes squint to brace from the angle of this question. I have all types of regrets. Which one is she trying to pull out of me?

"Sleeping with Kelly? Cheating on me? Giving up on us?" Her eyes narrow and she leans further away from me.

Ahh, those regrets. "I never gave up on us," I say, and I mean it. "I may have been unfaithful, but I never gave up on us. I love you. Always have and always will, not that that is for much longer."

She just stares back at me with a thousand-yard stare. I know she heard what I said, but it's not registering. She seems to be looking through me, to the wall behind my head as if I'm not really here. Or maybe it's her that isn't really here, and this is merely a phantom proxy of her. A projection of the person I wished would show up today of all days. She squeezes my hand an eighth time.

"I'm sorry for not being a better wife to you."

I snap back from my train of thought. *Where is this coming from?* She's not to blame for any of this. These were my actions. I caused all of this. I didn't commit murder but I did cheat. I did throw away what we had, carelessly like a piece of litter into a trash can I was passing. I can't leave this earth with her blaming herself for everything that happened. She is the only one who defended me through all of this. The only one who truly believed me. The last person on earth who loves me, aside from my mom. "Sarah... none of this was your fault. You were a wonderful wife. You worked hard and were the only person who believed me and defended me. You loved me during my darkest times. You did everything you could for me and my career. I don't blame you for anything. You have nothing to apologize for." I try to hold back tears. She squeezes my hand a ninth time. I squeeze back.

"You think I was good to you?" There's a peculiar lightness to her voice as if she is teasing me in a game on the playground.

"Of course you were, Sarah. Don't ever think otherwise. Someday you're going to make another man so hap—" At this point I can't hold back. The tears pour down my face and a small pool forms on the rough steel table. I shake my head and take a second to compose myself. "It hurts to say that. Because I wish I were that man. I wish I could still be that man. But I can't, my time is up. And even if it wasn't, I don't deserve you, I never truly did. I had you for a time, and you were mine to lose, and I fucked everything up."

"You did," she says pointedly.

"I know," I sob. "Not a day has gone by that I haven't thought about you these past eleven years."

The hard slam of steel hits the concrete wall as the guard re-enters. "Time's up." He smacks his gum loudly and is purposefully not looking at either of us to convey his disinterest.

She squeezes my hand for the tenth time. I squeeze back. She stands up, "Goodbye, Adam. For what it's worth..." She walks around the table to my side. Sarah leans over and plants a soft kiss on the side of my cheek. She then leans in, whispering into my ear, "I know for a fact it wasn't you."

I turn and look at her. She is smiling at me with no teeth. A sinister up-turn plastered across her face. There is a fire burning

in her eyes that I have never before seen, not in a human at
least.

"What does that mean?" My mind starts racing, trying to
piece together what I just heard. "Sarah, what do you mean?
Who was it then? If you know you have to tell me! You have to
get me out of here! Sarah!" I scream for an answer. The guard
grabs me by my shoulders, turning me toward the door.

Sarah keeps walking backward away from me, staring at me
with that fucking smile. "Adam, you will spend the rest of your
very brief life thinking about me, and I want you to know that I
will never think about you ever again." And just like that she
leaves, a cloud of hate and toxicity still hanging in the air.

I stand in a stupor as every sound leaves the room like a
vacuum. I don't even remember the guard escorting me back to
my cell. I thought Sarah still loved me or at the very least,
cared about me in some way. Not the way she had before but a
part of her must still, in some way. But who was that in there
with me?

I didn't ask her to forgive my errors. I am the root of all of
this. But why did she leave me with that? What did she expect
me to do? What the fuck does she want me to think?

I can't even control my own thoughts. They are like a
speeding freight train with a broken brake lever. Nothing is
going to stop it until the inevitable crash. So many words are
racing through my head and the more they race and repeat and
rearrange, the more they start to make sense.

About thirty minutes later, the prison guard comes and
escorts me into a new room with a brown gurney and several
pieces of health monitoring equipment. A doctor and a nurse
and two other prison guards are waiting for me, my last and
greatest surprise party. The gurney is facing a large blacked out
mirror that faintly shows my reflection. I know full well that on
the other side of that mirror, people are anticipating this

moment, anxious for what is about to happen. I don't fault their anger, it is just misplaced.

I lie down on the gurney and the guards strap me in. They hook me up to an IV and a heart monitor. The prison guard asks, "Would you like a priest or rabbi, or someone else brought in for your last rites?"

"No. That won't be necessary."

"Any last words then?"

Forgiveness. Vows. Broken. Cheating. Kelly. Fact. Kill. Sheriff Stevens. Jenna. Bob. Anne. Lake house. Jesse. Rebecca. DNA. End it. Matthew. Hudson. Scott. Sarah. Sarah. Sarah.

All of these words race through my head. I had hoped my last thoughts would be of the life I lived or the people I loved. Kind of poetic in a way that the struggling writer can't even think of a few good last words to say. The only thoughts swirling inside my brain are of my own demise. Something doesn't feel right. Something isn't right.

And then it happens. It's as if I can see right through the mirror in front of me and straight into Sarah. I see that smile and the look in her eyes. The counted out squeezing of her hand. Her curious parting words and her callousness. But why now? Why of all days did she need to say this, treat me like this? It's as if... wait. No, it couldn't have been...

I feel numb at first and think I might fall asleep. But soon I begin to flail and squirm, and then a stabbing heat starts to rip through my organs, and I scream. And then suddenly it stops. Everything stops.

I see nothing but a black canvas with the tiniest of holes punched in it, a white light growing from the center out, like an old tube television warming itself up. Images start to appear. Images of Sarah. Meeting her. Loving her. Marrying her. Watching her. And then everything I missed. They're almost like deleted scenes of a film. Except I didn't delete them. I just didn't pay any attention. Her planning, her plotting, her calculating, my demise.

Sarah controlled everything in her life, myself included.

I underestimated her. Like I did so many times before. This time it was just one too many. The images fade and then go black. Sarah is my last thought, my last image. She was right about everything... absolutely everything.

64

SARAH MORGAN

I'm looking through the one-way mirror at the scared man I once called my own. I had to be here for this moment, see it through to completion. A little to my surprise there is a familiar face. Eleanor, in all her seventy-something-year-old glory, has shown up to see her precious boy one last time. I haven't seen or spoken to her since the end of Adam's trial. Normally, I would detest the idea of having to spend even a second in her presence but for this moment, this event, I'm delighted to see her. I go over to where she is sitting, bringing along my most sober of moods and a pre-ordered set of tears ready to pool out of my eyes.

As I stand over her, she doesn't look up but simply says, "Sarah."

"May I sit?" I ask, politely this time around. She doesn't approve but nor does she decline, so I take a seat, returning my gaze to the room beyond. "Look," I say to her, "I know we were never the best of friends. I don't think today changes the past or the level of interaction we have going forward. But today, know that I am here."

Eleanor looks over at me with tears running down her cheeks, more welling up. "Okay," is all she says.

The proceedings continue as normal and then the time comes, the final piece of the day, the syringe. Eleanor sees it, and I can see her whole body go rigid. Nothing she can do now can stop this. All the mothering or money in the world can't save her son today, and that fact is paralyzing her.

Finally, the doctor says something to Adam, and Adam shakes his head. The doctor inserts the needle into the IV line, and Eleanor simultaneously inserts her hand into mine. As the lever depresses into the vial, she begins to squeeze my hand slowly. At first, it is quiet, like that small lapse of time after a lightning strike, waiting for the thunder to follow, and then it happens. Adam begins to convulse and scream on the table.

Eleanor wails "No! My baby boy!" and begins convulsing herself.

I squeeze her hand back and take her head into my chest, "Shh, it's over now. It's all over," I whisper into her ear as I run my fingers through her hair, a large smile plastered across my face.

When he finally goes limp, I lift Eleanor's head and stand. "Goodbye, Eleanor," I say as I turn to leave.

"Sarah. Wait," she quickly blurts out. I turn to look at her without saying anything. "I'm sorry... for everything." The words are almost a whisper as she is still crying heavily.

I stare back at her inquisitively, like a cat deciding what to do with a small rodent it just caught. "I'm not," I say and turn to make my exit.

In her state of hysteria the words don't even register and she returns to her sobbing.

His last thoughts were of me. I could tell by the stupid look on his face. I stand and exit, following Kelly's parents. They were weeping throughout the whole ordeal, pouring out the catharsis they came here to find. They probably think they witnessed some form of closure; the man who murdered their daughter being put to death.

I glanced over at them a few times and exchanged sympathetic glances. They knew who I was. The lawyer of the monster who took so much from them and not just the lawyer, but the wife of that very same monster. Yet, for some reason, they were kind to me. I don't know why. They seemed to see me as one of them, a victim, caught up in the mess left behind by the manifestation of evil on the other side of the glass. Something that just *happened* to all of us. This evil pit of toxic tar and sludge that we all were dropped into and couldn't free ourselves from. Not until the beast was slain.

They hold the door open for me, and I walk in front of them down the long hallway. I hear little whispers behind me, "I'm glad this is over" and "I'm happy he's finally paid for his crime" and "Kelly can rest in peace now." I nearly bite a hole through my tongue to stop myself from chuckling. From turning around and laughing right in their faces.

I push open the doors to the main security area where I had to relinquish my belongings. I check out and they hand everything back to me.

I have a text from Matthew.

John and I are leaving in two hours. Can't wait to walk you down the aisle tomorrow, and the kids are so excited to see their Aunt Sarah.

I text back,

Thanks, Matthew. Can't wait to see you guys! Love you.

I go through the rotating glass door at the mouth of the

building. Outside the sun is piercingly bright, each of its rays doing all it can to scorch everything in this world. I slide my Chanel glasses over my eyes and walk down the concrete steps.

I may have not been the most honest person. Not to Adam, not to Anne, not to Matthew, not to Sheriff Stevens, not with any of them, but I'll be honest with myself. Timing is everything and I timed everything out perfectly.

Adam always thought he was so smart, so well-read—the deep one, the introspective one. The warrior for justice and art and everything in between. And he was all those things. He just assumed I wasn't watching, and he was wrong.

I learned about Kelly and Adam long before she took her final breath. Bob had approached me with evidence of Adam's infidelities, which he had come across because he was looking to destroy Kelly's life after what she did to his poor brother. He thought he would kill two birds with one stone—that he'd blackmail me into resigning out of embarrassment or at the very least, that I would lose focus so he could swoop in and get my partnership while taking down Kelly at the same time. He was wrong too. When he brought this to my attention, my reaction was nothing like what he expected, but more than he could have ever hoped for.

We decided to kill Kelly and frame Adam. After all, they did have it coming. Bob was out of town when she was killed to ensure that when the connection between him and Kelly was found out, he'd have an alibi. I didn't want any loose ends.

We thought about hiring someone to do it, but like I just said about loose ends. There was only one person I could trust to do it and to do it perfectly... it's like they say, sometimes if you want something done right, well...

I wasn't pleased to learn that Anne knew Adam was cheating on me. As soon as I discovered the photo in Adam's desk, I knew it was her behind it. Think I wouldn't recognize my own assistant's handwriting? I ultimately did end up forgiving her, letting it all go. After all, we were both each other's alibis. That night we went out on the town, she didn't keep track of time or her own alcohol intake, and why would she? She idolized me. I was everything she aspired to be. Time with me was like gold to her. I knew that. I counted on that.

I also knew all of Adam's vices, and besides young pussy and self-loathing, his next favorite was scotch. Putting a handful of roofies in the decanter was as easy as, well... Kelly. With them both completely out for the evening, their memories on pause, all I needed was a quick detour from the bar at 10pm and a sharp knife. It was simple, like punching holes in a box so the animal inside can have air to breathe. But the opposite in this case.

Adam thought he was so smart. He thought Jesse was a real suspect. I knew Jesse was just a creep who was overly infatuated with Kelly, but following up on Jesse made it look like I was actually working on the case. Jesse was my decoy, just a way to look busy when in reality I was just waiting for everything I put in motion to play out.

That third set of DNA threw me for a loop, I will admit. It was honestly really starting to piss me off that I couldn't figure out whose it was. I thought I had studied Adam and Kelly well enough to know the details of who was and wasn't involved in their lives. I thought Bob and I knew everything about those two fucks. That was the only thing that worried me. So, who was this third guy? Had he seen anything? Thank God it ended up being that dipshit Sheriff Stevens. Yet another man who couldn't keep his dick in his pants. Once I figured it out, I made sure to keep that from the case, because I planned and pushed for a speedy trial and a guilty verdict, and I didn't need that muddying everything.

Sheriff Stevens ended up helping me anyway without

knowing it, thanks to his sloppy police work. Adam definitely had Rohypnol in his system. I know this because he didn't move, not even once, when I stabbed Kelly to death. The precious new love of his life, being ripped away from him one motion at a time, her blood splashing onto the clear plastic tarp I laid over him like a private little viewing window just for Adam, but he just lay there. So, either that half-wit sheriff didn't actually test Adam's blood, or he messed with the evidence to get the case closed quickly. I think it was the latter considering his involvement. It's also why I left that third set of DNA out of the trial. Sheriff Stevens unknowingly did me a favor, so I returned it in kind.

And what about Rebecca Sanford? The young wannabe journalist on whom Adam banked all of his hope. She was, in fact, a private investigator, but she wasn't hired by Scott. She was hired by Bob and when her job was done, she left town as arranged. Her job was to keep an eye on Adam, to steer him in the direction we wanted. We wanted him to find out about Bob's connection to Kelly, just so he'd have a small sliver of hope for a moment, just enough to make him crazy. We wanted him to put two and two together with Anne and her little threatening note. Another small glimmer of hope that would make him erratic and irrational. But most importantly, I wanted to remind Adam that he could only trust one person and that was me.

That overly-aggressive, small-brained ape of a human, Scott Summers, split on his own accord. I really don't think he wanted his whole "destroying evidence in the murder of Kelly's first husband" story getting aired out for everyone to see. Hmm, maybe he wasn't as dumb as I thought he was.

I'll never know what really happened between Kelly and Greg or Kelly and Scott. Was she a victim of the men in her life? Was she abused? Or was she a girl who cried wolf? I'll never know and neither will anyone else. That's the thing about relationships, you never really know what's going on in them, unless you're a part of them. Just like no one will ever know what happened between Adam and me. We all have our own truth and everything outside that truth is just a story.

Speaking of story, Adam did go on to write his tell-all. He titled it, *Innocence isn't Enough: The Adam Morgan Story*. Of course, he couldn't resist having his name on the cover... twice. It was a huge success, a *New York Times* bestseller, translated into forty different languages, and Netflix even made it into a four-part true crime documentary mini-series. The whole thing made millions and as an inmate on death row, Adam wasn't allowed to keep his portion of the proceeds, so he opted to donate it all to a justice nonprofit. He hoped that they'd be able to prove his innocence. Ironically enough, after reviewing the details of his proceedings, they declined to take on Adam's case. That one still makes me laugh.

Stabbed thirty-seven times. You might be wondering how I could do that to another woman. Easy. If someone came into your home and stole something of yours, would you defend yourself? You probably think I'm talking about Kelly Summers, but I'm not. I'm talking about Adam. There are always casualties in war: Kelly was just that.

A divorce would have given Adam half of everything I own. He didn't deserve that. He didn't deserve me. I vowed to never be like my mother. Allowing any man to take what I had earned and what I had worked hard for would make me just as weak as she was. In the end, Adam got the one thing he did deserve.

"How'd it go?" Bob asks as I climb into the passenger's seat of our Mercedes.

"Just as we planned." I smile and lean across the center console to kiss him on the lips.

"Mommy," Summer says from the back seat.

"Yes, sweetheart." I look back at her and smile at my beautiful eight-year-old baby girl.

She's the spitting image of Bob and me, perfect in every way, and I vowed when I found out I was pregnant that I would never make any of the same mistakes my mother made. Summer won't have to save herself from me like I had to save myself from my mother.

My mom didn't kill herself in the technical sense. One needle of heroin with her tolerance wouldn't do it, but the other three I stuck in her arm would. She was killing herself a little every day, I just helped speed up the process. I'll never put my daughter in that position.

"What's in there?" Summer points at the building I just came out of.

"Nothing, sweetheart... Absolutely nothing."

We drive back to the lake house in Prince William County. It's not just a lake house anymore though, now it's our permanent home. Bob and I didn't want to raise Summer in the middle of Washington D.C. and to be honest, this place is lovely. I never saw it the same way Adam used to, but maybe that's just because I always associated it with him. His insecurities and infidelities had coated a patina of filth across what is really a little slice of paradise.

My life is back to being exactly what I wanted it to be... and I intend to keep it that way.

ACKNOWLEDGMENTS

First, I'd like to thank the Bloodhound Books team for taking a chance on me and believing in The Perfect Marriage. Thank you to Betsy Reavley for plucking this book from the submission pile and helping me to achieve my dream of publication. Thank you to my editor, Clare Law, for refining this book and making it the best it could be.

My publishing journey took nearly five years and fortunately none of them was spent alone, as like any author, I had a family and a group of close friends behind me. They endured the highs and lows of pursuing publication, they sympathized with the rejections, celebrated the successes, and encouraged my pursuit. They put up with endless hours of me staring at a computer screen and rambling on about characters as if they were real people. A massive thank you to my family, my closest friends, and my in-laws for supporting me during this journey.

Special thanks to Noel Scheid, Austin Nerge, James Nerge, Kapri Dace, Hannah Willetts, Andrea Willetts, Mary Weider, Stephanie Diedrich, Emily Lehman, Rosemary Cariello, Kayla

Cariello-Becker, and Bri Becker for reading my first draft, i.e. my worst draft. A special thank you to my father-in-law, Kent Willetts, for not only reading it once, but also reading it a second time and providing editorial feedback.

Thank you to Matt Eckes for being the inspiration behind the character of Matthew Latchaw. Thank you to John Latchaw, Bari Weissman, and Katrina Nerge for reading more polished versions of The Perfect Marriage.

Thank you to my dad. You built me the writing desk I've now written two books at – a place where I plan to write many, many more.

Thank you to the authors that I've long admired for agreeing to read and blurb my debut. I'm forever grateful for your support and for your willingness to help out a new author. Thank you to Samantha Downing, Samantha Bailey, Allison Dickson, Sharon Doering, J.T. Ellison, Andi Bartz, and Wendy Heard. I would not only rate your work five stars; I'd also rate you all five stars. You are absolutely wonderful people, and I can't thank you enough for taking the time to read my book.

Thank you to my beta-reader, April Gooding, (aka @callmestory on Twitter). Your feedback was incredible, and you made this book so much better.

Thank you to my husband, Andrew, who believed in me when I didn't believe in myself. I literally owe this book to you. You made me write when I didn't want to (like Annie Wilkes and Paul Sheldon in Misery without all the violence).

Thank you to my mom who was the biggest champion of my writing. Every silly story or poem I wrote, she was the first to read and tell me how great it was, even when they weren't. She pushed me to keep going, and I did even after she passed when I was eighteen. I wish she were here for this.

Finally, thank you to you my readers for taking a chance on a new author. I hope you've enjoyed The Perfect Marriage, and if you did, I'd be forever grateful if you'd leave a review on Amazon or Goodreads. It makes such a difference in helping new readers discover one of my books for the first time. I love hearing from and connecting with readers, so feel free to get in touch with me on my Facebook page, through Twitter, Instagram or my website. Once again, thank you so much!

Facebook: Jeneva Rose Author
Twitter: @jenevarosebooks
Instagram: @jenevaroseauthor
Website: www.jenevarose.com

About the Author

Jeneva Rose is originally from Wisconsin. She spent a couple of years in Ithaca, New York and now calls Charlotte, North Carolina home. She lives with her husband, Andrew and English bulldog, Sir Winston. A lover of reading, cooking, board games, and wine, Jeneva also loves watching *The Office* on repeat and traveling every chance she gets. *The ~~Perfect~~ Marriage* is her debut novel. You can connect with her on Twitter @jenevarosebooks, Facebook Jeneva Rose, Instagram @jenevaroseauthor or via her website jenevarose.com.

Love this book?

Choose another ebook on us
from a selection of similar titles!

- OR -

Not loving this book?

No worries - Choose another
ebook on us from a selection of
alternate titles!

CLAIM YOUR FREE EBOOK